CLAY BRENTWOOD SERIES
BOOK SEVEN: OL' SON

I0585430

Creative Texts Publishers products are available at special discounts for bulk purchase for sale promotions, premiums, fund-raising, and educational needs. For details, write Creative Texts Publishers, PO Box 50, Barto, PA 19504, or visit www.creativetexts.com

CLAY BRENTWOOD: BOOK SEVEN: OL' SON
by Jared McVay
Published by Creative Texts Publishers
PO Box 50
Barto, PA 19504
www.creativetexts.com

ISBN: 9780692199855

OL' SON
By
JARED MCVAY

An imprint of Creative Texts Publishers, LLC
Barto, PA

This book is dedicated to:
Susan, Steve and Quincy Kenny.
Thank you Sue, for all your help.

ALSO BY JARED McVAY

Other works by Jared McVay

Jared McVay is an award-winning author who writes, Westerns: A western series: Historical Fiction: Action/Adventure: YA: Children's books: screenplays: teleplays: Short stories, and also does storytelling.

NOVELS:

Clay Brentwood western series:

Book 1 – Stranger on A Black Stallion

Book 2 – Unjust Punishment

Book 3 – Hammershield

Book 4 – Cinch Mountain

Book 5 – The Storm

Book 6 – The Chameleon

Historical Fiction: The Legend of Joe, Willy & Red – award winner

Historical Fiction: Silent Runner, Guardian Warrior

Western: Hacker's Raid – award winner

Action/Contemporary - Not on My Mountain – double award winner

CHILDREN'S BOOKS

Bears, Bicycles & Broomsticks – 11 short stories

Randal Gets A Hit

Santa's Magic Ring

SCREENPLAYS

The Hobos

Jared & the Warden

Talltree

Santa's Magic Ring

TELEVISION PILOT SCRIPTS

McClusky [6 episodes] - Drama/Comedy

ACT Acute Care Transport - Drama/Comedy

Melinda: Award winning short story

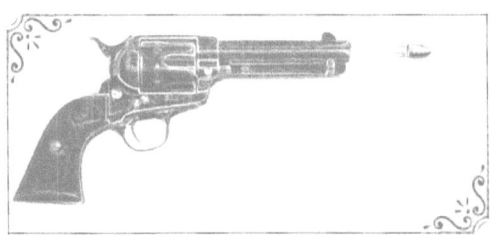

CHAPTER ONE

-

Clay Brentwood stood, hat in hand, next to his late wife's grave and talked quiet like, twisting his hat in his hands as he spoke, "It's been awhile now since the Beeler gang raided our ranch and took you away from me... There hasn't been a day go by that I haven't missed you. I reckon you'll always take up a big part of my heart."

Before continuing, Clay looked up at the sky and sighed, trying to build up the courage for what he had to say. Finally, after several minutes, he said, "I know you don't want me to go on living a solitary life any more than I would want you to had it been me who'd been killed," he stammered.

Clay was having a hard time saying what he wanted to say and swallowed. "The thing is, I've been doing some thinking lately, and with your approval, I'd like to maybe look around for a wife.

Not that anybody could replace you," he hastily added, "but I'm still a relatively young man and I'd like to have somebody to talk to; to do things for; and maybe even have a son or daughter like we used to talk about. Truth is, if I get myself killed doing ranger work, or maybe a mean ole bull, or a wild horse might stomp me to death and if there isn't someone to leave this place to..."

Clay was rambling on, but he couldn't help himself. It made him nervous talking to Martha about bringing another woman to the ranch. He was sure she would approve of Mrs. McIntyre, but Mrs. McIntyre was just the housekeeper and besides, she had recently become engaged to one of his two ranch foremen.

Clay chuckled. Most ranches had only one foreman, but he had two. His original foreman, Running Coyote was a full-blooded Comanche and could speak better English that he could. He was smart and ran the ranch efficiently. But he was still back at the ranch when Clay began his cattle drive from Wichita to the ranch and he needed a foreman. Riley fit the bill and when they got back to the ranch, the two men seemed to get along, so Clay left it that way – with them sharing the foreman's job.

What Clay hadn't told Martha was that he had been contemplating taking a trip to Tennessee on the pretense of buying one or more of Loralie's Walkers, knowing that wasn't the real reason for the trip. In her last letter, Loralie had informed him that she hadn't married the lawyer who had been unsuccessfully trying to court her and hinted that Clay should come to Tennessee to see her string of new two-year-old colts.

In Clay's mind, he could see the fiery red headed Loralie smiling at him and felt his heart begin to beat a bit faster. He knew Loralie had feelings for him and had, on more than one occasion, hinted at something more than just a friendship. He knew he was attracted to her, but he wondered if he was he ready to get married again. And was Loralie the one? He wasn't sure. He wondered if maybe he was just lonely for female companionship, but deep inside knew it was more than that.

He felt sure Martha wouldn't approve of him living alone. She'd want him to move on. She'd even made mention of that early on in their marriage, which he scoffed at, saying he would die long before she did.

"Just wanted you to know and see what you thought of the idea," Clay said to Martha's grave. After another moment of confusion over what to do next and getting no response from her, he slapped his hat on his head and headed back toward the ranch house.

He didn't know what he expected, but there had been no rumbling in the sky and he hadn't been struck by lightning, so he took that as a sign that it would be okay with Martha.

He'd just stepped onto the front porch of his Mexican styled ranch house when Riley, one of his ranch foremen called out to him. "Boss. Somebody's comin'."

Clay looked toward the road coming from town and saw a lone rider headed in their direction.

Clay stepped back off the porch and walked out next to the well in the center of the yard and waited.

When the rider got closer, Clay recognized the man and shook his head. "No. My answer will definitely be, no," he mumbled to himself.

Bill McDaniel, head of the Texas Rangers, rode through the open gate of the wall that surrounded the house, barn and outbuildings, at an easy lope. When he got close to the well, he pulled his horse to a stop and stepped down, handing the reins of his horse to Riley, who was the first person to greet him.

"Good ta see ya again, Captain McDaniel," Riley drawled.

"And you too, Riley," McDaniel replied before walking over and stopping in front of Clay.

Holding up his hands, Bill McDaniel said, "Now Clay, don't go saying "no" before you've heard what I have to say. I didn't ride all this way to not be able to say my piece."

The morning sun was already beginning to get hot and Clay knew he'd at least have to listen to what McDaniel had to say before he said, "no," or the man would pester him until he did.

"There's coffee on if you want a cup," Clay said, heading toward the house.

In the kitchen over coffee, Bill McDaniel pleaded his case stating he knew Clay had long ago completed his obligation to the rangers and had, in fact, taken on several jobs he wasn't obligated to take, including the last one that, as far as he was concerned, not another one of his rangers could have successfully done.

During their second cup of coffee, McDaniel promised this would be the last time he would ask for Clay's help. He even went so far as to raise one hand and put the other one over his heart.

The Marlow brothers were who McDaniel came to talk about. He told Clay they were as mean as the Beeler gang had been; maybe even worse.

Mentioning the Beeler gang was what did it for McDaniel, and Clay found himself agreeing to accompany McDaniel to Dallas and to meet with the sheriff there.

His trip to Tennessee was put on the back burner.

Three days later Clay and McDaniel marched into the sheriff's office in Dallas and met with a tired looking man of fifty who, at one time, had been a force to be reckoned with. But now was just looking to retire before some young hotshot came along and tried to build a reputation.

After introductions, Walt Brannon, the sheriff in Dallas, said, "Yeah, I had the Marlow brothers here in custody. They was to be hanged on the nineteenth. I even put on an extra deputy. They're as mean as rabid dogs – as mean as any gang I've ever encountered and bragged there wasn't ah jail strong enough to hold them."

The sheriff lit a small cigarillo and blew smoke into the air. "Our jail cells are on the second floor, and to the best of my knowledge, they didn't have any visitors, so I relaxed some, thinking they were just spoutin' off. But somehow, they got hold of a pistol and when one of my deputies brought their supper to them, they overpowered him and made their getaway. Purt near beat him to death," the sheriff said, shaking his head. "It'll be weeks before he's on his feet again. They stole all the pistols, rifles and ammunition I had here in the office, plus the petty cash – sixty dollars."

"Anything else?" Clay asked.

The sheriff rubbed his neck and said, "Like I said, they're as mean as they come. They went down to the livery and as well as I can figure, they was in the act of stealing some horses when Billy, the hostler woke up and inquired what was goin' on."

The sheriff looked down at the floor, then back up. "They cut his throat and left him laying on the dung pile."

It was quiet for a couple of minutes while they waited for the sheriff to continue.

"After asking around, Jake Larson, the bartender, said he was just leaving the saloon and saw 'em riding out of town, headed west."

The following morning Clay Brentwood, riding his black stallion and leading his buckskin packhorse, left Dallas in search of the Marlow brothers.

It took him two days to pick up a trail to follow and another long day in the saddle before he arrived in Mineral Springs, some fifty miles west of Fort Worth.

It was close to eight o'clock at night when Clay rode into the small town. Except for the saloon, the town had settled down for the night.

After he turned his horses over to the hostler at the livery stable, he inquired if the man had seen the three Marlow brothers.

The hostler spit a gob of tobacco juice onto the ground and said, "Yeah, I know who they are. Like ta beat me ta death afore I promised ta take care of their horses fer nuthin'."

Clay showed him his ranger badge and said, "I'm looking to arrest them. Any idea where they might be?"

"Over to the Night Owl saloon or maybe the hotel. I reckon it's one or the other. As they was beatin' on me, one of 'em was anxious to get some whiskey in his belly and ah whore in his bed. Guess that was the only reason I'm still alive."

The saloon was filled with locals, but Clay saw no one fitting the description he had of the Marlow brothers.

The bartender was a man of around thirty and looked more like a bouncer than a man who served beer and whiskey. He was well over six feet in height and had to tip the scales over two hundred pounds. His nose looked as though it had been broken more than once, and he had a scar over his left eye.

"What'll it be, stranger?" he asked, wiping the bar with a towel in front of where Clay stood.

"A beer, and maybe a little information," Clay said, laying ten dollars on the bar.

The bartender glanced at the money, then walked down to where he could draw Clay his beer.

Clay stood watching the man, wondering if the bartender could, or would, help him.

When the bartender retuned with Clay's beer, he asked, "What information are you looking for?"

Clay reached into his vest pocket and retrieved his badge and said, "Name's Clay Brentwood and I'm a Texas Ranger. I trailed the Marlow brothers to this town and I'm hoping they're still here. I'm guessing they came in here looking for whiskey and women."

The bartender got an angry look on his face. "Yeah, they were in here, acting all tough and trying to push their weight around, but I put a stop to that real fast," he said, reaching under the bar and pulling out a double-barreled shotgun, "with this and a promise to use it if they didn't calm down."

Clay grinned and asked, "And did they? Calm down?"

"Like young men at ah church social," he replied, then replaced the shotgun under the bar.

Any idea where they might be now?" Clay asked, shoving his empty beer glass across the bar, indicating he wanted another one.

When the bartender returned with the second glass of beer, he said, "You just missed them. They left and headed toward the hotel with three of our prostitutes less than fifteen minutes ago."

Clay downed his beer, thanked the bartender and turned to leave.

Near the door, the bartender called out, "Be careful, they're spoiling for trouble, specially the young one."

Clay waved his arm in the air and left.

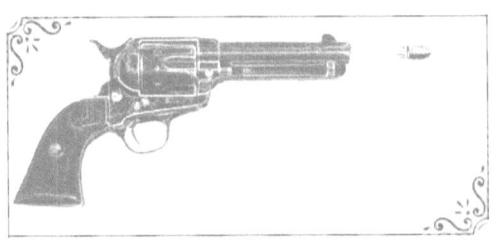

CHAPTER TWO

-

The man behind the counter at the hotel was sitting propped back in a chair, reading a newspaper when Clay walked in.

Hearing the door close, the man stood up and laid the newspaper on the counter, adjusted his glasses and asked, "Looking for a room?"

"Maybe later, but right now I need some information," Clay said.

The man was well over fifty, and the years behind the counter had not been good to him. His hair was gray and thin. He was frail looking and had a tired look.

"I'm sorry sir, but I can't disclose information about our customers if that's what you're after."

Once again, Clay pulled his ranger badge from his vest pocket, along with another ten dollars. Money always seemed to loosen people's tongues.

"Clay Brentwood, Texas Ranger and looking for three wanted men," he said, tossing the money on the counter.

The hotel clerk looked at the money then turned the register around for Clay to look at.

Clay read the names and room numbers of the three last entries, which were not the names of the men he was looking for, but assumed they'd used phony names in case anyone came looking for them.

Clay nodded to the man and turned for the stairs. As he started up to the second floor, the hotel clerk called out, "Remember, I didn't say a word."

Clay stopped in front of room 204 and listened. From inside came loud grunts and bedsprings creaking. He lifted his pistol from his holster, then knocked on the door and waited.

"Go away!" was what he got for an answer. He waited a moment, then knocked again – this time, harder and with more intensity.

Clay heard the bedsprings stop their creaking and a moment later the door was jerked slightly open and Clay could see a good-sized man with a pistol in his hand. The man fit the description of the oldest of the Marlow brothers, Matthew.

Clay kicked the door farther open, then slammed his gun barrel down against the hand holding the pistol and caused him to drop it.

Clay then stepped inside the room and kicked the man in the chest, sending him sprawling back across the floor, landing on his back at the foot of the bed.

The woman on the bed was middle aged but well preserved. She held the sheet up in front of her to cover her nakedness, but Clay could see one of her eyes was turning black and blood was running from a cut lip.

She didn't speak but stared at him with curiosity in her eyes.

Clay put two fingers to his hat and said, "Sorry for the interruption, ma'am, but I'm a Texas Ranger and I'm here to arrest this man."

The woman looked from Clay to the man on the floor and then back to Clay. "Thank you," she whispered.

With pieces of leather straps he carried in his belt for this kind of thing, Clay rolled Matthew Marlow over and tied him securely, then took a pillowcase and gagged him so he couldn't alert the others.

Clay then looked at the woman and asked, "The other two?"

Nodding her head, she whispered, "Next two rooms." She then stood up with the sheet wrapped around her and walked over and picked up a large water pitcher.

She smiled at Clay. "My name is Lilly - don't worry about him waking up and causing a fuss," she said, waiving the water pitcher back and forth.

Clay put two fingers to his hat again and said, "Ma'am," then eased himself out into the hallway.

At the second door Clay heard a woman's sobs and what sounded like a man's fist hitting raw meat, along with a man's laughter.

Clay tried the door easy like, and it opened. Clay stepped into the room as the man turned and stared at his intruder.

The young prostitute was laying on the bed – her eyes swollen almost completely shut and her skin was already turning purple. She was bleeding from her nose and mouth, and she was crying.

The man who was sitting astraddle her had a wild look in his eyes as he leaped off the bed and reached for his pistol, which was hanging from the end of the bed frame.

Before he reached his gun, Clay drew his pistol and clubbed the man, who he later learned was Mark, the middle brother, over the head.

Mark dropped to the floor and lay there unconscious.

As Clay tied and gagged the middle Marlow brother, he spoke quietly to the young woman, who, by now, was standing next to the bed, holding a bloody sheet up to cover her nakedness and sobbing uncontrollably.

"You don't need to worry any more. You're safe now. I'm a Texas Ranger and I'm here to arrest this man and take him away," Clay said, trying to soothe her fears.

After wiping blood from her nose and mouth, she said, "Loan me your pistol and I'll save you the trouble."

Clay could see the hurt in her eyes and felt sorry for her, but the truth was, and he hated it, this was not an uncommon thing in her profession. Why a woman would choose this kind of life he didn't quite understand, but for reasons only they knew, they did.

He looked up at the young woman and said, "I'm sorry ma'am. As much as I'd like to oblige you, I can't do that. And I'm sure you wouldn't want me to have to arrest you for killing him."

"It would be self-defense... and you know no court in the world would convict me," she said, defiance in her voice.

Clay shook his head, saying, "You might be right ma'am; it's not for me to say – but again, even though I agree he deserves to die, I can't condone you doing it. But you can rest assured once I get them back to Dallas the state of Texas will be happy to do it for you."

Mark, the middle brother, was slowly regaining consciousness and sat up, holding his head. "Who the hell are you, mister, and what right you got ta come bustin' inta my room? She yer wife or somethin'?"

"Name's Clay Brentwood. I'm a Texas Ranger, and you're under arrest."

Before Mark could protest, Clay gagged him, then pulled his pistol and pointed it at him and said, "You want to die here and now, you touch that gag and I'll grant you your wish. However, if you want to go on breathing for a while yet, you do as I tell you and you'll live a while longer."

Mark Marlow had fire in his eyes, but in the end, he nodded his head.

Clay said in a casual voice. "Get dressed."

When Mark was dressed, Clay tied him to the end of the bed then turned and said to the young woman, who was now also dressed, "He makes any noise or tries to get loose, you have my permission to hit him over the head with that water pitcher sitting on the table yonder."

"There are two others," she said.

"Already took care of one of them, going next door to get the last one, now," Clay said with a grin. "Just make sure this one stays quiet till I'm finished."

As Clay left the room he saw the woman reaching for the water pitcher and as he closed the door, he heard the pitcher break.

At the third door, Clay heard a muffled, "Help!" and reached up and kicked the door open, rushing in with his pistol in his hand.

The third brother, and the youngest of the bunch, Luke, had a knife in one hand and his other hand over the girl's mouth.

Clay could see several knife wounds on the woman's face and breasts.

"What the...?" Luke said, turning at the sound of the door crashing open. And when he saw a man standing in the doorway with a pistol in his hand, he threw the knife at him, then dove for his own pistol hanging on a nearby chair.

Clay turned sideways just as the knife went past him and lodged itself in the wall on the opposite side of the hallway.

"Touch that pistol and you're a dead man," Clay said as Luke was reaching for his gun.

Luke stopped and turned back, glaring at the man pointing a pistol at him.

By now the woman was standing next to the bed and when Clay stepped into the room, she darted out the door and disappeared down the hallway.

Clay explained who he was, tied Luke up, but didn't gag him since it made little difference now.

"You'll play hell gettin' us back ta Dallas," Luke said as Clay hauled him down to pick up his two brothers.

Once they were downstairs the night clerk wanted to know who was going to pay for whatever damages there might be.

Clay went through Matthew's pockets and found a twenty-dollar gold piece and handed it to the clerk. "This should take care of it," he said.

"Hey, you can't do that!" Matthew Marlow protested.

Clay shoved him toward the door and said, "Where you're going, I doubt you'll need any money."

Before leaving the hotel, Clay asked the clerk, "Where might I find the sheriff this time of night?"

Pleased at being paid for damages, since most of the time he wasn't, the clerk was glad to help. "He usually sleeps in a room behind the cells. He's a heavy sleeper and a mite hard hearing, plus, he's partial to a nip or two of whiskey before going to bed, says it helps him sleep - so you'll probably have to pound real hard on the door.

Clay thanked the clerk and then marched the three Marlow brothers over to the sheriff's office.

After pounding on the door for nearly three minutes and yelling, Clay heard someone from inside yell, "Hold your water, I'm comin'; and this better be important!"

The door was jerked open by a bull of a man who filled the doorway. He was wearing only his long johns and a holster strapped around his waist. His hair was a mess, his face was covered with several days of gray whiskers, and his breath reeked of whiskey. He had a lamp in one hand and a pistol in the other.

He looked Clay up and down, then eyed Clay's three prisoners who still had their hands tied behind them.

"What's goin' on?" he asked of Clay.

Clay showed the sheriff his ranger badge and then said, "Clay Brentwood, Texas Ranger." Nodding toward the Marlow brothers he said, "I've just arrested these three men and need a place to leave them until morning."

The sheriff shook his head in disbelief. "Do you know what time it is?" he asked.

Clay pulled his pocket watch out of his shirt pocket – held it up close to the lamp and said, "According to my timepiece, it's ten-forty-four pm." Stepping back, Clay said, "I apologize for the lateness, but you have to apprehend outlaws when the occasion presents itself."

The sheriff stared at Clay for a moment, then rubbed the stubble of whiskers on his chin and stepped back. "You might as well com'on in. The cells are in the back and the keys are hangin' on ah peg by the door. They're all empty and you can use one of 'em ta sleep in if that suits your fancy; but me, I'm goin back ta bed and pretend none of this happened.

And with that, he set the lamp down on the desk and marched toward the room in the back, mumbling to himself.

After locking the Marlow brothers in two of the cells, Clay took one look at the cot in the next cell and shook his head. Two large cockroaches were walking slowly across the mattress.

As he headed for the office, Clay called over his shoulder, "You boys get some rest if you can. We'll be leaving for Dallas, come morning."

"Where do you think you're goin', Ranger? These accommodations not good enough fer ya?" Matthew shouted.

Clay stopped just short of the doorway and said, "I've had a long day in the saddle. My horse needs tending to, and I'm in need of something to eat and a good night's sleep. If I hear you've caused any trouble, any trouble at all, I'm going to bring those women you beat up on over here and give each one of them a loaded pistol."

The inside of the cells suddenly got quiet. Clay nodded his head and left.

The hostler at the livery stable, a man in his forties, heard Clay approach and came out of his room to greet him. He had a lantern in his hand.

"Howdy. Kinda late, ain't it? You just get into town?" the man asked pleasantly.

"Sorry about it being so late, but yes, I did just get into town, and my horses are in bad need of some grain and a good rub down," Clay said, stepping down from the saddle.

"Be ah dollar each," the hostler said. Bucket of oats, fresh hay, water and ah rub down. Anything else?" he asked.

"That should do it," Clay said. "And my appreciation for what you're doing this late at night, here's two dollars each."

"Yes sir!" the hostler said as he took the money. "Bert's the name, and rest assured, Mister, they'll be treated real good.

Clay grinned and stuck out his hand, "Clay Brentwood."

After handing over the reins of his two horses, Clay patted the black stallion's neck and said, "This man is going to take real good care of you, so you behave yourself, you hear?"

"You talk to that horse like he can understand you, Mister Brentwood," the hostler said with a grin.

Clay looked at Bert and said, "I know it sounds crazy, but I think he can."

Changing the subject before Bert could respond, Clay asked, "Any place open where a man might get a bite to eat?"

"The saloon's the only place open this late at night. Might be she can have her Chinaman fix up ah plate of somethin' for ya."

"Much obliged," Clay said as he turned and headed toward the light shining through the window of the saloon.

Surprisingly, the saloon was still doing a thriving business Clay noticed as he walked in. In most towns this size the saloons closed shortly after the town did.

As he stepped up to the bar, Clay nodded to the bartender, who recognized him and nodded back. "I'll bring you a beer as soon as I finish taking this whiskey to the table over there," he said, motioning his head toward a table in the back.

As he waited, Clay looked around and saw the three prostitutes he'd saved from the Marlow brothers. They were in clean clothes and had on makeup to cover the bruises.

The oldest of the prostitutes walked over and touched him on the arm and asked, "Are you all right?"

"Yes ma'am," Clay responded. "And you?"

Just then the bartender walked up with a cold glass of beer and set it in front of Clay.

"This is the man I told you about, Sam," she said, then looked back at Clay. "We never got a chance to say thank you. They may have killed all three of us," she said. "I'd like to repay you somehow. It would be on the house," she said with a wink. "And to answer your question, "We're going to be fine, thanks to you.""

Clay looked down at her and saw the look of appreciation for what he'd done on her face. He reached out and patted her arm and said, "Thank you. Maybe some other time. I've been on their trail for several days with very little sleep and right now all I'm looking for is something to eat, a bath and a good night's sleep."

The woman smiled knowingly and stuck out her hand. "Sure, any time. Lilly's my name and I own this joint. With that said, she looked at the bartender and said, "Have the cook fix up a steak with all the trimmings. We'll be at my table and bring him all the beer he wants to drink – on the house."

"Yes, Miss Lilly," the man behind the bar said as he turned and headed for the kitchen.

Lilly walked behind the bar and drew two tall glasses of beer, then led Clay to her private table.

When they were seated, she asked, "What did you do with those no-good bums? I hope they're where they can't bother us again."

Clay wiped the beer foam from his mouth and said, "Woke up the sheriff and put them in his jail for the night," Clay said with a grin that fell short when he saw a worried look on Lilly's face.

"Something wrong?" he asked.

Lilly started to take a drink of her beer, then set the glass back down on the table. "Maybe, maybe not. I don't know."

"I don't understand," Clay said, looking directly at her.

Finally, Lilly took a drink of her beer, then gave out with a sigh. "He's a drunk with a tin star pinned on his chest, and in my opinion, he's none to reliable. The only reason he hasn't been fired is because he can be mean and has the town council buffaloed. They're afraid he'll burn the town to the ground if they get rid of them, or worse, kill them all."

"You think I should pull them out of the jail? And if I do, where can I put them?" Clay asked, feeling confused.

"To be honest, I can't say for sure. The sheriff was pretty drunk when he left here tonight, so, hopefully, he'll sleep through the night."

"And if for some reason he does wake up?" Clay queried.

"He'll probably wonder who those men are. I doubt if he'd even remember you coming to the door."

As Clay sat there, pondering her words, a small framed Chinaman came running up with a tray of food. He sat several plates on the table, then bowed and said, "My name, Ham Sing. I get out of bed to fix this for you. You eat now, before it gets cold."

When Clay hesitated, Ham Sing shouted, "Eat! Now!"

"Yes sir," Clay said looking down at a big steak, fried potatoes, green beans, and a large slice of fresh bread with butter melting on it. On another plate was a huge slice of apple pie.

With a mouthful of food, Clay grinned at Lilly and said, "I'll go over and check on them after I've eaten."

The little Chinaman grinned and bowed several times before turning and hurrying back to his domain.

Lilly sat and watched him eat. In her heart she knew this was one of the good ones, but there was also a sadness about him. As she sat there she wondered what made a man like him take a job tracking down outlaws. He seemed more the rancher type. Had there been a woman in his life that had hurt him or died at the hands of men like the Marlow brothers? Something stirred inside her as she wondered what might have happened if they'd met some years back, before she had been driven into prostitution by a man she thought she loved.

After swallowing the last bite of pie, Clay shoved his chair back and said, "That is the best meal I've eaten in a coon's age."

Reaching into his pocket, Clay pulled out two silver dollars and laid them next to the plate. "Will you see that Ham Sing gets this with my compliments?"

"You really don't have to do that. Maybe you were just really, really hungry," she said.

Clay nodded his head. "I reckon I was mighty hungry, but no matter, he deserves the money for getting out of bed to fix my supper."

Lilly could only smile and think to herself, 'Yes, he is one of the good ones.'

After thanking Lilly for the beer and steak, Clay left the saloon and walked quietly down the alley behind the jail, where he could listen through the open window.

Standing in the darkness, all he could hear was loud snoring. After a minute or so he turned and headed for the saloon, never seeing Mark who was watching from the side of the window.

Clay was tired and with his stomach full of steak, he was ready for a bath and some much needed sleep.

When Clay entered the hotel, Mark turned and grinned at his brothers, saying, "He just went inta the hotel."

Matthew stood up and stretched, then picked up a tin cup from the small table and began to beat it on the bars. "Sheriff, sheriff, get in here!"

CHAPTER THREE

The following morning while Clay was having breakfast in the hotel restaurant, he made arrangements for food to be taken over to the jail for his prisoners.

Clay was half way through with his ham, fried potatoes, and three eggs when the man from the restaurant came rushing up to his table with the plates of food still on the tray.

Clay looked up and noticed the still full plates. "What's wrong? Wouldn't they eat?" he asked with a grin.

The man swallowed and said, "Mister Ranger, sir, there aren't any prisoners over there to feed. All the cells are empty!"

"What?" Clay said, jumping to his feet.

The man stepped back, his eyes wide, not knowing what to expect. "The sheriff told me he turned them loose around midnight. He said they told him you really aren't a Texas Ranger. They told him you are a jealous husband whose wife was a loose woman, and you caught her making love to all three of them. They said you planned to take them out in the desert and murder them and leave their carcasses out there for the buzzards and other critters to feast on."

The man swallowed again, then said, "They said you already killed your wife."

Clay sat back down in his chair and took a sip of his coffee, wondering how a man wearing a star could be stupid enough to believe hogwash like that. Why didn't he come talk to him before turning them loose?

Before he could give it any more thought, the sheriff stormed into the restaurant and walked directly over to Clay's table.

He pulled his pistol and pointed it at Clay. "You're under arrest. Now get up real slow like and put that hog leg of yours on the table with two fingers and no funny business – and I won't tell you twice."

Not quite comprehending what was happening, Clay stood up and with two fingers, lifted his pistol from his holster, and laid it on the table. "Just for the record, my name is Clay Brentwood, and I am a Texas Ranger. The Marlow brothers were my prisoners, and you turned them loose. Now tell me why you're arresting me?" Clay asked, trying to keep his temper under control.

The sheriff's eyes were bloodshot, his face was unshaven and his clothes were dirty and rumpled, but the gun hand was steady. "I'm arresting you for the murder of your wife. Now turn around and head for the jail, and remember, I'll shoot you down like the dog you are and spit on your grave. I got no use for women killers," the sheriff said, waving his pistol toward the front door of the hotel.

"You do understand you'll be arresting a Texas Ranger – a lawman just like yourself. Well, maybe not like you, but one who would not have made the blunder you're making. I didn't murder my wife or anybody else. You've been taken in by the Marlow brothers, and now they're getting away because of your stupidity."

Instead of making the sheriff think about what he was doing, like Clay wanted, it only inflamed the sheriff's anger.

When they reached the jail, Clay tried again to talk to the sheriff, but the sheriff already had his mind made up and shoved Clay into one of the cells and locked the door and left without a word.

Clay looked at the bed, remembering the cockroaches and decided to sit on the wooden bench under the window. He was angry and beginning to shake. He lit a cigarette and pondered his situation and sighed. The Marlow brothers had to have done something other than make up that stupid story for the sheriff to turn them loose. And he had to find out what it was and then find a way to get out of here before the trail got cold. He'd just finished his cigarette when the sheriff came back in.

"Texas Ranger, you say? And you're stickin' to that story, are ya?"

"That's right," Clay said, standing up and walking toward the bars.

The sheriff gritted his teeth and spit on the floor, then said, "That's not the way I heard it, and it's three of them against one of you."

"If I'm not who I say I am, why did I ask you to hold them in your jail over night? Why didn't I just take them out into the desert like they said I was going to do and kill them and ride away? No one would have known for days, weeks, or ever," Clay said with a finality that made the sheriff lose a little of his fluff.

Clay could see he'd struck a nerve and was about to continue when the sheriff turned and stormed back into his office.

Clay turned and stepped up onto the bench and looked out of the barred window.

He could see part of the street and watched as people went about their daily business.

Anger caused him to grab the bars and shake them. They were solid, and there didn't appear to be any way to pry or pull them loose.

Clay reached into his pocket and withdrew his pocketknife. This hick sheriff hadn't taken the time to search him – big mistake on his part.

Using his pocketknife, Clay tried to dig out around three of the bars but finally decided to give up. They were planted deep into the wall.

An hour and a half later Clay heard someone enter the jail, and he quickly put his knife back in his pocket and sat back down on the bench and rolled a cigarette, wishing he'd been able to get at least one of the bars loose. At least he'd tried.

The sheriff came in looking somewhat better. He'd had a bath and a shave and was wearing clean clothes. Stopping in front of Clay's cell, he shook his head and said, "I have to say, pretending to be a Texas Ranger is a pretty good ruse. Where'd you get the badge? You kill a ranger, too?"

Clay stiffened. He could smell whiskey on his breath and said, "Like I told you, sheriff, I am a Texas Ranger and you can verify this by telegraphing Austin and asking for my boss, Bill McDaniel."

"Already done that," the sheriff lied. "Said they never heard of you. Now, you want ta tell me the truth?"

Clay sighed. He knew the sheriff was lying about contacting Austin. Bill McDaniel would never deny him being a ranger.

Trying to calm his anger, Clay said, changing the subject, "I can't believe you could be bamboozled by that pack of lies the Marlow brothers made up. There had to be something else. How much did they give you to turn them loose?"

Before he could catch himself, the sheriff said, "A hundred dollars." But when he realized what he'd just said, he turned and headed back toward his office.

Clay looked at what used to be a man but was now, nothing more than a drunk. Matthew Marlow had realized this and knew the man could be bought. A hundred dollars would buy a lot of whiskey.

It took Clay no more than a moment to know he had to do something or the sheriff would wind up hanging him on trumped up charges. As the sheriff reached for the door, Clay called out, "Sheriff, I need to go visit the outhouse."

The sheriff turned and looked back at Clay and saw him holding himself and dancing around.

The sheriff reached around the doorsill and grabbed a ring of keys, then walked up and unlocked the door to Clay's cell.

When Clay was sure the cell door was unlocked, he kicked the door as hard as he could and drove it into the sheriff's forehead.

The sheriff dropped to his knees, and then toppled over like a tree that had just been cut down.

Clay dragged him into the cell and tied him to the cockroach-infested bed, then gagged him.

After locking the cell door, Clay went into the sheriff's office and retrieved his gun and holster - and for good measure, took a box of ammunition.

Before leaving, Clay dropped the ring of keys into the wastebasket and threw some paper in on top of them. It would be awhile before anyone found them.

Once outside, Clay walked directly to the livery stable and asked the hostler to get his horses ready, then went to the hotel and gathered up his gear. At the front desk, Clay paid his bill.

Less than thirty minutes after escaping from the jail, Clay was headed west, out of town, hoping to pick up the Marlow brother's trail.

As he rode past the saloon, Lilly was standing on the sidewalk, and when she saw him, she smiled broadly and raised her hand and waved. "Next time!" she called out.

Clay put two fingers to the brim of his hat and rode on. He could feel the muscles of the black stallion ripple against his legs. The big horse was rested and ready to make some tracks.

Near the edge of town Clay reined in and tied up in front of the mercantile store and went inside.

The owner quickly put Clay's order together and helped him carry it outside where Clay loaded it into the packs on the buckskin. Clay paid the man, and they shook hands just before Clay swung his leg over the black stallion and led the buckskin west.

He left Mineral Springs, hoping to never have an occasion to return.

The first night, Clay camped off the trail near a small spring that had good, cold water and plenty of cover. If a posse happened to pass by he was sure they'd ride on by. He'd eaten lightly and then read for a while by the light of the fire. When his eyes got tired and he'd heard no one prowling around, he put the book in his saddlebag and went over to his bedroll, ready for a good night's sleep.

Just as Clay started to bend down, he heard the rattle and stood back up. In the middle of his bedroll was a huge rattlesnake, and it was not happy about being disturbed. Clay jerked the end of his blanket up just as the snake struck and got his fangs stuck in Clay's blanket.

Clay grabbed the four-foot rattlesnake by the tail and jerked it loose from the blanket, then stepped on his head and held it down while he pulled his knife and cut its head off.

His first reaction had been to shoot it, but if a posse or the Marlow brothers were anywhere in the vicinity, they would be alerted, and he didn't want that.

As he skinned the big snake, Clay thanked the gods for providing him with meat, just as the Indians did when bringing down a buffalo or deer, or any other critter that provided them with food, clothing or weapons.

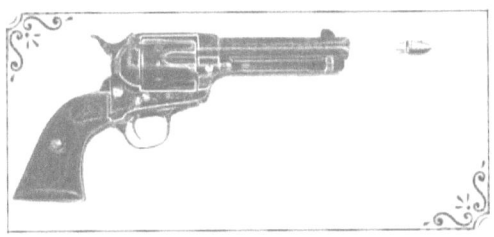

CHAPTER FOUR

-

Three months later and a trail of murders, rapes and thefts across Texas and New Mexico, Clay felt he was finally closing in on the Marlow brothers. They had eluded him at every turn, staying just a step or two ahead of him by stealing horses when theirs were worn out, making any tracks hard to follow. Sometimes it took a day or more to figure out the new tracks and by the time he'd caught up with them, they'd changed horses, again. It was the small towns where they had committed their crimes that kept him going in the right direction.

A week and a half ago the Marlow brothers had crossed over into the Arizona territory, making their way over the White Mountains and across the Salt River. In the northern end of the Gila Mountains they had broken into a ranch house and was beating up on the man who owned the small spread, and more than likely would have killed him if the man's wife had not taken up a pistol and began putting holes in the walls near where they were.

Fortunately for the Marlow brothers, the woman had never fired a pistol before and was not the best of shots, and they escaped to the barn where they stole fresh horses.

Clay arrived the following morning and spent most of the day helping the woman care for her husband.

The man would be layed up for some time with a broken jaw, broken ribs and a multitude of bruises and abrasions. He couldn't speak to thank Clay, but his wife made sure Clay had plenty of food for him and his horses before he left.

East of Phoenix, in the small town of Mesa, Arizona, Clay caught up to them when they broke into a general store and was in the act of stealing food, guns and ammunition.

Clay got the drop on two of them, but it was Matthew, the oldest brother who was in another part of the store and threw a lantern at Clay, catching his shirt on fire. Matthew threw down on him and barely missed shooting Clay, when Clay dove behind a large pile of sacked beans, beating the fire out and trying to shoot back.

During the shootout, the owner of the general store mistakenly thought Clay was the thief and sneaked up behind him and threw down on him with a shotgun, then shaking like a leaf in a hurricane, ordered Clay to put his pistol down.

Fearful that the man would accidentally shoot him, Clay tossed his pistol to the floor.

As the Marlow brothers made a hasty get-away, Clay was explaining to the local sheriff who he was, along with describing the men he was chasing. Fortunately, the sheriff had a wanted poster on the Marlow brothers and turned him loose.

Crossing the Salt River was an experience Clay would never forget, of that he was sure. The river ran through the bottom of a canyon that was so deep he wasn't sure there was a way to cross. He guessed the canyon had to be close to eight or nine thousand feet deep.

It took him half a day scouting before he found a trail leading down the wall of the canyon. It was a zig-zag trail made by animals and was fairly easy to follow.

That night he made camp on the bank of the river and caught a fish for dinner.

The following day was bleak and overcast. The trail going up the opposite side of the canyon was much the same as the one coming down on the other side and Clay was worried about his horses making the climb. Walking ahead, with the horses following him, it took them most of the morning to reach the top. He'd never experienced a climb like that before, and he was exhausted.

He made a small fire and a pot of coffee and spent the next hour drinking coffee and thinking about where the Marlow brothers might be headed, while his horses grazed on lush, green grass. Phoenix was his best guess.

To get there, they still had to get out of the mountains and then cross a stretch of desert that held broken down wagons and the bones of people who weren't prepared. Even though some were prepared, they hadn't taken into consideration the Indians who didn't care much for white people crossing their territory.

On his second day after leaving the mountain range, Clay could see their dust trail in the desert air no more than a mile ahead of him.

Unless they'd swapped horses recently, which they seemed to do on a regular basis, he was sure it was them. His biggest problem was, he wasn't positive. They would ride their horses until they were exhausted, then steal new ones from whatever ranch or farm they happened to come upon, which made it difficult to track them.

This last set of tracks he'd been following hadn't changed in several days now, presumably because they hadn't happened onto any pastures with horses in them.

Clay's own horses were tired, but still in decent shape because he hadn't ridden them to death. He made sure they had rubdowns every night before turning them loose to graze. He never shackled or tethered the black stallion because he knew the big horse would stay close by – they had that kind of relationship. And the buckskin stayed close to the black stallion. They could wander around and find grass or take a roll, unencumbered by a rope around their neck, or shackles on their feet.

In this part of Arizona, the bleak desert was dotted with mesas that seemed to come up out of the ground. Farther north they loomed out of the desert even higher and wider, but here, not quite so high. Even so, the Indians liked to use them because they could see for miles all around.

Clay was tired and let his eyes close for a few minutes - a careless thing to do because the Marlow brothers caught sight of him trailing them and took positions on top of the mesa and waited for him, hoping he would come within rifle range.

The first shot put a hole in Clay's hat and sent it flying off his head. Lucky shot or not, it had been way too close as far as he was concerned.

Instinct and several years of being shot at by outlaws caused Clay to grab his rifle and dive for a nearby ditch that, as it turned out, was just deep enough to give him some protection as long as he didn't raise his head.

Without being able to see him, the shooters laid down random shots; some in front of him and some behind him, some close, like the last one, hoping one of them would find a target. Clay figured that as long as he didn't raise his head, he was relatively safe – or at least he hoped he was.

A bullet kicked up dirt just in front of Clay's head causing him to stop and lay very still, hoping the next shot would not be the one that ended his life. His one and only consolation was that the men shooting at him were high up on the mesa some distance away, and he was laying in a shallow ditch. Hitting your target from that height and distance would, at best, be a lucky shot. He hoped none of them were lucky today.

Fortunately, the black stallion had the good sense to run away from the shooting and out of rifle range, with the buckskin packhorse following close behind. Both were now leisurely eating what little grass they could find in small clumps here and there, not caring about the dealings of humans who went around shooting at each other.

The scorching Arizona sun beat down on the desert making the sand so hot it burned Clay's arms and the front of his body as he tried to inch his way along the shallow ditch. The temperature was over a hundred and getting hotter by the minute.

Clay was hoping the ditch would get deeper where he might have a chance to shoot back. Sweat ran down his forehead, and into his eyes, causing them to burn, making it difficult to see. His back felt so hot he guessed you could fry an egg on it. Such was the life of a Texas Ranger.

"This is definitely my last job," he said to himself for the hundredth time during the last few years.

-

"I can't find no target ta shoot at," Luke Marlow said, glancing over at his two brothers who were also concealed behind boulders atop a small mesa a little less than two hundred yards from the ditch Clay had dived into.

"Just keep watchin' that ditch," Matthew, the oldest of the three Marlow brothers said, wiping sweat from his eyes with the back of his hand. "He's bound to show himself sooner or later."

"But what if he don't? What if he somehow sneaks up on us? I've heard stories. They say rangers ain't like normal lawmen. They say they got more lives than ah cat, and this'un is the worst of the bunch," Luke complained.

"Them's just old wives tales ta make idiots like you fearful of 'em," Mathew said with a snarl.

"I ain't no idiot!" Luke yelled at his older brother. "Just cause you're the oldest don't make you the smartest."

Before Matthew could respond, Mark, the middle brother jumped in. "Shut up, both of ya! I'm sick and tired of your bickerin'. While you're throwin' insults at each other that ranger down there could be gettin' away, or sneakin' up on us."

Matthew and Luke glared at each other for a moment, then turned their attention back to the ditch and the man they were trying to kill.

-

Their mother had been a god-fearing woman, and had named her sons after men she held in high esteem, Matthew, Mark and Luke; all from the bible her father had given her. Being named after men from the bible, she hoped they would grow up to be honest, decent men. Sadly for her, that never happened.

Before the boys were born, their father, Samuel Marlow, worked as a clerk in a store in St. Louis, Missouri and had dreams of going west to make his fortune. At a church social he'd met Marlene Curtis. Marlene's father was the minister of the small church and liked Samuel, giving his consent for him to court his daughter. The idea of going west excited Marlene and two weeks after they were married they headed into the unknown with dreams and visions filling their heads.

In Oklahoma, Samuel met a man who convinced him to buy his farm and settle down there. Over the next three years Samuel worked from sunup to sundown, trying to make the farm work, while Marlene gave birth to their three sons and also worked from sunup to sundown, trying as best she could to help.

As it turned out, Samuel didn't know much about farming and was too stubborn to ask for advice. Each year his dreams of making his fortune grew less and less. After six years of struggling he'd had enough. One day he told Marlene he was going into Enid, the closest town to them, to buy some supplies and that was the last she ever saw of him.

With three small boys to raise on her own, and a farm that lost money every year, Marlene went to the bank in Enid to see if they would buy it from her, only to find out that Samuel had borrowed against the land and not one payment had ever been made.

"I have no choice but to call the note," Angus Whitehead, the bank president told her. "Nothing personal you understand. It's just policy."

"But what am I to do?" she asked, clutching her three boys close to her. "I have no money, no place to live and three boys to raise," she said as the tears dripped from her chin onto her lap.

"Do you have people back where you came from?" Angus asked.

Angus Whitehead hated this part of his job and he felt sorry for her, but he had people he had to answer to, and they said, "Call the note."

After wiping the tears from her eyes, she nodded her head. "St. Louis. My mother and father live there."

Angus Whitehead looked across his desk at Marlene and her three young sons, and came to a decision unlike he'd ever made before.

Because of the circumstances, and the fact that he felt sorry for this woman who was trying to raise three sons all by herself, he gave her one hundred dollars out of his own pocket.

"Here, take this" Angus said, pushing a small stack of money across his desk. "It should be enough to get you and the boys back to St. Louis."

Having no other choice but to take the handout, she thanked him and put the money in her handbag and left his office, her three small boys trailing along behind her, complaining about being hungry.

Out on the street, her first thought was to use the money to go home as the bank president had suggested, but quickly changed her mind. Before leaving St. Louis, she'd boasted about one day having a place for her mother and father to come to where they could spend their later years in comfort. She wouldn't allow herself to go home broke, destitute and humiliated, and have everyone whispering behind her back.

What she was going to do she wasn't sure, but returning to St. Louis was not an option. Standing on the sidewalk, she looked around and a short distance down the street, she spotted a church steeple. Gathering the boys, she hurried down the sidewalk to the church and went inside, hoping to find the minister so she could ask his advice on what she should do, but the place was empty.

Even though she read her bible daily and prayed in private, Marlene hadn't been inside a church since she'd married Samuel, and was feeling a bit intimidated. She left the boys at the front door and made her way down the center aisle to the front of the church where she knelt down on her knees and prayed for help and guidance.

Leaving the church with her three sons in tow, Marlene headed for the business district of town. After a lot of prayer and weighing her options, she decided the only thing she could do was to stop at each and every store in town and ask if any of them needed help.

Tugging on her dress, Matthew, the oldest, said, "Mama, we're hungry."

With tears in her eyes, Marlene said, "We'll eat very soon, son. I need you boys to be patient for just a little bit longer."

The boys scuffed their feet on the sidewalk, knowing they would have to wait, but not liking it.

A block from the church she saw a sign in a restaurant window that caused her heart to speed up. It read, COOK NEEDED IMMEDIATELY - INQUIRE WITHIN.

Looking upward toward a cloud that reminded her of an angel she whispered, "Thank you." To Marlene it was divine providence. The one thing she was good at was cooking, which she loved to do, and here was someone needing a cook.

The owner of the restaurant was a forty-year-old man by the name of Henry Crooker who reluctantly admitted his cooking abilities were less than desirable. Over the last five years he'd worked as a cook on cattle drives where bacon and beans and maybe a pie once in a while was all the skill he needed. Not only was he a bad cook, and since he'd never eaten in a real restaurant, he had absolutely no idea of what the menu should include, so his menu consisted of eggs, bacon, biscuits and gravy, fried potatoes, and beans, and that was it.

Hating the cattle drives with the long days and constant bickering of the cowboys about his cooking, he'd saved every penny he could get his hands on, and six months ago had put a down payment on the restaurant.

The first week, business was good. People came in out of curiosity.

Henry tried hard, but after a while his only business consisted of a few diehard cowboys who didn't mind beans for supper - which wasn't enough to allow the place to pay for itself. He finally decided he had only two choices, sell the place and lick his wounds, or, hire a good cook, if he could find one, and hope people would return.

By the time Marlene showed up, he'd turned down four people who couldn't cook any better than he could and he was just about to give up and sell the place.

When she walked in with three young boys trailing behind her, his heart sank. First, she wasn't attractive, which didn't make a lot of sense. It made absolutely no difference what she looked like if she could cook. Second, she was fairly young and had baggage in the form of three young boys. And third, he wondered if a woman her age knew anything about cooking in a restaurant?

"I was sorta hoping for an older, experienced person," he told her, not mentioning her baggage.

Marlene suggested he let her cook the evening meal and if he wasn't satisfied she would move on.

The kitchen was a mess and the supplies were next to nothing, and Henry knew it. It would be a real challenge for her to come up with something enticing.

Even with two strikes against her, so to speak, Marlene was able to put together a stew from what was available and make some dried apple pies. Between the stew and the pies, the restaurant was filled with aromas that made Henry's mouth water.

The evening crowd was small, but to the person, each one praised the food and said if this was the way it was going to be, they would return.

Henry was more than satisfied with her skills and happy that he'd finally found a cook and wouldn't have to sell. He felt being a business owner was much better than being a chuck wagon cook.

"You're just the one I've been looking for," he told her. "Now, if we can work out some terms, you've got yourself a job."

Henry lived in the three rooms above the restaurant but had recently acquired the ownership of a two-bedroom house on the edge of town, from a young man who recently inherited it from his distant aunt who had no other relatives to leave the house to. The young man came to Enid with the intention of selling the house and moving on, but after three weeks, he'd had no takers and was running low on funds.

The young man entered the saloon and saw several men playing poker. After only a moment's hesitation, he decided he would replenish his funds by relieving the locals of whatever money they had to offer.

The young man drank too much and was not the poker player he thought he was. He lost not only all of his money, but also the small house on the edge of town.

Henry gave him back forty of the eighty dollars he'd lost so he could go back to where he came from, but kept the house.

Instead of moving into the house he let Marlene and her boys live there as part of her wages, along with allowing them to eat their meals at the restaurant. With the house and food he allowed them to eat, he wound up paying her only ten dollars a month in cash money. Any tips she might receive would be hers to keep.

Life was tough on a single woman with three small boys to raise, but she felt the job as the cook in Henry's restaurant was a godsend. In a manner of minutes she not only had a job, but also a place to live and food to feed her family, which made the boys very happy. After returning the money he'd loaned her, she thanked the banker for his kindness.

In a short time, word got around about Marlene's cooking and Henry's restaurant was suddenly the best place in town to eat, and the tips outweighed her salary.

Marlene's days at the restaurant were long without much time to devote to her family and somewhere along the way they became lost souls, running wild and getting into trouble with the law.

By the time her oldest son, Matthew, turned seventeen, all three boys had spent short terms behind bars for petty theft and other charges, including beating up on other boys and making them pay to be left alone.

It was the rape charge of a young lady named Becky Sue Lambert that caused the boys to flee Enid just ahead of the law and an angry mob bent on hanging all three of them.

Battered and bruised, with her clothes in tatters, with tears streaming down her face, she staggered through her family's front door and collapsed.

After being administered to by the doctor, she told the sheriff and her father, "The Marlow boys dragged me into an alley, tied me up and took me out in the country in a buggy, where they beat me and told me if I told anyone, they would kill me. They took turns raping me. Even though they had flour sacks over their heads, they called each other by their names and I knew who they were."

Before leaving town, the boys stopped by their mother's house and took two hundred and sixty-three dollars from the vase where she kept her life's savings.

Marlene was tired, worn down, sick, and embarrassed by what her sons had done. She went to the Lambert house and told Becky Sue and her parents how sorry she was and asked what she could do?

Mister Lambert told her, "What's done is done. There's nothing you or any of us can do at this point. Hopefully, time and love from the family will help Becky Sue put it in the past and move on with her life."

Everyone in Enid knew how hard Marlene had tried. They grieved for her, but there was not much they could do. "Those boys are just wild," one of the women had said.

From the day her sons left town, Marlene began to go downhill and a few weeks later when she didn't show up for work, Henry went to the house and found her laying in bed. She'd passed sometime during the night. Whether it was by her own hand was never talked about in public. The house was tidy and she'd left a note that had only two words... "I'm sorry."

When the local newspaper reported her death, it said, the poor woman died of a broken heart. Close to half of Enid's population showed up for her funeral, which was paid for by Henry Crooker.

The three Marlow brothers went on to become murderers, cattle rustlers, bank robbers and more. If they knew of their mothers passing, they never talked about it.

CHAPTER FIVE

Clay was inching his way along the ditch and saw that it was curving to his right. From his position, it looked to be getting deeper, giving him cause for hope. As he belly crawled around the curve in the ditch, he froze. Not five feet in front of his face was the biggest Gila monster he'd ever seen – close to two feet long and even from five feet away, Clay could smell the lizard's putrid breath, which almost made him gag. Even though many people thought the Gila monster's bite to be deadly, Clay knew that wasn't true. If bitten by a Gila monster, it would be painful and make him very sick for several days, and easy prey for the Marlow brothers, but he doubted he would die from the bite - but for sure the Marlow brothers would shoot him where he lay if they found him unable to defend himself.

Clay also knew the Gila monster was a very slow mover, which allowed him time to draw his pistol and point it at the lizard. He really didn't want to fire his pistol because it would give his location away, plus, he had nothing against the lizard other than the lizard had stinking breath and was blocking his escape route.

The Gila monster and Clay stared at each other for close to a minute before the big lizard turned and slowly moved away, climbing up the shallow embankment and disappearing.

Clay gave a sigh of relief then put his pistol back into his holster and continued crawling around the curve.

-

"I ain't waitin' up here much longer in this heat," Mark, the middle brother said with conviction. "I'm for movin' on and headin' fer Phoenix where we can get some decent grub and have ah few drinks. Hell, I might even bed me one of them prostitutes." he said with a wide grin.

"You'll stay here as long as it takes ta get rid of that ranger down there," Matthew said, giving his brother a scowl.

"Hell, he might already be dead," Luke, the youngest of the three, said. "We ain't seen no movement for ah long time now. Maybe one of our bullets found ah home. I agree with Mark, we've been here long enough. I vote we move on."

Matthew sighed. If these two idiots weren't his flesh and blood, he would have shot them a long time ago. "This ain't no votin' situation. We ain't goin' nowhere til we know for sure the ranger's dead and that's the end of it," Matthew said matter-of-factly.

"If you're so blamed eager ta head for Phoenix, then go down there and check for yourself. You bring me his scalp and we'll head for Phoenix," Matthew hissed at them. Neither brother left their hiding place.

Sometimes Clay's wishes seemed to come true and his hope for survival grew as the ditch became deeper and turned downward toward a small pool of cool water seeping from a crack in the wall of the rocky ditch.

The pool wasn't deep and was formed by a natural bowl in the rock. Where the water came from, Clay wasn't sure, but it was like many small water holes hidden here and there all over this part of the country – mostly only known by the Indians who lived here. The water was cool and sweet, and after drinking his fill he washed his face and splashed some over his head.

Looking around, Clay discovered he was in a fairly deep, rocky depression that would allow him to stand up; which he did, then brushed the dirt and sand off the front of his shirt and pants as best he could.

Clay checked his rifle and then made his way to the top of the bank, but stayed just below the edge.

Off to his left, he saw a small piece of brush that had turned brown and blended with the ground. He quickly moved over behind the small bush. His hair and sun-tanned skin wasn't much darker than the desert or the bush, which allowed him to raise his head up behind the bush to check his surroundings. He was several hundred feet from where he'd been shot at and first entered the rocky crevice.

In the distance he could see the top of the mesa and saw the glint of three rifle barrels, but not the men themselves. "At least they're smart enough to stay hidden behind the rocks," Clay muttered to himself. Although he wasn't positive, he was relatively sure it was the Marlow brothers up there. If he stayed patient, eventually one of them would make a move. He just hoped he could get a good shot.

Glancing around for other signs to help tell him who might be on top of the mesa, he felt confident it wasn't the feared, Apache Indians up there. Apaches were noted for their guerilla fighting tactics and were some of the most fearsome fighters in the world. If it had been them, they would have known about this water hole and would have had it protected or made their stand there.

If they had let him make it this far, it would have been on purpose so the ones who were waiting nearby could make an easy kill. No, if it were Apaches he would be a dead man by now with his scalp hanging from one of their spears or bows and he would be staked out over and ant hill or laying on his back, facing the sun with his eyelids cut off.

Looking toward the mesa, again he saw the sun glinting off what appeared to be rifle barrels. Long ago, Clay learned about the sun glinting off rifle barrels and had wrapped his own rifle barrel with canvas. This did two things; one, the barrel was never too hot to hold onto and second, the sun would not glint off the barrel and give his location away.

Very slowly, Clay eased his rifle barrel above the top of the ditch and waited.

-

"I'm thirsty," Luke said. "Where's the canteen?"

Matthew sighed. It wasn't one thing it was another. "Right here next ta me," he said with disgust.

"Toss it over ta me," Luke said, wiping his mouth with the back of his hand.

"I ain't tossin' nothin'. You want it, you come get it," Matthew said after taking a drink and smacking his lips.

Luke looked down toward the ditch and weighed his options. He didn't want to get shot, but he was awful thirsty. They hadn't seen hide nor hair of the ranger in quite a while now. The lure of water got the best of him and he stood up and began to run across the short distance.

-

Clay noticed the movement and took aim at the moving target. He took a deep breath and as he let out the air, he slowly squeezed the trigger on his Winchester thirty-caliber rifle.

Luke Marlow felt the jolt and excruciating pain as Clay's bullet dug its way into his shoulder. He let out a scream that could be heard for miles in any direction as his rifle went flying over the side of the mesa.

"I'm hit! I'm hit!" Luke screamed, grabbing his shoulder - forgetting about his thirst.

Before Matthew could tell the middle brother, Mark, to stay where he was, Mark jumped up and ran toward his brother, yelling, "Hold on Luke, I'm comin'."

Mark had taken only two steps before he was knocked backward as Clay's second bullet entered Mark's left side and plowed its way out his back.

In a matter of seconds, Clay Brentwood had evened the odds in his favor.

CHAPTER SIX

Matthew fired three quick shots at where he thought the ranger's shots had come from, which was nowhere close to where Clay actually was, then yelled at his two brothers in a loud whisper, "Crawl back away from the edge! Get outta sight!"

Matthew watched as his two brothers made their way, painfully back onto the middle part of the mesa, then, after firing three more rounds, he belly crawled over to where his brothers were sitting.

Neither of the shots were life threatening, except for maybe bleeding to death if not bandaged.

"Am I gonna die?" Luke asked.

Matthew was frustrated by their stupidity and said, "No. Neither of you two imbeciles is gonna die. I can't be that lucky. Now sit still while I put your neck kerchiefs on your wounds ta stop the bleedin'."

Even though they had shot several people, none of them had ever been shot before so they had no idea what it felt like. Now, both Luke and Mark were whining like schoolboys.

"Now can we go ta Phoenix? I need ah doctor, real bad," Mark complained.

Matthew sighed. Looking back over his shoulder toward the edge of the mesa, he said, "I reckon we don't have much choice. You two crybabies ain't gonna give me no peace til we do."

"I reckon if it had been you that got shot, then you'd be ready ta get outta here," Luke said.

"I wasn't the one that stood up and made ah target of himself," Matthew snarled.

"How else was I supposed ta get the canteen? You wouldn't throw it to me like I asked ya to," Luke yelled.

"You could'a crawled on your belly. That way you wouldn't ah give the ranger somethin' ta shoot at and you could'a got yourself ah drink of water without gettin' shot!" Matthew said, his face getting red from frustration.

Both Mark and Luke lowered their heads and stared at the ground.

"Now," Matthew continued, "While I make sure the ranger stays put for a while, you two stay outta sight and make your way back over to the horses, Wait for me there and try not ta get yerselves inta any more trouble."

And with that, he belly crawled back to the nearest rock and peeked down at the ditch, but saw nothing but a roadrunner chasing a snake. He watched as the long-legged bird grabbed the snake in its bill and ran off.

-

Clay was tired of staring at the top of the mesa and was missing his hat that would have at least shaded his eyes somewhat. He'd just wiped sweat from his eyes with the heel of his hand when he noticed a slight protrusion at the side of one of the boulders at the top of the mesa – a protrusion that hadn't been there a moment ago.

Several years' back one of the Indians that worked on his ranch had taught him how to look at the land. "Never stare at one place. Look at the land as one big picture and if anything changes in the picture, you will notice. That is the Indian way."

With that in mind, Clay saw the protrusion move ever so slightly, and smiled.

Clay picked up his rifle - took careful aim and when he was satisfied, he slowly squeezed the trigger and watched as rock chips flew off into the air next to the protrusion.

Matthew jerked his head back and cursed the ranger.

After a moment to calm his nerves, Matthew pushed the rifle barrel around the edge of the rock and pointed it down toward the ditch. Keeping himself hidden, he pulled the trigger four times, then turned and belly crawled back toward where his brothers and the horses were waiting.

In the desert area of Arizona, as in other similar places, sound can be heard for long distances. Thus was the case when the Marlow brothers rode hell bent for leather off the mesa and headed for Phoenix with Mark and Luke complaining about their wounds.

"Just shut up and ride," Matthew yelled. "Do your complain' ta the doctor in Phoenix!"

Clay listened until he could no longer hear the sound of horses running or men's voices, and then stood up. The fact that they had given up and headed in the direction of Phoenix suited him just fine. He was tired of being shot at, and even more tired of shooting people. He could have killed either or both of the Marlow brothers but elected not to. If he'd killed them, then the one that was left would have hightailed it off the mesa and more than likely run for the Mexican border thinking Clay wouldn't follow him there. But, by wounding two of them, the third brother would have to see his brothers got medical help and the closest place was Phoenix.

The first thing he needed to do was find his hat, then he would bring his horses to the water hole and let them drink.

Looking up at the fading sun, he decided to wait until morning to go into Phoenix and hunt down the Marlow brothers. He was tired and hungry and this being possibly the only water hole between here and Phoenix that he knew of, made it a good place to camp.

With two of them wounded, they would still be in Phoenix when he got there. The third brother could possibly head for the border once his brothers were seen to, but he doubted it.

Clay found his hat and beat it against his leg to get the dirt off, then set it on his head. The black stallion had its head up and was staring at him.

Clay put two fingers to his lips and blew.

At the sound of Clay's whistle, the black stallion reared up on his hind legs and let out a shrill whinny, then raced toward his master, leaning his head across Clay's shoulder when he reached him. Clay stroked his neck, and when the buckskin he used as a packhorse and second mount, came to a stop next to the black stallion, Clay reached out his other arm and did the same thing to her.

Both horses liked the attention Clay gave them along with the sugar cubes he sometimes had for them. Clay dug in the pack and came up with two withered apples, and gave one to each horse.

Even though he didn't have all the comforts of home, he made a decent camp and fixed himself a pot of coffee and a small pot of beans with beef jerky, and some fried potatoes for his supper.

After supper, Clay read from a copy of Mark Twain that his wranglers had given him for his last birthday until he felt his eyes drooping. Sleep came quickly.

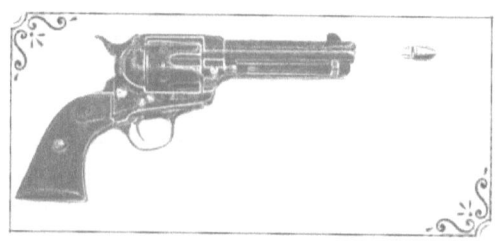

CHAPTER SEVEN

Raymore Gains was a man who played both sides of the fence, depending what suited his fancy at the time. He'd run with the Marlow brothers for a time and had been a deputy sheriff in several small towns in Missouri and Kansas. In Texas, he'd ridden with the Biggs gang and rustled cattle.

A year ago, just a few steps ahead of the law, he'd taken the job of deputy sheriff in Phoenix and when someone standing in the alley mysteriously shot the sheriff in the back, Raymore Gains stepped in and took his place.

As Gains was headed for the bar for his nightly drink he saw the Marlow brothers ride down the street and stop at the doctor's office.

He hurried over and helped Luke off his horse while Matthew helped Mark down from his.

The Marlow brothers were surprised to see their old friend – especially in the role of sheriff.

"What happened?" Gains asked.

"Got us ah Texas Ranger on our tail. He shot Mark and Luke from ambush and we just barely got away. What'er you doin' wearin' ah tin star? You gone and turned honest?" Matthew asked.

"It's a long story. We can discuss it later. Right now, we need to get these two into the doctor's office so he can patch them up. As much as I'd like ta hash over old times, you boys know I can't let you hang around town too long, especially with a ranger dogin' your trail."

Matthew eyed Raymore Gains for a second, then said, "You're right we need ta get these two inta the docs, but then you and me are gonna palaver some. It seems ta me you owe us a favor or two. As I recall, we broke you outta jail twice when you was waitin' ta get your neck stretched.

"I remember," Gains said. "What do you plan on tellin' the doctor?"

Matthew grinned and said, "Why we was way-layed out on the desert by some owlhoot wantin' ta steal what little money we have. We returned fire and barely escaped."

While the doctor was patching up Luke and Mark, Gains and Matthew went next door to the saloon and found a table in the back corner. Caroline, one of the ladies of the night who worked the bar, brought over a bottle of whiskey and three glasses, but the sheriff gave one of the glasses back and told her they needed some privacy. She huffed back to the bar like she'd been insulted and waited for the next rube to come through the batwing doors.

When Gains explained how he'd become sheriff, Matthew shook his head and said, "And you say you never caught the shooter?"

"Nope. Whoever it was just up and disappeared," Raymore Gains said with a straight face as he poured his second glass of whiskey.

"And you're stickin' with that story, I suppose?" Matthew asked.

"And why not. Caroline will vouch that I was with her when the sheriff got shot," Gains said with a grin.

Matthew looked over at Caroline and saw a young woman of about twenty or so who, in his opinion, would say anything the sheriff wanted her to.

After a moment, Gains asked, "How long do you boys plan on staying here in town? Not long I hope. I got the mayor and town council breathin' down my neck already and don't need more trouble."

Matthew drank his second glass of whiskey with one gulp, then looked at his old riding companion. "We'll be ridin' on as soon as the doc says Mark and Luke is well enough ta ride... maybe ah couple of days. But in the meantime, you've got ta do somethin' bout that ranger."

And just what is it you want me to do?" Gains asked with a frown.

Matthew shrugged his shoulders and poured himself a third drink. "Don't care what ya do as long as he can't bother us. Once we're gone, we'll need at least three days head start. Think you can do that?"

The sheriff poured himself another drink and gulped it down, his mind whirling, trying to think of some way to tie up the ranger.

"When do you expect him to ride in?" Gains asked.

"Probably sometime tomorrow," was Matthew's answer. "I reckon he'll spend the night out on the desert and head this way at first light. Took us four hours of hard ridin' ta get here."

The sheriff poured himself another drink.

Matthew signaled Caroline for another bottle.

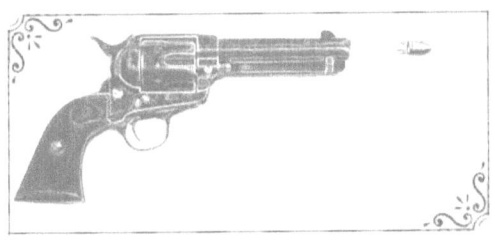

CHAPTER EIGHT

A blazing sun came creeping over the eastern horizon of the Arizona desert, promising another scorching day as Clay rolled out of his bedroll and checked his boots for critters. Snakes and scorpions liked to climb into a man's boots at night and when he tried to put them on in the morning, the critters took umbrage. Many a cowboy had died from not being careful, or wound up with a swollen foot for several days. Clay Brentwood was not one of those men.

After a quick breakfast of bacon, hardtack biscuits soaked up with bacon grease, and coffee, Clay watered his horses, packed up the buckskin, saddled the black stallion and headed west, hoping to end his chase of the Marlow brothers by sometime this very afternoon.

As Clay rode along at a brisk pace, taking advantage of the morning coolness that was getting hotter by the minute, he wondered how his ranch was getting along, knowing full well that other than major decisions it was running smoothly.

Even so, he missed being there, just in case a major decision was needed to be made.

He was anxious to get to Phoenix and get his business over with, but after nearly an hour, he slowed the pace to conserve the horses. A man who didn't take care of his horse in country like this was likely to find himself stranded. A man on foot out here was asking for more trouble than he could handle. If the heat and lack of water, or one of the deadly critters didn't kill you, the Apaches probably would.

Being caught by the Apaches was worse than being snake bit. With a snakebite you'd probably die an agonizing death within a few hours but the Apaches, who had come to hate most white men, delighted in seeing how many torturous days a man could last. After a day or so most white men pleaded and begged to die. The Apache had no respect for a man who could not die with honor and would drag a whiner's death on as long as he could.

Around noon Clay stopped the horses under the lea of an overhang – a slab of rock protruding out from a good-sized outcrop boulder. It wasn't much shade, but a man took advantage of whatever he could find out here.

He took the pack off the buckskin, then unsaddled the black stallion and let them roll while he enjoyed a smoke and a few sips of water, saving most of it for his horses. He carried two, small canvas bags that he put a little grain in and fed his horses, then refilled the canvas bags with water and allowed each horse a drink.

Two hours later, Clay saw the outskirts of Phoenix in the distance and allowed the horses their own pace.

Seeing the promise of food and water, the horses increased their speed to a nice lope.

Clay guessed the first place to check would be the doctor's office. If he got lucky he might find all three of them there.

Clay rode into town on the only road coming from the east and saw a man with a star pinned on his chest, sitting astride a paint horse. Next to him were what he guessed to be three deputies with rifles laying across their laps.

Clay reined in and asked, "You expecting a bunch of outlaws?"

Raymore Gains looked at the man facing him and asked, "You the man who claims to be a Texas Ranger?"

Clay suddenly got a chill up his spine. Why would a sheriff and three deputies be waiting for him at the edge of town? How would he even know of his arrival? The Marlow brothers! What story they had concocted and told the sheriff, he had no idea, but guessed he was soon to find out, and doubted it would be good.

Clay slowly reached into his vest pocket and removed his badge and held it up for the sheriff to see. "Name's Clay Brentwood and yes, I'm a Texas Ranger. I've been trailin' the Marlow brothers all the way from Texas. They're wanted back there for cattle rustling and murder, along with a few other things. They tried to ambush me from on top of a mesa east of here, yesterday. Of course, I shot back and I'm pretty sure I wounded two of them. They snuck off the backside of the mesa and headed this way, hunting for a doctor. I'll only be in town long enough to arrest them, pick up some supplies, and then we'll head back to Texas."

The sheriff had a jaw full of chewing tobacco and spit a stream of brown liquid off to the side of his horse. "Ain't quite the way they tell the story," Gains said.

Clay watched the four men facing him and knew there was trouble brewing, but wasn't quite sure what to do about it. "So, they are here," Clay said. "And if I might ask, what kind of story did you hear, sheriff?"

The sheriff spit another gob of brown liquid onto the road and after wiping his mouth on the back of his shirtsleeve, he said, "They said they was havin' their noon meal when you rode up and began blastin' away, meanin' to rob them of what little money they had. They said it was only a stroke of luck that they got away and have no idea why you'd want to rob them, and have no idea why you'd be trail'in them in the first place, if that's what you were doin'?"

"That's a lie," Clay said, his eyes growing hard.

Raymore Gain's eyes instantly took on a cold hardness of their own that gave Clay the impression he would enjoy pulling his gun and shooting Clay off his horse. The man had a short temper and didn't like being talked back to. He was used to people he could ramrod, but Clay Brentwood was not one of those men and it bothered him to no end.

The stare lasted only a moment before the sheriff regained control. "Is it now?" Gains said. "I've known the Marlow brothers for several years and have always known them to be upright citizens; but I don't know you from Adam, so why should I believe you?"

"I told you who I am. I'm a Texas Ranger in pursuit of the Marlow brothers for crimes committed in Texas," Clay said, "and I'm not in the habit of lying."

Clay saw the look flash back into the sheriff's eyes again and for just an instant thought the man might go for his gun and readied himself for a shootout, but once again, the man pulled in the reins on his temper and let the hint of a grin appear on his lips.

"Or so you say," the sheriff said, slowly drawing his pistol and pointing it at Clay's chest. "How do I know you really are who you say you are? Maybe it's you who is the murderer and cattle thief. Just maybe you killed the real ranger and took his identity and claim to be him when it suits your purpose, like right now. Put your hands in the air real slow like and keep 'em there mister whoever you are."

Clay wondered if he could draw and shoot the sheriff before the sheriff could fire, then knew the folly of that thought because all three deputies had their rifles trained on his chest and he couldn't shoot all of them before they put lead in him.

After a long moment, Clay raised his hands in the air and said, "You're makin' a big mistake, sheriff. While you're wastin' time over me, you're letting three really bad men run free to murder and steal from more innocent folks. If you want ta know the truth about me, send a wire to Captain Bill McDaniel, head of the rangers back in Austin, he'll confirm who I am."

Raymore Gains never took his eyes off of Clay, but said, "Grant, get his pistol and rifle and be careful about it."

Grant Everheart was a young man of around twenty. He had mean eyes and an attitude that showed Clay he was only a couple of steps ahead of being an outlaw himself. He was in bad need of a haircut and shave and as he got close, Clay could smell whiskey on his breath.

Clay sat very still as Grant rode over next to him and lifted Clay's pistol from his holster and pulled his rifle from its scabbard. The young man was hoping Clay would try something, anything. Just a twitch would set him off. Clay could see murder in Grant's eyes and knew he needed to sit quietly – at least for now.

"Well lookie here," Grant said, holding up Clay's rifle so all could see the canvas covering the barrel. "Looks like he likes shootin' people from a ways off without the sun gleamin' off his rifle barrel and warnin' his victims."

Raymore Gains stared at Clay for a long moment, then said, "Now ain't that interesting. Covering your rifle barrel like that appears to me to be somethin' ah back shooter would do, don't it?"

Raymore Gains had been searching his mind for some way to delay the ranger to allow his friends to escape; something other than the slim excuse he had, which could be cleared up with a wire to Austin. The canvas on the rifle barrel was what he'd been looking for. It was enough for him to say that even if he was a ranger, maybe he was a ranger gone bad. It was not hard evidence, but enough to hold him for the few days the Marlow brothers had asked for.

"Guess your bluff ain't workin' quite like you thought it would mister whoever you are. Lock your fingers together on the top of your head and don't try nothin' stupid," the sheriff said, then turned his head. "Gabriel, take the reins of his horse and lead him into town. I want him behind bars til I can get this figured out."

Gabriel was an overweight man of about thirty who was in need of a bath and a shave, along with some clean clothes. The ones he had on needed burning. Clay could smell him as he rode over and took the black stallion's reins. If this was the best the sheriff could do for deputies, he felt sorry for the people of Phoenix.

The black stallion didn't like the pungent odor of the man and jerked back, almost pulling the reins out of Gabriel's hands.

Gabriel fought for control and Clay had to speak to his horse before it would allow the man to lead him.

All four men admired the black stallion. They each thought he would be a horse to ride the river with, and wondered how they could figure a way to have him for themselves.

As they rode toward the jail, the sheriff wondered if there was a way he could kill the ranger and get away with it? He could then claim the horse for his own.

CHAPTER NINE

From the side of an upstairs window of the hotel where he couldn't be seen from the street, Matthew Marlow watched as the sheriff and his deputies came riding into town with the ranger in tow. He watched until he saw them enter the jail then stepped back into the room.

"Shake ah leg!" he yelled at his two brothers who were nursing a bottle of cheap who shot john. Pain medicine they'd called it.

"What'er you so riled up about?" Mark asked with glassy eyes and a bit of a slur.

"Yeah, what?" Luke, who was well on his way to being pie-eyed, asked with a stupid look on his face.

By now, neither of the brothers were feeling any pain.

"Gains just brought that ranger inta town and put him in jail. I'm goin' down ta the saloon and meet him and see how long of ah head start we'll get. Get your gear together and I'll see you down at the livery stable – and be quick about it."

Mark shook his head. "You heard what the doc said, we's ta rest up ah couple of days before we can do any serious ridin'."

Luke drunkenly nodded his head in agreement.

"Fine," Matthew said as he grabbed up his gear and headed for the door. "You can stay here and wind up with your neck in a noose when Gains has ta turn that ranger loose. And good riddance to the both of ya as far as I'm concerned."

"Now wait ah minute," Mark said, jumping unsteadily to his feet. "You ain't gonna leave us here alone, are ya? We're the Marlow brothers and we stick together. You said that way back when we were just young'uns."

Matthew had his hand on the doorknob when he turned and looked back over his shoulder at his two brothers. "Brothers or no brothers, I ain't stickin' around here ta face that ranger. Now make up your minds. Either come with me now or face the consequences on your own."

Mark looked at Luke, who in reality, was in no condition to ride, then back at his older brother. "I'll need help ta get him down ta the livery."

Matthew thought for a moment, then said, "Alright. I'll come back as soon as I meet with Gains. But he'd better be ready or we leave without 'im.

-

Clay took one look at the cell and decided the inside of his horse barn was cleaner.

The sheriff opened the cell door and ushered Clay inside. "I know it ain't much but owl hoots don't deserve ta be treated like this is some fancy hotel," he said as he turned the key and locked the door.

"Food ain't much ta brag about, either, but supper's somewhere around six," the sheriff said as he walked back to his office.

Clay picked up the straw mattress and filthy blanket and tossed them into the corner of the cell, as far away from the bed as he could get them and watched as bedbugs scampered around the heap, then ran back to the mattress.

Clay sat down on the wooden framework where the mattress and blanket used to be and rolled a cigarette and lit it, wondering if the sheriff was in cahoots with the Marlow brothers. He said he'd known them for some time and thought them to be upright citizens, which anyone who knew anything about them, knew that was a lie.

It was the only reasonable explanation he could come up with. Otherwise, the sheriff would have no reason not to believe he was who he said he was.

Now that that was set in his mind, how he was going to get out of this jail was his next consideration.

Clay stood up and walked over to the window, which was nothing more than an opening in the wall with steel bars to prevent anyone from climbing through. Next to the jail was an alley that was wide enough for him to see the street and the front of the saloon.

In less than half a minute, Clay saw the oldest of the Marlow brothers come down the sidewalk and enter the saloon. A few minutes later, he saw the sheriff hurry across the street and enter the saloon.

Coincidence, Clay wondered shaking his head? He thought not. If he needed any proof that they were more than acquaintances, this had done it for him.

Anger welled up inside Clay and he grabbed the bars and began to shake them.

One of the bars moved slightly. Not a lot, but enough for Clay to take notice.

Clay looked back toward the office and saw two of the deputies' playing cards. Where the third one was he didn't know, but guessed him to be gone. Turning back to the window, he reached into his pants pocket and pulled out his pocket knife. They'd taken his guns, but had not searched him further - their mistake.

Being as quiet as he could, Clay stuck the point of his pocketknife into the adobe wall next to the bar and began to chip away small pieces. The building was old and the work was not difficult – and after half an hour, the bottom of the bar was loose enough to pull out. He was about to start of the top part of the bar when he heard a noise and hurried over and sat down on the bare bunk.

"We just made ah fresh pot of coffee," the deputy called Gabriel said from the office doorway. "You want ah cup?"

"Sure," Clay said with a slight grin.

Gabriel grunted and turned back into the office.

Clay looked toward the barred window, but couldn't see any evidence that he'd been chipping at the adobe or that the bar had been tampered with.

When the deputy came back with a cup of steaming coffee, Clay started to get up but the deputy waved him back. "Stay seated. I ain't takin' no chances with you. I'll set the cup on the floor near the bars and you can get it after I'm back in the doorway. You understand?"

Clay nodded his head and waited.

When Gabriel had stepped back a few feet, he waved his hand at Clay, indicating he could approach the bars. Clay stood up and walked over to where the coffee sat. It smelled good and as he stooped down and reached through the bars to grasp the cup, Gabriel ran back over and kicked the cup, sending it across the room, then stomped down on Clay's hand.

Clay jerked his pain-ridden hand from under Gabriel's boot and clamored to his feet, reaching through the bars with his good hand, grabbing for Gabriel's throat.

Gabriel stepped back just inches from being strangled. His eyes were wide with fear and he hurriedly retreated to the safety of the office.

Clay walked over and sat back down on his bunk, flexing his fingers. They hurt like hell, but none were broken. How men like him and the sheriff ever got their jobs was a mystery, remembering a few years back when he was unjustly thrown in jail back in Texas and what had been done to him there. He had almost died that time.

Clay heard a noise and looked up. Gabriel was standing in the doorway with a sneer on his face. "Don't go askin' for no supper cause you ain't gettin' any, but you're free ta eat all the cockroaches you want," the deputy said as he closed the door between the cells and the office. Clay could hear him laughing.

By now it was beginning to get dark outside and Clay figured he could go without a meal or two and still survive. After all, he'd done it before. The good part was, he could work on the window bars without being bothered, or at least he hoped he could.

-

Matthew was sitting at a table toward the back when the sheriff came in through the batwing doors and looked around. They made eye contact, but instead of coming back to where Matthew sat, the sheriff walked over and leaned against the top of the bar and said, "Whiskey."

Matthew waited while the sheriff had two whiskeys before he stood up and made his way over to the bar and stopped, casual like, next to the sheriff and ordered a beer. He would not be doing any serious drinking until they were far away from Phoenix and safely away from the ranger.

Looking straight ahead, Matthew took a swallow of beer, then quietly said, "I see you have him in custody."

"For the time being," Raymore Gains said, "but I don't know how long I can hold him."

"We'll be leaving within the hour," Matthew said. "And thanks."

"Don't thank me yet. Just get the hell outta Phoenix as quick as you can, and I don't want to know where you're goin'."

Matthew finished his beer and turned for the door. "Until we meet again, my friend, until we meet again."

The sheriff poured himself another shot and made a, "harrumph," sound.

-

Clay was picking at the top bar when he saw three riders go past the alley – two of them were slumped over, riding awkwardly. He had just blown some small chunks of adobe chips and dust off the windowsill where they landed in the dirt outside the jail when he heard a noise coming from the office. Reacting to the noise, Clay walked over and sat down on his bunk.

He'd been there only a few seconds when the door opened and the sheriff came in with a plate in one hand and a cup of coffee in the other.

"Stand up and walk over and face the window and don't turn around til I tell ya to, the sheriff ordered.

Clay did as he was told and heard the cell door open, then close. Next, he heard the sheriff walk back toward the office.

"Okay, you can turn around now. There's supper and coffee there if you want it. If you don't, one of my deputies will eat it."

As Clay turned around, the sheriff closed the door, leaving the cells in darkness. The only light was what little came through the window.

Clay looked down and could see a tin plate of pinto beans and fried potatoes and a cup of coffee sitting on the floor just inside the cell. Next to the plate was a hard tack biscuit.

Although it wasn't a big steak with all the trimmings, it tasted good and he cleaned the plate before turning it sideways and sticking it through the bars where he sat it on the floor outside the cell. When he'd finished his coffee, he did the same with the cup, then called out, "I'm done."

The young deputy with the mean eyes came in and retrieved the plate, fork and cup, without a word, and closed the door behind him.

Clay grinned. He guessed Gabriel hadn't informed the sheriff he was to get no supper, or maybe he had and the sheriff overruled him.

Clay rolled and lit a cigarette and considered his situation. He could sit here for god only knew how long, waiting for the sheriff to contact his boss, which would allow the Marlow brothers to make their get-away. They could go in most any direction – California was to the west, Nevada to the north and Mexico to the south. Or, he could try and get at least three of the bars loose enough to pull out so he could escape.

The big problem would not be finding the Marlow brothers trail, but out distancing the posse the sheriff was sure to put together. He would be hard pressed to find the Marlow brothers trail and shake the posse at the same time.

First things first, he thought as he stood up and walked back to the window. He only needed to loosen one more bar. He was fairly sure he would be able to squeeze through the opening without much trouble or noise.

Clay figured it was close to ten o'clock when he eased himself down onto the alley and moved off through the darkness in the direction of the livery barn.

The hostler had long since gone to bed when Clay entered the barn through the back door. The interior was dark but when Clay got close, the black stallion smelled him and nickered.

Clay rubbed his nose to quiet him down, and then found his saddle and retrieved the extra pistol he kept there. After sticking the pistol in his waist belt, he saddled the black, and loaded the buckskin as quietly as he could.

Clay was just leading his horses out of the stall when the hostler stepped into the barn and asked, "Who's there?" He was holding a rifle in his hands.

Clay drew his pistol and walked up to the old man who ran the livery and pointed it at him.

The old man's eyes went wide and as frail as he was, he wasn't about to put up a fight. He'd never actually shot anybody. The rifle had just been for show.

"Stay real quiet like and you won't get hurt. I've got no truck with you, so I'm going to tie you up so you can say you tried to stop me but, I got the drop on you. I'm also going to leave you forty dollars for your trouble and that rifle. Do you understand?"

The old man swallowed, licked his lips and nodded his head up and down.

Clay pulled some money from his pants pocket and counted out forty dollars and stuffed it into the man's shirt pocket before tying him to one of the poles that supported the barn. When he'd finished, Clay untied the kerchief from around the man's neck and then tied it around his mouth as a gag. "Just to make things look good," Clay, said.

The old man nodded his head and made the semblance of a smile. "Bust ob luk," the old man mumbled through the gag.

Clay smiled and said, "Thanks."

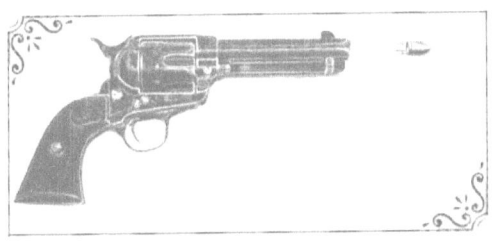

CHAPTER TEN

-

A little after six the following morning, the sheriff strode into his office and stood with his hands on his hips. Grant, his youngest deputy was leaned back in a chair with his feet propped up on the desk, filling the room with his snoring. The front door hadn't even been locked.

The sheriff walked over and opened the door to the cells to check on his prisoner and stopped dead in his tracks. The cell was empty and three of the bars from the window were missing.

Raymore Gains was an angry man when he approached his sleeping deputy and kicked the chair out from under him.

Grant landed on his back and his head made a thudding sound when it hit the wooden floor.

Grant climbed slowly to his feet, rubbing the back of his head. "What'ya do that for?"

"Just wanted to ask you a question," the sheriff said, calmly.

"Well you didn't need to kick the chair out from under me to do that, did ya?" Grant asked, wiping sleep from his eyes.

When the sheriff said nothing, Grant asked, "So what's your question, sheriff?"

Raymore Gains worked hard at holding his temper and when he thought he had it under control, he said, "Oh, I was just wondering how our prisoner was doin'? Wonderin' if he got ah good night's sleep?"

Grant got a questioning look on his face and asked, "How would I know? Last I saw of him he was sittin' on the edge of his bunk with the mattress and blanket layin' over in the corner. If I was to guess, I'd say, none to comfortable. Why do you ask?"

The sheriff looked down at the floor and said, "Why don't you go have a look for yourself, then come back and tell me."

Shaking his head, Grant ambled over to the doorway and looked in at the cells, then yelled, "He's gone!"

"Your dammed right he's gone. While you were sittin' here with your feet propped up on the desk, dreaming about whiskey and prostitutes, your prisoner, the one you were supposed to be guarding, somehow tore the bars out of the window without waking you up - and escaped!" Raymore Gains yelled.

-

They found the hostler tied to the one of the posts inside the barn, with a gag in his mouth and both the ranger's horses, gone.

"What happened, Homer?" the sheriff asked after untying him and removing the gag.

The old man rubbed his arms where he pretended the rope had cut into them and then rubbed his mouth. "I need some coffee before I do any talking," Homer said heading for the front door of the barn.

In the restaurant, Homer sipped his coffee, smacked his toothless lips then said, "It was sometime in the middle of the night when I heard ah noise in the barn and when I went to see, that ranger fella stuck ah pistol under my nose and tole me ta keep my mouth shut. He looked like he meant business, so I did. Then he tied me up and gagged me, and went out the back door. Don't know where he went after that."

Grant scratched his head and asked. "Where'd he get a gun?"

"How would I know?" Homer said, taking another sip of coffee and waving to the waitress. "I'm hungry. You mind if I eat my breakfast in peace, sheriff? It's been a long night."

Looking back at the sheriff, Homer said, "And by the way, he took my rifle and all my ammunition."

The sheriff stood up and grabbed Grant by his shirt, yanking him to his feet, then looked down at the hostler. "Do whatever you want; we're leaving."

"But sheriff," Grant wailed. "What about us havin' some breakfast too?"

"After what you did, you don't deserve any breakfast. In fact, I don't think I'm gonna let you eat again until we've got that ranger back in a cell. Now go round up the others and get our horses saddled. We've got a long day ahead of us."

-

At the edge of town, Clay woke up the owner of a small Mexican cantina and bought some basic supplies from him to fill out what he already had, explaining why he needed them in the middle of the night.

The small man who came out to see who was knocking on his door was not unhappy to be awakened to make a sale, especially to a gringo who had outfoxed the sheriff and had money to pay for what he bought.

The sheriff looked at Mexicans as though they were to be treated like animals and extorted protection money from the storeowner every week.

Being a slight built man of fifty-eight years of age, he was no match for the evil sheriff, but wished someday someone would come along and do away with him, and here, standing in front of him, was the answer to his prayers.

"We'll just keep this under our hat," Clay said to Raphael, the owner of the cantina. "If the sheriff comes around asking questions, you've never seen me, right?"

"Si, Senor. I have been sleeping through the night. How could I have seen or heard anyone?"

"One more question, my friend," Clay said before leaving. "Yesterday, three mean looking hombres left town riding in this direction. Did you happen to see them?"

Raphael thought for only a moment before frowning. "Si Senor, I know who you speak of. They came into my cantina and ordered whiskey and something to eat and told me to be quick about it. Two of them were wounded and bleeding. They ate my food, drank my tequila and then the older one, Matthew, I think the others called him, knocked me down, pulled his *pistola* and pointed it at my head while the others emptied my money box. I will not forget those three, Senor."

"That would be the three men I'm after," Clay said, nodding his head. "How much did they take?" Clay asked.

"My small cantina does not make a lot of money, Senor, maybe twenty dollars?"

When Clay paid for his supplies, he put and extra twenty dollars on the counter.

Raphael eyed the money and said, "You do not have to do this, Senor."

Clay ignored the response and asked, "They didn't happen to mention where they were headed, did they?

Raphael grinned and said, "Si, Senor. I heard them talking about how the sheriff was holding a Texas Ranger in his jail so they could escape and the older one said they should leave a.... how did he say it...? A false trail for when you came looking for them.

"One of the others said they should make it look like they were going to Mexico, then when the time was right, turn and go to California. Yes, I'm sure that's what they said."

"Thank you, mi amigo, you've just saved me ah lot of riding," Clay said, pulling an extra ten-dollar gold piece out of his pocket and handing it to Raphael.

The small, Mexican man looked at the gold coin and his eyes grew wide. "Oh no, Senor, I cannot take this just for telling you what I heard; this is too much."

"Keep it," Clay said with a grin. "Maybe it will help make up for what the sheriff takes from you – and remember, not a word to the sheriff about my being here."

"He will get no information from me, *Senor*, and *muchas gracias*. May you catch the bad men and no harm come to you," Raphael said, sticking out his hand.

Raphael stood watching as Clay mounted the black stallion and rode away. He was about to go back inside when his wife walked out and stood next to him.

"He is one of the good gringos," she said, staring into the darkness.

"Si," Raphael said, putting his arm around his wife's shoulders. "He is one of the good ones."

When Clay was out of sight, they turned and, arm in arm, walked back into their small store.

"Make some coffee, I think the sheriff will be here, soon," Raphael said, grinning.

CHAPTER ELEVEN

-

Raphael and his wife, Francisca, were just cleaning up from the breakfast crowd when Raymore Gains and his thug deputies came in, ordering something to eat.

Francisca looked at her husband and he rolled his eyes and shrugged his frail shoulders as if to say, 'Did I not tell you?'

Francisca also knew she had to do as the sheriff said, or he and his men would beat up Raphael and maybe even kill him.

While Francisca was preparing food for the sheriff and his deputies, Raphael served free tequila to them, hoping they would eat and leave.

Raymore Gains looked around and said, "Big breakfast crowd, Raphael?"

"Not so big, Senor Sheriff," Raphael said, trying not to look the sheriff in the eyes.

Raymore Gains stood up and walked over behind the bar and pulled out the moneybox. "I'll just have ah look-see for myself, if you don't mind?"

"Of course, Senor Sheriff, see for yourself. There is very little. Three gringos came by yesterday and took all the money I had," Raphael said - glad he had hidden the money the Texas ranger had given him in a place where the sheriff would never think to look – deep in the barrel of raw pinto beans.

Raymore Gains knew who the three gringos were that had taken Raphael's money and was not surprised. "Well, it ain't much, but it'll have ta do," he said, stuffing the few dollars into his shirt pocket.

While they were eating, Raymore Gains motioned for Raphael to come to the table and when he got there, Raymore said, "Ah gringo might have come ridin' past here during the night. You see or hear anything?"

Raphael knew he'd promised not to say anything but couldn't help himself. "It is funny you mention it, Senor Sheriff. I was outside having to relieve myself. The moon was up and as I stood there, a man, I could not tell if he was a gringo or not, but he was leading a pack horse and riding very fast like the devil himself was chasing him."

"Did you see which way he went?" Raymore Gains asked, a gleam of anticipation in his eyes.

"As I said, Senor Sheriff, the moon was very bright and there were many stars. At the fork in the road, he turned and rode away in the direction of Nogales."

Raphael watched the sheriff, hoping he would believe his lie.

-

The truth was, Raphael was not lying. Expecting the sheriff and his posse to be on his trail, Clay had taken the fork toward Nogales, just as the Marlow boys had done.

Being Indian trained as a tracker by one of the Indians who worked for him; Clay was able to distinguish two tracks that kept showing up on the dirt packed road. One had a scar like mark on the left rear side of the shoe and the other had an x mark on the front of the shoe, probably put there by the blacksmith who made the shoe. Many blacksmiths put marks on the shoes they made to identify their work.

In addition to tracking what he believed were tracks made by the Marlow brothers Clay also kept an eye on his back trail, looking for a dust trail to let him know if a posse was coming after him. He also looked ahead and to the sides for a place to fort up in case he had to fight, but so far, the only thing he could see was tall saguaro cactus and desert brush to hide behind, which wasn't much.

It was getting late in the afternoon when Clay suddenly realized the tracks he'd been following were no longer to be seen.

Turning around, Clay studied the far distance behind him and thought he saw evidence of a small dust cloud, but it was still a long way behind him. He urged the black stallion into a steady walking pace as he studied the ground.

Clay had gone close to half a mile when he spotted where the tracks turned off toward the west. He looked in that direction and saw a group of hills in the far distance.

His gut told him this is where the Marlow brothers had turned off. In the distance, still far behind him, the dust cloud was growing larger. That would be the sheriff and his deputies, Clay thought to himself.

Clay found it ironic that as a lawman, he was having to dodge the law just like a criminal would do. Of course, this would never happen if all law enforcement officers were on the up and up. The sorry truth was - there were far too many like Raymore Gains, men who were former outlaws themselves and had no problem using the law for their own gains.

Clay climbed down and rummaged through his pack on the buckskin until he found what he was looking for, some precut pieces of sheepskin and some rawhide straps.

With the wool side down, he covered each of the horse's hoofs and tied them in place. Next, he picked up a piece of brush and using it like a broom, erased his tracks for a good hundred feet, then mounted the black stallion and headed toward the western hills with the buckskin following close behind – leaving virtually no tracks for the posse to follow.

Clay had disappeared behind a low hill and was viewing his back trail through his binoculars when the posse reached the spot where he turned west - and watched as they kept on going. He chuckled to himself. If only everyone who had ever tracked him had been so easy to lose. They would ride south for a bit longer, but knowing the kind of man the sheriff was, he would soon call a halt and turn back. He couldn't afford to be away from town for long periods of time. Besides, he'd somewhat held up his end of the bargain he had with the Marlow brothers.

As sure as Clay predicted, he watched as the sheriff come to a stop and hold up his hand.

"Hold up men," he said. This is as far as we go."

"But what about the prisoner?" Grant asked feeling guilty about being the one who had allowed the ranger to escape. "He's gettin' away!"

"So, let him," the sheriff shrugged as he turned his horse around. "I told the Marlow boys I would hold him as long as I could and that's just what I did. He's their problem now."

Clay watched as they rode back north and when they were only a trail of dust in the sky, he put the field glasses away and climbed aboard the black stallion and followed the tracks of the two horseshoes headed west, toward the mountains.

Clay was searching for a place to make camp for the night when he heard a whimpering sound and pulled back on the reins of the black stallion. The horse's ears were standing straight up and Clay knew he'd also heard the sound.

A yellow-red sun was gracing the far horizon giving a burnt look to the desert and Clay almost didn't see the dog until he was right up on him because of the dogs coloring. His fur was brownish-tan and dirty white. Clay didn't know much about dogs but guessed it to be a mixed breed of maybe Collie and Shepard along with some coyote thrown in, but he wasn't sure.

The dog looked up at Clay and whimpered again. He was lean and had a gaunt look. There was an arrow sticking out of his hip and Clay's nerves immediately went on alert. The apaches were known to eat dogs and horses, and it was said they were particularly fond of mule meat, but right now, Clay was interested in whoever it was that shot this dog.

Clay felt his adversary before he actually saw or heard him and that reaction was what saved his life.

The Apache brave had crawled up close enough to leap from the ground and attack Clay with his knife.

Clay turned just as the brave made a downward thrust with his knife, and the blade made only a thin slice down across Clay's left shoulder.

Clay stepped to the side and drew his own knife. He could have easily pulled his pistol and shot the brave but didn't for two reasons. First, there might be other braves nearby and he wanted no part of fighting a bunch of bloodthirsty young Indians looking to take a scalp. And second, the Marlow brothers might be in the vicinity and be alerted by his gunfire. Either way, Clay was forced to fight this brave with only his knife.

Clay and the young brave circled each other, each looking for an opening. Clay didn't want to kill him; he had nothing against him, but for some reason he didn't want to see the dog die and wind up in the brave's belly.

The young Apache brave made several slashes at Clay, which he avoided.

Clay saw several openings where he could have killed the inexperienced brave, but chose not to end his life - his mind racing for another solution.

Clay stopped his circling and stood up straight, placing his knife back in its sheath then raised his hands, palms forward. He knew most Apaches could speak Spanish from having so much contact with them through the Mexicans and Comancheros. And since he didn't speak Apache, which there were several dialects, he decided to give Spanish a try. "You are a very brave warrior and I do not want to die today; nor do I want to fight over this dog. Look at him - he is far too skinny to make a decent meal. I will buy him from you. I have silver."

The young brave looked at the white man and shook his head. "This is not your dog. He is a mongrel who has been around our camp for many weeks, looking for scraps. Yesterday he stole a piece of meat from my son's hand and ran away. I will feed this mongrel to my family to teach him not to steal from me."

Clay sighed and said, "But then you will have nothing. If you let me buy him from you, just think of the things you can buy for your family – things that will last, like new blankets or coats to keep away the cold. Your family will look up to you for being such a good trader," Clay said, hoping the brave would rather have money than the dog."

To Clay's disappointment, the brave shook his head and said, "I do not want your white man's money."

"What then?" Clay asked.

"I will take your guns and bullets," the brave said, pointing toward Clay's stomach where the pistol rested in his waistband.

Clay looked the young Indian in the eyes and said, "This I will not do." Clay pulled his badge out of his vest pocket and held it up so the brave could see it. "I am a Texas Ranger and I am following three very bad men, and I need my guns, but I do have a sack of sugar you can have. I'm sure your wife and children will be happy with you for bringing back a sack of sugar."

"How big is bag?" the brave asked, staring at the white man with the badge.

Clay walked over to the packhorse and rummaged around until he came up with a two-pound sack of sugar. He pulled it out and handed it to the young brave along with a small sack of salt. "I will also give you this salt."

The young Apache brave poured some sugar into the palm of his hand and put it in his mouth and immediately, grinned. Next, he tasted the salt and nodded his head. "You may take skinny mongrel dog. I will take the sugar and salt," he said, feeling he had made a good trade. After all, the dog wasn't really his anyway and if this white man was stupid enough to give away salt and sugar for a dying dog he would take it. "Dog too skinny to eat, anyway," he said as he turned away.

By now the sun had set and the moon was coming up in the eastern sky. Clay looked down at the dog and back up, but the Apache brave had already faded into the darkness.

After seeing to his horses, Clay made camp and put some water on to boil then carried the dog over and laid him next to the fire. After a careful examination, he saw the arrow was stuck in the dog's hind leg, but not buried deep.

"Easy boy," Clay said, rubbing the dog's shoulder and side. "This is gonna hurt a bit and I hope you don't try to bite me, but that arrow has got ta come out."

The dog looked up at Clay as though he understood every word and only made a small whimpering sound.

Clay swallowed and took hold of the arrow with one hand and patted the dog's shoulder with the other, then jerked upward and pulled the arrow out of the dog's leg.

The dog let out a yelp, but didn't try to bite Clay.

"Good boy," Clay said as he tossed the arrow onto the fire.

By now the water was hot. Clay cleaned the wound and then poured some purple horse liniment on the wound and said, "I reckon that's going to have to do ol' son. You lay here and rest while I put some grub on and we can both have ourselves a bite to eat. How does that sound?"

The dog reached his head over and licked Clay on the back of his hand. Clay, in turn, scratched the dog's ears.

Clay made fried potatoes, a small pot of beans, and threw in some dried beef for good measure and when it was ready, he made up two plates – one for him and one for the dog.

He placed the plate near the dog's head and said, "Don't know if man food is to your liking, but it's all I have to offer right now."

Clay walked over and picked up his plate and as he ate a mouthful; he glanced over at the dog and saw him standing on three legs, eating from the plate.

Clay smiled and continued to eat his supper. He guessed the dog wasn't going to die after all.

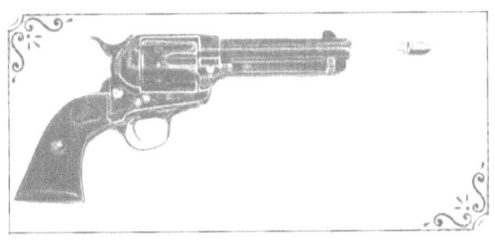

CHAPTER TWELVE

-

While Clay was rescuing a mongrel dog of questionable breeding from a young Apache brave, several miles further on, the Marlow brothers were not faring so well.

Phoenix sits in a bowl called, the Valley of the Sun, surrounded by a mountain range on the north and east. To the west for many miles, it's a dry, arid place where only the hardiest of people can survive. The Apache stay mostly in the mountainous areas far to the west, but know the desert like the back of their hand, and love to prey on whites who try to settle here or cross the barren desert without the protection of the blue coats.

Due to the high heat, most travelers prefer not to stop here. Instead, they dream of California and the ocean where the days are pleasant and the nights are cool. However, if not part of a wagon train, your chances of making it are slight.

Leaving Phoenix, the Marlow brothers had ridden south toward Nogales which is the border town between Arizona and Mexico, hoping to mislead the ranger when he was finally released and came looking for them, which Matthew figured he would do.

Late in the afternoon, they turned west and into the Sonora desert filled with giant saguaro cacti, snakes, reptiles, very little water, and Apaches.

Both Mark and Luke begged their older brother to slow down so they could tend their wounds and get some much-needed rest.

"We'll make camp when we reach those mountains, yonder," he yelled over his shoulder, urging his horse to run faster.

Traveling in the desert can be very misleading since sometimes things look a lot closer than they really are. The mountain range Matthew was indicating was still more than a two-day ride, although it looked much closer – at least in Matthew's mind.

By the time the sun disappeared over the horizon and the moon had climbed into the sky, the temperature had dropped considerably. The fast pace Matthew was setting was somewhat easier on the horses, but not much. The animals were in desperate need of food, water and rest and running for hours on end was slowly taking its toll.

When Mark's horse stumbled and nearly fell, Mark yelled at his brother. "We've got to stop. My horse ain't gonna last much longer and if he goes down, we'll be stranded out here in the middle of nowhere!"

"Do what you want," Matthew yelled over his shoulder, "but I'm goin' on," and kept on riding.

Less than a quarter of a mile later, Matthew's horse gave up and fell, sending Matthew sprawling onto the ground.

Matthew came to his feet and ran over and kicked his horse and yelled, "Get up you no good critter. I ain't done with you, yet!"

His yelling did no good because he was yelling at ears that could no longer hear. The poor horse had run itself to death.

When Luke came to a stop next to his brother, he asked, "Your horse die on you?"

Matthew looked up at Luke and said "Get down."

Luke got a bewildered look on his face and asked, "Why?"

"Cause I need your horse, that's why! Now get off, dammit!"

"No!" Luke yelled.

Matthew was out of his head and reached up and pulled his younger brother off his saddle and tossed him to the ground, then climbed onto Luke's horse and put his heels into the horse's sides.

The almost done in horse moved forward as fast as he could, leaving Luke standing in the desert staring after his horse and his brother.

Within minutes Mark came walking up to Luke, leading his own worn out horse. He stopped and looked down at the dead horse, and in the moonlight couldn't tell that it was Matthew's horse. "Your horse die on you, did he?"

"No," Luke said, staring wearily at his brother.

"If that ain't your horse, then whose horse is it?" Mark asked belligerently.

"It's Mathew's horse," Luke said matter of factly.

"Well, if that's Matthew's horse, where's yours?"

After a long pause the answer filtered its way into Marks head and he said, "He didn't do what I think he did, did he?"

"If you're thinkin' Matthew took my horse and left me stranded out here, you'd be guessin' right, big brother," Luke said, shrugging his shoulders.

The two brothers looked at each other and knew they had no other choice but to keep going. Side-by-side with Mark leading his horse, they began to walk toward the mountain in the far distance.

The two wounded Marlow brothers had been struggling across the desert for close to two hours when they saw the glitter of a small fire in the distance. They stopped and stared at the glow for some time before deciding to move on, hoping it was their brother's fire and not an Indian's campfire.

A little over an hour later, Mark and Luke saw their older brother Matthew sitting next to a small fire. Luke's dead horse was laying nearby with a slab of meat cut off the hindquarter and roasting over the fire.

As they walked closer, Matthew looked up and said, "Well, look what the dogs dragged in. My two younger brothers have come ta pay ah visit. I suppose both of ya are hungry and want me ta share my meat with you, don't ya?"

"That meat came from my horse, the one you stole from me, big brother!" Luke yelled.

Matthew stood up and for the first time noticed Mark's horse standing close to the edge of the firelight. "Well, well, well," he said with a grin building on his face. "I see you brought me transportation, so's I can get outta here."

"That's my horse and you can't have her," Mark said, reaching for the pistol on his hip, but did so an instant too late.

Matthew had always been the fastest draw of the three of them, and saw what was coming and outdrew his younger brother.

Matthew stood looking at his two younger brothers, pointing his pistol in their direction. They looked like they were on their last legs. He could see red spots on their shirts where their wounds had started to bleed again and their skin was burned from the desert sun.

"You can't both ride that horse in the condition you're in. You'll be lucky ta last through the night, so neither of you will be needin' transportation come mornin', anyhow."

Motioning with his pistol, he told his brothers, "Now, real easy like, and with only two fingers, lift them peashooters out of their holsters and toss 'em over here near my feet – and no funny tricks. You might be my brothers but out here it's the law of the fittest that survives, which at present is yours truly."

In unison, both brothers lifted their pistols from their holsters and tossed them at their brother's feet.

Mark and Luke looked at each other and wondered if their brother was going to shoot them.

"Not that it'll be doin' ya much good," Matthew said, shaking his head. "but I suppose you should get ah last meal."

Matthew saw the looks on their faces and laughed. "Go on over there by the fire and get somethin' ta eat and some coffee too. I don't reckon I need ta shoot ya, that ranger already took care of that."

Matthew sliced off another piece of horsemeat and put it over the fire, then poured a cup of coffee and waited for the meat to cook.

When they finished eating, Mathew turned them back-to-back in a sitting position and tied them together.

"Nothin' personal, you understand; just ah precaution so you can't jump me durin' the night while your horse and me get some rest," Matthew said with a chuckle.

When he was sure his brothers were tied securely, Matthew dropped down on his makeshift bedroll and pulled his hat over his eyes and was soon snoring.

-

A ray of light sneaked under Matthew's hat brim and drove its way directly into Matthew's left eye.

Opening his right eye, he saw it was morning and felt the urge to relieve himself.

He reached up and lifted his hat from over his eyes and saw his two brothers, still sitting back-to-back and still tied together. The only thing different was, they both had gags in their mouths - gags he hadn't put there.

Looking around, his heart began to pound. Staring back at him was at least a dozen Apache braves. They were all eating horsemeat.

Matthew had met only three Indians and that had been back in Oklahoma. They were reservation Indians and had been friendly, but these braves didn't look friendly. He was pretty sure they were the dreaded Comancheros or Chiricahua he'd heard so much about, and felt wetness in his pants.

One of the braves noticed his condition and nudged the brave next to him who pointed a finger and said something Matthew couldn't understand, but whatever it was, it caused the other braves to look at him and laugh.

After what seemed an eternity, one of the braves stood up and walked over to Matthew and stared down at him. His face was covered with red and black markings. He was wearing only a piece of cloth around his waist that hung down to his thighs. He wore moccasins that laced up to the calf of his legs. His chest was bare and showed both bullet and knife scars on the upper part of his body. Under the war paint, his skin was beginning to wrinkle and the hard years were beginning to show.

When the brave finally decided to speak, he said, "I will speak the white man's tongue so you will understand me and know who I am. When I rode beside my cousin Geronimo, I was called, JUH, which you whites spoke as Hoo. I was a great and fearless warrior that caused terror in the whites throughout this part of the world and now I am their chief."

Matthew watched in silence as the Apache chief waved his arm all around, "It was your blue coats who chased me down into Mexico. When they thought to capture me, I eluded them by pretending to fall off my horse and drown in the Casas River down in Chihuahua. You whites are so easy to fool. I never fall off my horse," he said shaking his head. "It was then my braves renamed me, He Who Did Not Die. They call me this because I am still alive and still taking scalps from you whites."

The old warrior turned and looked at Mark and Luke for a moment, then turned back to Matthew. "I understand those two men are your blood brothers, yet you have them tied up and according to what they told me, you plan on leaving them here to die of their wounds which they received honorably, fighting one of your law dogs."

Matthew couldn't find his voice and sat there, staring at this terrifying Apache chief. Matthew knew the Indian in front of him planned on killing him and there wasn't a damn thing he could do about it.

He Who Did Not Die studied Matthew for a long time, then spit on him and said, "The Apache are strong and do not turn on their brothers, but you, white man, have done this most dishonorable thing. For this, you will die a long, slow, painful death while your brothers will die a quick, honorable death. That, I have promised to them."

A whimpering noise emitted from Matthew's open mouth and he felt him wetting himself, again.

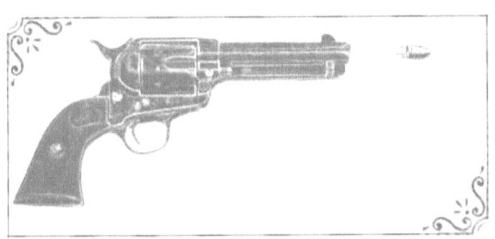

CHAPTER THIRTEEN

-

Clay woke up feeling somewhat rested for the first time in a long time. Looking down at his feet, he grinned when he saw the dog resting there. After checking his hat and boots for unwanted critters, he put them on and stood up, stretching to get the kinks out.

There were still a few hot coals from last night's fire and he added dried grass and small twigs to get the cook fire going again before adding larger pieces of dry wood. He was hungry and decided to fix pan bread to go with the bacon, beans, fried potatoes and coffee.

"Hope you're hungry ol' son," Clay said to the dog who had limped over and was sitting on his haunches, staring up at him.

The dog wagged his tail, but made no sound when Clay checked his wound and put more blue medicine on it.

When everything was ready, Clay sat a plate filled with human food in front of the dog, who waited until Clay took his first bite, then wolfed the human food down like it was to be his last meal.

Clay studied the far mountains and knew he still had a lot of desert in front of him and wondered how the Marlow brothers were faring with two of them wounded?

After loading the pack horse and saddling the black stallion, Clay looked down at the dog and asked, "What am I gonna do with you, ol' son? I don't reckon you can just go your own way and let me go mine, can you?"

The dog stood up on his three good legs and wagged his tail, then sat back down again.

"That's about what I figured," Clay said as he reached down and lifted the dog in his arms. "And you ain't in any condition to be running across the desert with me. At least not yet."

With that being said, Clay sat the dog on top of the packhorse between the two packs. The dog stretched out on his stomach like it was the most natural thing for him to do.

Clay mounted the black stallion and headed west at an easy pace with his new companion. Unlike Matthew Marlow, Clay Brentwood took care of his animals.

-

Two days later, Clay was nearing the lower part of a mountain with the dog now trotting beside him, his leg healing nicely. Clay was scanning the ground with a frown growing on his face. For over an hour now, he had seen the tracks of at least a dozen horses, but none of them belonged to the Marlow horses.

From the way they were scattered Clay guessed they belonged to a small band of Apaches. He was about to turn around and backtrack to find the Marlow horse tracks when he heard the scream.

He hauled back on the reins and looked around. The dog had also heard the scream and was standing, facing the lower part of the mountain – a growl in his chest and the hair on his back standing on end.

"I heard it too, ol' son," Clay said as he stepped down and rolled and lit a cigarette, all the while studying the lower part of the mountain.

It took him nearly a minute before he spotted it – a small trail of smoke, barely visible to the untrained eye. Next, came a second scream, much like the first and Clay was fairly certain he knew where the Marlow boys were.

Clay leaned against his saddle and pondered the situation. If the Apaches had them, they were going to die a slow, painful death and he could turn around and go home. His report would show they had been killed by a group of Apaches and that would be the end of it; but as he stood there, something inside his brain asked if he should try to rescue them, to which he had no immediate answer.

Looking down at the dog, Clay said, "If I was to try and save those no-goods, I just might get myself captured and end up dying a slow, painful death, myself."

The dog sat with his tongue hanging out of the side of his mouth and stared at Clay, wagging his tail, slowly.

"On the other hand," Clay said, blowing cigarette smoke down toward the ground in between his horse and the mountain so it wouldn't be seen if any of them were watching, "it would bother my conscience some to know I'd just left them there at the mercy of the Apaches and didn't try to do anything."

The dog made a whimpering noise as though he was sympathizing with Clay.

"You're right, ol' son, I've got to try," Clay said, snubbing out what little was left of his cigarette, then lifted his foot and stuck it into the stirrup, swung onto the saddle and headed for the Apache camp somewhere up above him.

-

He Who Did Not Die came out of his wickiup and looked around. The two brothers with gunshot wounds were still hanging naked by their wrists from a piece of log laying across the top of two boulders, just high enough so the prisoners' feet didn't touch the ground. The leather was cutting into their wrists and blood was running down their arms. Their wounds had opened and also were bleeding. He watched as squaws walked past and poked them with sticks, shoving the ends into their wounds and sometimes hitting them in their private parts.

Each time they did, the men screamed and pleaded for them to stop, which only urged them to do more. The squaws would laugh and poke them in their private parts, again, giggling as they tried to wiggle away.

Luke had already passed out from the pain, but he would wake up soon and the squaws would go back to torturing him.

He Who Did Not Die sauntered over and looked down at the oldest brother who was staked out naked on the ground; his arms and legs spread wide.

Next to Matthew a small fire was burning and one of the squaws walked up and looked at He Who Did Not Die. The chief looked at her and nodded his head.

Matthew watched the squaw take a piece of spoon shaped wood from a small pile of firewood and then, carefully scoop up some of the hot coals. He began to writhe around when he saw what she was going to do, but none of that helped. He was secured with leather straps tied around his wrists and ankles to wooden stakes driven into the ground. He tried to close his fingers into a fist, but a second, older squaw pulled his hand open and held it in that position.

From a second nod from He Who Did Not Die, the woman dumped the hot coals onto Matthew's open palm.

Matthew felt excruciating pain from the hot coals burning into his skin and try as hard as he could, he could not stop the scream that came out of his mouth. He was on the verge of passing out when a second pain down near his crotch roared into his brain. The squaw had dropped hot coals onto his skin right above his manhood. Everything went black as Matthew went to the place where extreme pain takes you.

-

All of this, Clay witnessed through his field glasses, as he stood propped behind a large rock some distance away.

He'd found a shadowed place to leave his horses and had put on his moccasins for the climb up the mountain toward where he'd first heard the screams. The dog stayed by his side all the way.

It had taken him nearly an hour before he was able see their camp and was surprised that he had not run into a lookout. In truth, the camp was well hidden in a small valley and this was their territory. Clay thought they were probably comfortable with the fact that not a lot of white people would be coming across this part of the mountain.

Clay was looking at the camp and taking note of how many people there were, including men, women and children, when the dog let out a low growl and the hair on his back stood up.

Clay laid his hand on the dog's head and whispered, "Quiet, ole son."

The dog immediately stopped growling and dropped to his belly, but kept staring off to the left. Probably a lookout, Clay thought to himself.

Clay looked down at the dog and marveled at his understanding of commands. "He must have had a lot of training or he's an exceptionally smart dog," Clay muttered to himself. "Or maybe, both."

Clay reached for his rifle that was leaning against the rock, but changed his mind and pulled his knife from its sheath. Easing away from the rock, Clay headed in the direction the dog had indicated, moving just slightly above where the lookout might be.

He'd gone no more than a few hundred feet when he saw the lookout. He was an old man who was spending more time cutting his toenails than looking for a white man and a dog to come sneaking up the mountain.

Clay looked down to see what the dog was doing, but he was nowhere to be seen.

Clay was still a good thirty feet from the old brave and was wondering if he could make a quick rush over to him before the old man could yell and alert the tribe.

As it turned out, he didn't have to make a decision. The decision was made for him when the dog, who had circled around to the other side of the brave, came walking out from behind a boulder and stood, growling at the old warrior.

The old man was shaken and dropped his knife. As he bent to pick it up, Clay rushed from his hiding spot and clubbed the old man on the head with handle of his knife before he had a chance to make a sound.

Clay quickly tied and gagged the old warrior who opened his eyes as Clay placed the gag in his mouth. He squirmed around and tried to spit out the gag, but Clay pulled it tighter and tied it behind the old man's head.

To keep the old man from belly crawling down to the camp, Clay tied him to a small, nearby tree.

The old man kept looking from Clay to the dog and it was obvious he was more afraid of the dog than the white man.

Back at the rock overlooking the Apache camp, Clay lifted the binoculars to his eyes and the first thing he saw was, several squaws building a new wickiup. They had the wooden framework put together and was covering it with hides.

He swung the glasses to his left and saw Mark and Luke hanging by their wrists and being beaten on by passing squaws. Small children were throwing stones at them and laughing.

A scream filled the air and Clay swung the glasses further to his left in time to see the squaw putting hot coals onto Matthew's hand and crotch area, again.

Next to Matthew stood a man who Clay immediately knew was their chief. He stood rigid and had his arms folded across his chest. He was dressed in buckskin pants and wore a union army jacket. His laced moccasins came up above the calves of his legs.

He watched as the squaws looked to him for instructions and noticed the nod of his head.

Since he'd not had much experience with the Apache, he had no idea what the chiefs name might be, but knew he stood in high status with the people and would be a man to be wary of.

How he would go about trying to rescue the Marlow brothers eluded him for the moment. There had to be close to a hundred people in the camp and two thirds of them were males, not counting the children, who could be just as dangerous as the adults.

"Got any suggestions?" he queried of the dog who just wagged his tail and sat looking up at Clay.

Clay wanted a cigarette to help him think but knew that was out of the question. They would see or smell the smoke and he'd have more trouble than he could handle.

Just before dark, Clay saw an old woman look up toward where he'd tied the old warrior, and after a moment, she lifted her skirt and headed up the mountain.

Clay hurried back to where he'd tied the old man and waited behind a tree until she walked past him, then stepped out and grabbed her, placing his hand over her mouth.

At first, she squirmed and tried to get away. She even tried to bite Clay's hand but his large hand held her jaw closed tightly.

Clay spoke to her softly, in Spanish, and told her if she would be quiet and not cause any trouble, he would not have to kill her.

The dog stepped in front of her and growled, barring his teeth and the woman stopped moving. After a moment, she nodded her head that she would make no noise or cause any trouble.

Clay loosened his hold on her and slowly removed his hand from over her mouth.

She looked up and glared at him but made no sound.

Clay led her over to where her mate was sitting tied to the tree and when she saw him, she rushed over and checked to make sure he was alive and well.

Clay sat her next to a tree across from the old man so they could see each other, then tied and gagged her as he had done to the old man, then returned to his place behind the rock, a plan beginning to form in his mind.

Taking his time, Clay circled around the camp to the north side and found what he was looking for.

In a grassy area north of their camp, some sixty or more horses were grazing lazily – a few of them were already laying down for the night.

Clay kept moving until the wind was blowing in his face, which as luck would have it, placed him behind the herd, with the horses in between him and their camp. The dog must have sensed what he was about to do and moved on a few more yards then dropped down on his stomach.

The moon was high overhead and the camp was quiet when Clay fired his pistol and let out a loud yell, startling the horses and causing them to race toward the camp.

The dog began barking and chasing them, encouraging them to run faster.

As the horses ran through the village causing havoc, Clay followed them, and in all the confusion, quickly cut down Mark and Luke, then cut Matthew loose, urging them to follow him away from the camp.

Injured like they were, it was slow going and Clay had to keep prodding them to keep them moving. The dog helped by nipping at their legs.

At the bottom of the hill, Clay found several of the Indian ponies had stopped and were grazing on the spotty sections of grass.

At first, they shied away from him, not recognizing his smell, but a few gentle words in Spanish made them allow him to approach them. He selected three that looked like they could run and brought them back to where he'd left the Marlow brothers with instructions not to move or he'd turn them back over to the Indians.

"Who are you and why did you risk your neck ta save ours?" Matthew asked when Clay came walking up, leading three Indian ponies.

"Clay grinned and said, "I'm the ranger you tried to kill and then had your friend the sheriff, try and hold in his jail until you could get away.

"Mark, who had now recovered some, asked, "Why didn't you just let them dirty redskins kill us and be done with it?"

Clay looked up at the moon. "It's this dammed ranger code I swore an oath to," he said, then turned back to them. "I swore to bring you back so they can hang you. Now get on these horses and let's get out of here. We don't have much time before they'll gather up the other horses and come looking for us. Make up your mind, it's them or me."

Clay mounted one of the Indian ponies, and rode down the mountain, heading for the spot he'd left his own horses.

Grudgingly, the Marlow brothers followed Clay, figuring he was less of a threat than being tortured by the Apaches.

Once they were out of danger from the Apaches, they would find a way to kill the ranger and head for California where hopefully no one had heard of them.

The problem with that kind of thinking was the fact that they would continue their lives by stealing, raping and murdering, with a trail of wanted posters in their wake. With that kind of growing reputation, not only would they be chased by the law, but every bounty hunter with a wanted poster would also be looking for them.

After stopping and collecting the black stallion and the buckskin packhorse, Clay rode out toward the southeast.

Matthew noticed the direction and asked, "Wouldn't it be quicker ta go a little northeast and go through Phoenix where them redskins cain't foller us?"

Clay just shook his head, but said nothing. Riding into Phoenix with the Marlow boys in tow was definitely out of the question.

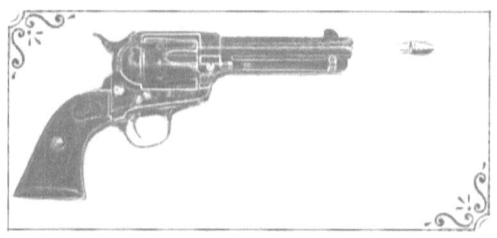

CHAPTER FOURTEEN

-

When the stampeding horses raced through the camp, causing it to look like a tornado had roared through it, He Who Did Not Die rushed out of his wickiup and was immediately knocked down by the horses and stomped on by several of them.

Needless to say, he did not survive the stampede and when he was later found during the clean up, the entire tribe wailed with grief.

He Who Did Not Die had no sons to take his place so they had neither a leader, nor horses to pursue the white men for what they had done. For the moment, everyone but one hotheaded buck who was called, Idandi, forgot about the white men and went about preparing for their chief's burial. Idandi did not participate.

With a fierce hatred for the white men who came unwanted to their lands with their blue coated soldiers who raided their camps in the middle of the night, and killed anyone who resisted, Idandi made himself ready for war.

In white man's language Idandi means, Thunder. He was called that because of the deep rumbling sound in his chest when he talked and the fierceness of his fighting skills. Idandi was also a Spirit Dancer and whenever he was about to go to war he danced the Killer Of Enemies dance in honor of the brave who taught them all they knew about war. Killer Of Enemies was the one who taught them to take scalps to prove they had conquered their enemy.

As the body of his chief was being prepared for burial, Idandi danced around the central fire, preparing himself to go after the white men and make them scream for mercy before killing them and taking their scalps for what they did.

When he'd exhausted himself from dancing and praying to the great spirits, he went to his wickiup and lay down to get some rest.

By the time the sun came over the horizon, Idandi was up, his face, chest and arms covered with war paint. He was armed with a rifle and what few bullets he was able to borrow from the others, his best knife, a bow and quiver of arrows - then after eating his fill, he said his goodbyes and set out on foot to find a horse so he could pursue the white men.

Several members of the tribe were there to see him off and assure him if he brought back the scalps of the white men who did this, he was sure to become their next chief.

-

Clay had no idea He Who Did Not Die had been killed by the stampeding horses, nor did he realize they would be followed by only one Apache brave and not half the tribe.

The sun was beginning to disappear beyond the western mountains. It had been a long, hot, miserable day beginning late last night. The Marlow brothers were elated when Clay called a halt, but said nothing.

Although he didn't mention it, Clay was also feeling the strain of the past twenty-four hours; plus, the horses wouldn't go much farther before being all in and Clay knew it.

Allowing the black stallion his head, he was the one who smelled the water hole in among some rocks. The water pool was hidden behind a clump of boulders just off the trail they were following and if not for the horses, they would have ridden on past, never knowing the lifesaving liquid was within thirty feet of where they rode.

The area also gave them shelter so a fire could be lit and not be seen unless you came within the circle of the boulders. There was grass here and after letting them drink their fill, the Indian ponies were tethered along with Clay's horses, and left to eat and rest.

The Marlow brothers were no help with setting up camp. Matthew's hands were burned and Clay gave him some salve to put on them to help the healing and the pain, along with two pieces of rag to use as bandages.

Both Mark and Luke washed their bruised and bloody wrists with water in a canvas bucket and complained about their shoulders aching, along with snide remarks about their bullet wounds caused by the ranger.

Fortunately, Clay had plenty of supplies on the buckskin packhorse he used from time to time as a second mount to give the black stallion a breather.

After seeing to his prisoner's wounds, Clay put a pot of beans over the fire to cook, and then cut bacon strips and put them in a skillet to fry. Next, he made dough for pan bread, then sliced up four potatoes to be fried in the bacon grease. From a small pouch, he took four jalapeno peppers and tossed them into the pot of beans for seasoning.

On the far side of the fire, a pot of coffee was brewing and when it was ready, Clay dug out four tin cups and gave each of the Marlow brothers a cup.

"Got anything ah mite stronger ta put in this here coffee? You know, for medicinal purposes?" Matthew asked, hopefully.

"Nope," Clay lied.

He always kept a bottle of whiskey in the bottom of the pack but he wasn't about to give any of it to these no-goods. The last thing he needed was a bunch of drunken outlaws to deal with. Them and the Indians he was sure would be on their trail soon, was enough problems.

Supper was a quiet affair as the Marlow brothers wolfed down the best meal they'd eaten in some time. Only Luke complained about having to share a plate of food with the dog. "What if one of us wants seconds?" he grumbled.

Clay looked at Luke and said, "If it wasn't for me and that dog, you wouldn't be sitting here. You'd still be hanging by your wrists in an Apache camp, waiting to die, so keep your complaints to yourself."

Luke filled his mouth with a spoon full of beans and potatoes and said nothing – but glared at Clay with hatred in his eyes.

When they'd finished eating, Mark said, "You sure you ain't got ah bottle stashed in that pack of yore'n? Ah nip or two sure would take off the chill come nightfall and that's ah fact."

"As I said before, I don't carry whiskey out on the trail. Numbs the brain, and out here that can mean your death. I'm guessing we'll have company sometime tomorrow and I want ever'body alert and wide awake," Clay told him.

After cleaning up the camp and allowing each man to go off to relieve himself before settling down for the night, Clay tied each man, separately to a boulder. He was tired and needed rest. He hoped the black stallion and the dog would awaken him if anyone or anything came sneaking around.

When he felt comfortable with the situation, Clay rolled out his bed sheet.

"Hey, you ain't gonna make us sleep all trussed up like this are ya? It's gonna get cold and we need ah blanket. Sides, I don't sleep well sittin' up like this." Matthew barked.

"I reckon I could stake you out on your back like those Indians did if it will make you more comfortable," Clay said, starting toward Matthew.

"You just stay away from me," Matthew yelled. "Just ferget I said anything. I'll be just fine right where I am."

Clay grinned and after adding more fuel to the fire, he rolled up in his blankets and closed his eyes. A minute later, he felt something against his feet and opened one eye and saw the dog settling down.

Clay slipped into a worriless sleep, knowing the dog was there.

CHAPTER FIFTEEN

-

Idandi hated walking and hated the whites for making him walk. He was a horse soldier – a warrior of the great Apache Chiricahua nation, not some woman who walked behind and carried her young or a pack.

It was close to noon before he came upon a lone horse standing in a small patch of brown grass, eating. It was dirty white in color with dark gray hips and forelegs, and a black mane and tail.

Idandi recognized the horse to be one owned by He Who Did Not Die, and since he was no longer among the living, the horse was free to anyone who captured it.

Three times Idandi approached the horse and three times the horse shied away. Idandi had not thought to bring a rope that he might use to capture a horse if he found one, and was perplexed. Absentmindedly, he reached into his pouch for a hand full of corn to munch on and saw the horse's ears go up as he turned his head and looked at Idandi, then walked over and ate the corn from Idandi's hand when he held it out toward him.

Idandi stroked the horse's neck and spoke softly to him, then took a handful of mane in his hand and swung up onto the horse's back.

The horse shivered slightly, then followed the knee command he was given.

Idandi looked at the sky and thanked the great spirits for coming to his aid.

The trail made by the four white men was easy to follow as he headed southeast.

Stupid white men, he thought – leaving a trail a child could follow. He would catch them within another day and be headed back with their scalps proudly hanging from his spear the following morning.

He also thought about what he would do when he was chief. He would make hit and run raids on the whites, taking many scalps while driving them from the land.

He would be as feared as Geronimo, Cochise, Victorio, or even Nana. When he was chief, he would be the most powerful warrior of them all.

That night, Idandi made a dry camp and fed his horse some of the corn he had with him and gave him a small amount of the water he carried in a gourd. He slept on the ground, rolled up in an army blanket he taken during a raid on a small group of blue coats who came looking for them. Unaccustomed to fighting Indians, especially Apache Indians, they found more than they bargained for.

Idandi remembered killing the young guard standing his night watch. He cut his throat before the young soldier even knew he was up next to him. He took his cap, his coat, his rifle and ammunition, his boots, his knife and the blanket he'd had over his shoulders. There was still a bloodstain on the blanket as a reminder of that fine night. He Who Did Not Die had praised him for his cunning.

The next day, Idandi found where the white men had camped and filled his gourd with fresh water, wondering how they had found this place? As far as he knew it was only known to the Apache. It had to have been the man who rescued them. None of the three captives were smart enough to find water if they were standing in it.

He studied their tracks and saw he was gaining on them. Now that he had water, he would set a good pace and come upon them by nightfall.

Less than an hour later he captured a second horse who had a rope hanging around his neck and moved slowly, afraid he would trip on the rope. Idandi felt he now had the advantage and by changing horses ever few hours, he would gain considerable time.

Idandi rode at a high lope, watching the horizon for a trail of dust rising in the sky.

-

Clay knew he could have been making faster time had he been alone, but with three wounded, whining, men who balked at the pace, he did the best he could.

During their noon meal of pan bread and bacon, Clay studied his back trail and saw a dust column in the far distance. He studied it with a lot of curiosity. It was a small dust column, not the wide one he expected to see. He was sure half the tribe would be on their trail by now, but as far as he could tell, there was only one or maybe two braves following them.

"Now why would they send only one or two braves to capture four men?" he muttered to himself.

"What was that?" Matthew queried.

"Nothing," Clay answered. "Eat up, we need to get moving."

"I ain't in no mood ta keep on ridin' at the pace you're settin', especially in this heat. Hell, it's got ta be more'n ah hundred degrees out there," Luke said pointing to the desert around them. "I vote we rest here til mornin'," he said, nodding his head at his brothers.

"Clay stood up, gathered the coffee pot and cups and put them on the pack horse, then went over to the black stallion and tightened his cinch.

"You do what you think you have to," Clay said, putting his foot into the stirrup and swinging himself onto the saddle. "Feel free to deal with those braves coming up behind us. If you're lucky and they don't take your scalp, you can tell us all about it when you catch up to us down the trail."

Clay touched his feet to the black stallion's sides and the horse moved out - the dog trotting next to him. He'd gone no more than forty feet when he heard the three Marlow brothers coming up behind him. He swung to the side and let them pass so he could keep an eye on them and his back trail.

It still worried him that only a couple of braves were pursuing them.

Idandi saw the column of dust suddenly rise into the air some distance ahead of him and knew it was the white men. The tracks he was following headed straight for the dust column. He smiled. He would soon have their scalps on his lance and be headed back to show his people what Idandi was capable of.

"I will deal with you before the moon has reached its high place in the sky," Idandi said into the hot wind that was blowing across his face.

Only a few hundred feet in front of him was an overhang jutting out from a large boulder. It wasn't much, but enough to give him some relief from the blistering heat while he rested and ate some of the jerked meat he carried in a sack tied around his waist. He was saving the corn for the horse.

While Idandi sat in the shade, chewing a piece of jerked meat and thinking about how he would be honored when he returned with the white men's scalps, he glanced at his back trail and noticed a large column of dust headed his way, and stood up to get a better view.

Instinct told him to disappear until he could find out who was making such a dust cloud. If it was blue coats, or other white men, he might have to reconsider his quest to track down the white men who were responsible for his chief's death – and wait for a better time. This he would do if he had to, but he would not give up his desire for the white men's scalps.

Idandi led his horses around behind the boulder and tied them to a bush, then went back and wiped out his tracks leading from the main trail to the overhang with a piece of brush. Then, dragging the piece of brush behind him, he went back to where his horses were tied and waited.

From his position, Idandi could see the land behind him without being seen by whoever was making the large dust column, and unless they were exceptionally good trackers, they would ride past him without realizing how close he was. He levered a shell into firing position in his rifle, just in case he had to fight.

"Maybe, if it is only two or three whites, I may choose to kill them and take their horses, food, guns and scalps," Idandi told himself with a wicked smile.

Idandi didn't like letting the men he was chasing get further away, but he had no choice until he could discover who was coming up behind him.

When the riders got closer, Idandi stepped over and put his hand on his horse's noses to keep them from whinnying at the other horses and giving his position away.

When he could hear the pounding of the horse's hooves, he peeked around the boulder and smiled with relief.

As the riders came abreast where he'd been camped, Idandi stepped from behind the boulder and raised his arm. "Hola!" he said with a wide grin.

The six Apache braves pulled their horses to a halt and jumped down.

Stands Alone was the first one to greet his friend, Idandi. "Hola, my friend. I am so happy we were able to catch up to you before the fun has begun."

Idandi looked at his friends and asked, "Why are you here? How did you get horses to ride and come after me? What about the burial of He Who Did Not Die? Did you see him to the great beyond?"

"One question at a time, brother," Bear Chaser said as he came walking over. "The burial will not be for several days yet. As you know there must be a time of mourning before he is allowed to go to the great beyond."

"We did as you did; we walked down the mountain and to our surprise, we found the horses coming back toward our camp," Three Fingers piped in.

He was called Three Fingers because two fingers on his left hand had been chopped off during a skirmish between them and the blue coats. An officer had swung his saber at him and he raised his hand to ward off the long knife and for his efforts, he'd lost two of his fingers. The officer then lost his life when Idandi's spear pierced his back. Before being renamed Three Fingers, he was called, Walks Softly. He was eternally grateful to Idandi for saving his life.

Three Fingers continued. "We did not want you to have to face the white men alone. We are not only your friends; we are your brothers and like you, warriors. We will stand with you now and when you become chief.

"Together we are unbeatable!" Bear Chaser said with great enthusiasm. "When you become our new leader, the whites will flee in terror," he proclaimed.

Idandi smiled. It would be easier to bring down the whites with more braves than trying to do it by himself. Plus, he would have witnesses when he took their hair.

Idandi pointed to the south and said, "Below the column of dust are the men we seek. At first, I was in a hurry to catch up to them and kill them all, but now that you are here, we do not have to be in a hurry. They will know we are coming and their hearts will be filled with fear. When the moon fills the sky, we will capture them and make them scream and plead to die - but we will wait for the sun to be high overhead before we grant them their wishes.

"And remember," Idandi said, looking at each of his followers, "I want them to be alive when we take their scalps so they will know it was Idandi and his brave warriors who do this to them. Then when they are begging to die, we will allow them their wishes, but it will not be the quick death they beg for. We will kill them, slowly and painfully, one at a time, making the others watch. The strongest of them will be the first to die. It will be entertaining to watch the weak ones scream with terror."

The six Apache warriors raised their rifles, bows and spears in the air, cheering their new leader.

CHAPTER SIXTEEN

-

Idandi looked over his shoulder and saw the dust column had disappeared and decided they had stopped to rest. He didn't have to be in any hurry, he could let them sweat and worry until he was ready to strike. The Apaches were known for their patience. It was something they did to drive their opponents crazy with worry. The more worried their prey was, the more likely they would make mistakes and then the Apache would strike. This was just one of the many reasons they were such fierce guerilla fighters, maybe the best in the world.

Clay pulled on the reins of his horse and turned it around. A frown creased his face as he studied a new column of dust. It was larger than the one that had been following them earlier.

"Damn..." Clay said to himself. It had to be the group of the Apache braves he'd expected to be coming after them. Not knowing for sure, he guessed the first brave had been sent ahead to find their trail, while the rest came along after rounding up their horses. Any way he looked at it, he would need to find a place to hole up – a place they could fight from, which meant arming the Marlow brothers, which he was not happy about doing.

He knew they could fight off the Indians, sure enough, but when it was over he had no doubt the Marlow brothers would turn on him and he wasn't sure he could best all three of them if they were coming at him from three different directions.

"If I get out of this, this will definitely be my last job as a ranger," Clay promised himself.

How many other times he'd said these words he couldn't remember, but this time he really meant it.

Clay pulled on the rein and turned the black stallion around, then reached over and made sure the pack on the buckskin was secure before chasing after the Marlow brothers, who were suddenly in a big hurry to put space between themselves and the Indians following them.

As Clay rode to catch up, he surveyed the area in front of him and sighed. There was nothing but desert in all directions and what he saw was a huge piece of land the creator had turned his back on. No one in their right mind would try to live out here – except for a few crazy prospectors in search of the elusive threads of silver that was said to be hidden beneath this barren land. Even the Indians shied away from this part of the desert, preferring to live in the higher elevations where it was cooler - where there was game and water.

Clay rode up next to Matthew and said, "Keep a lookout for a place to make a stand. Our friend has picked up some more braves and it looks like we'll need to find a place to stand them off."

Matthew jerked his head around and saw the large column of dust.

He turned his head back around and glared at Clay. "And just what do you suppose me and my brothers are gonna use ta fight 'em with, rocks?"

Clay sighed, knowing what Matthew would do when the fighting was all over if he had a gun in his hand.

"Let's find a place where we can defend ourselves and see how many we're up against, then we'll talk about arming you and your brothers," Clay said, putting his heels against his horse, urging him into a gallop.

-

As long as Idandi could see the dust column made by the whites, he was in no hurry. They would know they were being followed and that alone was enough to cause them to make mistakes like pushing their horses too hard. If they rode their horses to death and were on foot, they would be easy to ride down.

The blistering hot sun would also be a big factor. The whites were known to be stupid and drink all their water without knowing where the next waterhole could be found.

He would take his time and let their minds, stupidity, and the sun god do most of his work for him. He laughed and talked with the other braves about what they would do with the whites once they had taken them.

Three Fingers liked the idea of staking them out naked on the hot desert sand by laying them on their back, arms and legs spread apart, then cutting off their eyelids so they couldn't close their eyes against the menacing sun. This had been known to drive a man crazy and causing him to bleed through his eyes.

Bear Chaser thought it would be good to find some wild honey and pour it over their heads, which would attract the ants. They would crawl up their noses and into their ears. He could already hear them screaming.

At first, Stands Alone thought it would be fun to find some rattlesnakes and place one on each of their stomachs to see how long it would take for them to start screaming, but decided they were probably weak and would scream and try to wiggle away causing the snakes to bite them and then they would die too soon.

"I think it would be a good way when we are finally ready to kill them," he said with conviction.

The others agreed and wondered how many bites it would take to kill each one. They would make wagers.

-

Clay had to force the Marlow brothers to slow down. They were in a panic and wanted to get as far away as fast as they could, which was exhausting their horses far too quick.

"You're doing exactly what they want you to do. They want you to be afraid and run your horses to death, leaving you afoot. Once you have no horses, no food or water and beaten down by the heat, you'll be no threat and easy to take captive."

"Why don't they just kill us and be done with it?" Luke asked.

"Because that's not their way," Clay said. "They believe in torturing their captives to see how brave and strong they are. The weaker you are, the longer they'll take to kill you. A brave man who makes no sound, no matter how much pain he's in, will be honored with a quick death."

"Well now that's just plumb stupid," Mark said. "Savages. Savages, the whole lot of 'em. They ain't nothin' but ah bunch of savages. I say we kill 'em all."

"Yeah," Clay said, "It's that kind of thinking that made them the way they are. Before the white man came with his murdering ways, Indians were pretty docile for the most part. They counted coup by touching each other in battle. Many a horse was stolen back and forth between the tribes. Stealing from one another was a game they enjoyed and no one got killed for it."

"Well that's stupid, too," Matthew said. "Ah man steals from me, he's gonna die."

This from a man who made his living by stealing. Clay rode ahead, looking for a place to make a stand. Talking to these idiots was beginning to make him angry enough to leave them here for the Apache braves to find and do with - whatever they wanted. It would serve them right.

It was what he wanted to do, but knew it wasn't what he would do. He would stand and fight and if he won, he would take them back to Texas to stand trial for their crimes and more than likely, be hung.

Up ahead was a rock formation that he wanted to investigate. It looked large and formidable, but as it turned out, a den of rattlesnakes shared his opinion and had gotten there first. Plus, there was no water or grass for the horses that he could see.

Moving on, Clay glanced over his shoulder and saw the dust column was about the same distance as it had been the last time he looked and decided they were doing just as he'd told the Marlow brothers; waiting for them to run their horses to death. They might even let them wander on foot for a day or so before closing in on them.

Clay looked around and sighed. If there was a more desolate place in the world he couldn't imagine where it would be. It was so hot he could cook the evening meal on a rock. Looking closely at the black stallion, he could see lather on his shoulders and foam beginning to drip from his mouth. He pulled back on the reins and said, "Whoa, big fella." Clay stepped down and patted his neck, then loosened the cinch on the saddle.

He poured some water from his canteen into his hat and was giving the black stallion a small drink when Matthew Marlow rode up next to him.

"What'ya doin'," Matthew asked. "We ain't got time for lollygaggin'; not with them heathen redskins breathin' down our necks!"

"Get down, all of you," Clay said as the other two rode up. "Loosen the cinches on your saddles and give your horses a small drink of water. We'll walk for a while and give the horses a breather."

"Are you crazy?" Luke yelled. "Them bloodthirsty redskins are not far behind us and you want ta get off your horse and walk. Well not me mister lawman. I'm gettin' the hell outta here and if you want ta shoot me in the back, go ahead."

And with that he kicked his horse in the sides and with great effort the horse lunged forward at a high lope.

"You just gonna let him go?" Mark asked as his younger brother rode away.

Clay was giving the buckskin a drink of water from his hat as he watched the youngest of the Marlow brothers ride away. He looked at Matthew and Mark and said, "Each man has a right to choose the way he wants to die. Luke obviously wants to die of thirst and on foot out here in the desert or at the hands of the Apaches; I'm not sure which, but either way, he keeps going the way he is, he won't have to worry about going back to Texas to hang."

"Well I'm goin' after him," Mark said, but before he could, Matthew reached over and grabbed the reins of his horse. "You ain't goin' nowhere. As much as I hate ta admit it, the ranger is right. We keep goin' like we have been, we'll be afoot and at the mercy of them heathen redskins back there."

"Ain't we gonna do nothin' about Luke?" Mark shouted.

Matthew shook his head. "Like the ranger said, he made his choice."

"But he ain't thinkin' straight," Mark said with anger in his voice.

"Maybe so," Matthew said. "But if we go chasin' after him, we'll wind up just like he's gonna wind up and I ain't ready ta die – not just yet anyway."

All the while, Clay had been studying the dust column and noticed it had stopped.

"They've stopped. They're probably waiting to see what we're going to do," Clay said, pointing back toward the Apaches. "I suggest we start walking. They won't wait much longer."

"What makes you think that?" Mark asked.

"As long as they think it's to their advantage, they'll hang back and just watch to see what we're going to do, but if whoever is in charge gets impatient, they'll make a move - and out here in the open like we are, we won't stand much of a chance. This is their land and they're some of the best desert fighters in the world."

With that, Clay pulled his rifle from its scabbard, then turned and began to walk on across the desert, with the black stallion and buckskin following along a few feet behind him.

After a couple of hours Clay's shirt had turned white from losing so much salt and his skin was dry and burning. His tongue was beginning to swell and his lips were cracked and bleeding. His whole body ached. The blistering sun was drying his sweat as fast as his body could produce it, which was getting slower and slower. He knew they needed to find water soon. He was losing strength by leaps and bounds. If he had been able to see a thermometer, it would have read one hundred and sixteen degrees and climbing.

From behind him, he heard Mathew say with a much-labored voice, "I can't go on much farther. I've got ta have some water and rest."

Clay knew how he felt because he felt the same way. "Just a little bit farther," he said in a scratchy sounding voice. "There's bound to be a water hole and a place where we can make a stand somewhere nearby."

Even as he said the words, he wasn't sure he believed them himself. He knew there were water holes out here, but finding them was next to impossible.

Thirty minutes later they found Luke sitting next to his horse. The horse was dead and Luke was wild eyed. His face looked like a cooked piece of meat. His mind was somewhere other than here and he looked up at them and said, "Have you come for dinner? We're havin' steak and taters with big pitchers of beer ta drink."

Clay watched as Matthew and Mark walked over and helped their brother to his feet, brushing the dirt from his clothes as best they could.

Trying to pacify his brother, Mark said, "Sure. Sure. But first we need ta get ah bath and ah shave and inta some clean clothes. We can't go ta dinner lookin' like this."

Luke looked at his brothers and said, "I do believe you're right, brother. Yes, a bath and some clean clothes would be just the ticket."

Not wanting to give Luke's saddle to the Indians, Clay was tempted to pull it off and put it on top of the pack for the buckskin to carry, but changed his mind. The buckskin was already about to fall down and any added weight would do it for sure.

Ten minutes later, all of them were ready to drop to the sand and let whatever was to happen, happen. All three of the Marlow brothers had stopped and were bending over at the waist, gagging with dry heaves.

At the sound of their gagging, Clay turned around and watched, knowing they were done in. They could go no farther. They would have to make their stand, here in the open.

The way Clay figured it; it wouldn't be much of a stand. They were in no condition to fight and they had no protection. Once again, with patience, the Apaches had won.

Clay was looking back toward the advancing dust cloud when the black stallion, followed by the other horses came trotting past him with their ears up and making funny noises in their throats.

Turning, Clay saw they were headed for a small outcrop of rocks a quarter of a mile or so, further on.

"Water! The horses smell water!" Clay said with a raspy whisper. "Pull yourselves together, we've got to follow them!"

The horses and the dog were all standing next to a small pond of clear, cool water with their noses deep into the cool liquid when they arrived.

Pulling the black stallions and buckskins heads up, Clay said to the Marlow brothers, "Don't let your horses drink too much at first; just a little to cool them down for now. Later, they can drink their fill. The same with us – otherwise we'll all get sick.

The Marlow brothers were already laying flat on their stomachs with their faces in the water, but reluctantly stood up and moved their horses back a few feet from the waterhole.

After taking a small drink and then pouring a hatful of water over his head, Clay looked around at his surroundings. He couldn't ask for a much better place to make their stand against the Apaches. They had good-sized rocks all the way around them like a small fort. They would have a wide field of fire. There was plenty of water and some grass for the horses to eat, along with food for them in the packs. Unless more warriors showed up, or they ran out of ammunition, he felt they stood a good chance of surviving.

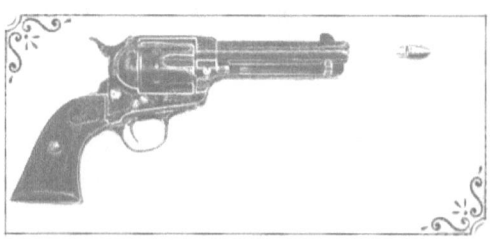

CHAPTER SEVENTEEN

-

The white men's dust trail stopped moving and Idandi made a frown as he called for a halt. Standing up on the back of his horse, he stared into the heat waves that danced on the desert floor ahead of him.

Idandi was tired and hungry and in need of water. They had run out early that morning. Had the white men found water? Were they now drinking their fill, he wondered? The heat and lack of water was causing Idandi's mind to not think clearly. He tried licking his dry, parched lips but could make no saliva.

"What do you see?" Stands Alone asked.

Idandi dropped back down on his horse and looked at his companions. "Nothing but desert," he said.

Bear Chaser wiped sweat from his eyes and said, "They have to be in worse shape than we are and since they are much weaker, I believe they can no longer go any farther. I believe now is the time to ride in and take them."

Everyone, even Idandi thought this might be true and nodded their heads.

Like the white men's horses, the Indian's horses were lathered and foaming at the mouth. But unlike the white men, an

Indian will ride his horse until he drops, then eat him and go on, afoot.

So, thinking only about their anger and wanting to capture the men in front of them, the Apache braves urged their horses forward, knowing they had a little over a mile to go before coming face to face with the men they sought.

The Apache horses were down to a stumbling walk and no matter how hard the braves kicked them or yelled at them, they refused to go any faster.

In the distance, in the middle of the dancing heat waves Idandi saw the small stand of rocks and knew in his gut this is where he would find his enemies.

Pulling his horse to a halt, the horse stopped and stood there, shaking. Idandi slid down from his back and motioned for the others to do the same. "The whites are not far ahead. I believe they are hiding behind those rocks just ahead of us," he said, pointing toward the circle of rocks.

By now, Three Fingers was almost out of his head from his need for water and wild-eyed he asked, "Do you think they have found water?"

"If they have, we must take it from them," Bear Chaser said and started to walk toward the rocks, with the others following him.

Idandi, though he wasn't in any better shape than his warriors, was still able to think more clearly than they did, but barely.

"Wait," he said with authority, and the braves stopped and turned back to look at Idandi.

"I agree with Bear Chaser, but if we try now, in the daylight, they will see us and shoot us before we can reach the rocks they hide behind like the cowards they are."

"Then what are we to do? Are we to stand here and die from the heat and need for water while they have plenty to drink and are laughing at us?" Three Fingers asked.

Idandi looked at them for a long moment, trying to clear his mind, which at the moment was not thinking rationally. Finally, his mind cleared some and he said, "We are Apache warriors, Chiricahuas, stronger than any whites. We will take them captive, but on our terms, not theirs. They are weak, and even if they have water, they are tired and in need of sleep. We will rest and wait for night when the darkness will protect us. We will surround them and sneak up on them and catch them while they sleep." Reaching down, Idandi picked up several small rocks and passed them to his followers. "Put a stone in your mouth and suck on it. It will help with the thirst."

The braves muttered amongst themselves and agreed to the wisdom of what Idandi said.

"What you say makes sense," Three Fingers said. "We will do as you say. We will rest and dream of our victory over the whites."

The others all nodded their heads in agreement.

-

The top of the boulder was too hot to put his elbows on, so instead, Clay leaned against one of the rocks to steady his trembling body, then lifted the field glasses to his eyes. In the far distance, he could make out the images of the Indians and saw that they were sitting in a circle with their heads bowed. All their horses were down on their sides.

Clay presumed the horses were all still alive or there would be a fire and the Indians would be eating one of them. He also knew they were in bad need of water. He figured they knew about this water hole and were not pleased the white men had found it, and were discussing what to do about it.

"What'a ya see?" Matthew asked as he stumbled up and stood next to Clay.

Clay took his eyes away from the field glasses and looked at Matthew. "They're all sitting down in a circle," Clay said, taking the makings from his shirt pocket and rolling a cigarette.

"What'er they doin' that for?" Mark asked as he walked up and heard what Clay had said.

Clay stuck a Lucifer against the rock and lit his cigarette, and to the aggravation of the two outlaws, took his time before answering. Clay took a puff and blew a smoke ring then said, "They're sitting around in a circle discussing what to do when they capture us," he said, after blowing a second smoke ring in their direction.

"So, you don't reckon they're gonna give up and leave us alone?" Mark asked.

Clay shook his head and said, "No. I seriously doubt that's what's on their mind."

"Well that's just plumb crazy. They know where we are and that we've got water, right?" And they half'ta be needin' water too. So, I don't understand what they're doin'?"

Clay studied his cigarette for a moment, then said, "They're resting and talking. And yes, they know where we are and that we have water."

Clay looked up at the sun and saw it was on its downward thrust toward the west.

"They're waiting for night to come," Clay finally said. "Sometime before midnight when it's cool and dark I believe we can expect an attack. They think we're too tired to fight and need rest. They believe they can sneak up on us and catch us while we're asleep. That's why they're resting now."

"How will they come at us?" Mark asked. "Will they come on horseback, ah screamin' and ah hollerin', or will they come ah belly crawlin', real quiet like?"

Clay scratched his sunburned ear and said, "If it was me, I'd surround this place and belly crawl up next to the rocks and take a look-see at what I was up against.

If everybody is asleep like I thought they should be, then I'd slip in real quiet like and do whatever it is I was planning to do. We're too well forted up for them to come at us with a frontal attack."

Matthew looked at Luke, who was sitting, propped up against one of the rocks, then said, "They'll only be three of us that's able ta fight if it comes to it. Luke won't be of no help. Not only is he out of his head, but he's dog tired and sound asleep."

"What about guns? You got any ta spare?" Mark asked, "so's me'n Matthew can defend ourselves? I don't hanker fightin' injuns with my bare hands."

There was a long silence before Matthew finally said, "You haven't givin' us no guns cause you're wonderin' if one of us might shoot ya durin' the fight, ain't ya?"

Clay looked him square in the eyes and said, "That's exactly what I was thinking."

Matthew gave a big sigh and lightly touched his sunburned face. "Can't say as I blame ya none for yer way of thinkin' bout it, and I can only speak for myself, but the way I see it, it's gonna take all three of us blastin' away at them red devils if'n we're ta have ah fightin' chance. So... shootin' you afore the fightin' is done with, don't make no sense."

Clay looked over at Mark.

Mark shrugged his shoulders, rolled his eyes and nodded his head. "I'll go along with whatever Matthew says," he said with a sigh.

"And what about Luke?" Clay asked.

Matthew and Mark looked at their brother. His snoring was loud enough to wake the dead.

"You ain't got ta worry none about him. He'll probably sleep right through it all if'n it comes to ah shootout," Matthew said. "Sides, he ain't no hand with ah gun."

"And what about after the shootout? If we come out on top, what happens then?" Clay asked them both, straight out.

"I reckon we'll half'ta cross that bridge when we come to it. I don't plan on goin' back ta Texas ta get strung up." Matthew said with a sigh. "And if them heathens come after us, there ain't no way in hell you can stand 'em off all by yourself, no sir, not by a long shot. Even with the three of us, it's gonna be tough. You said you counted seven of 'em."

"I reckon that puts you between ah rock and ah hard spot, don't it?" Mark sneered.

Clay knew Matthew was right. He would need their help when the Apaches came calling. He also knew if they were all three still standing when it was all said and done with, he would have to face down the two of them.

"If I get out of this, this will definitely be my last ranger job," Clay muttered to himself.

"What was that?" Mark asked.

"Nothing worth repeating," Clay said, shaking his head.

"Well, what's it gonna be, Ranger?" Matthew asked.

Clay lifted the field glasses to his eyes and looked toward the Indians. They were still sitting in a circle. The horses were now standing on wobbly legs and looking in toward the rocks, but other than that, nothing had changed. The blazing sun had dropped over the horizon and heat waves were no longer dancing before his eyes.

Clay was about to lower his binoculars when he saw the Indian ponies begin to run as best as they could in their direction. They'd smelled the water.

Clay watched as the Indians jumped to their feet and tried in vain to catch them, but were a mite too slow.

They stopped and watched as their horses, on stumbling legs, ran into the rock formation and water, knowing the white men would let them come.

"What the hell," Matthew exclaimed as the Indian ponies ran up to the pool of water and began to drink.

"Just a little at first," Clay reminded Matthew and Mark as he walked over and began to move them away from the water.

Between the three of them, they moved the Indian ponies over to where their own mounts were grazing.

Clay lifted his field glasses to his eyes to see what the Apache braves were doing and saw that they were grouped together, staring at the rocks.

He knew it wouldn't be long now. They were getting desperate.

Clay lowered his field glasses and walked over to his pack that was laying on the ground near the pool of water. After putting the field glasses down on top of the pack, he took a tin cup from the pack and dipped it into the pool. The water felt cool on his parched tongue and throat and he drank thirstily. When he finished, he watched as Matthew and Mark walked toward him.

"Well, what's it gonna be?" Matthew asked, dropping down on his knees and drinking directly from the pool.

Clay stood up and backed away two steps. He didn't want to be in an awkward position if they decided to try and take his gun away from him before the attack.

Clay looked at the sky and then around their camp. What was left of the setting sun was making long shadows across the ground and he knew it wouldn't be long before they would come.

"Like you said, I'm between a rock and a hard spot and don't have much of a choice, do I?" Clay said.

With that, Clay walked over to the opposite side of the pack, all the while, keeping the two Marlow brothers in sight. He dug into the pack and pulled out two pistols and two boxes of ammunition.

"I only have one rifle, and I'm keeping it. I'm probably the better rifle shot anyway. You'll each have a pistol and one box of ammunition between you. It's gonna be dark when they come and they'll be hard to see, so make every shot count," Clay said tossing the pistols down on top of the pack, next to the tin cup.

Clay could see the eagerness in their eyes. They wanted to rush over and pick up the pistols and shoot him, but held back because they didn't know if the guns were loaded or not. If they weren't and they tried to shoot him, they knew he would shoot them down, then ride out of here and not look back. By himself, he would get away, especially if he took their horses with him. The Indians would come and drink the water, but wouldn't try to follow him on foot, not with it getting as hot as it did.

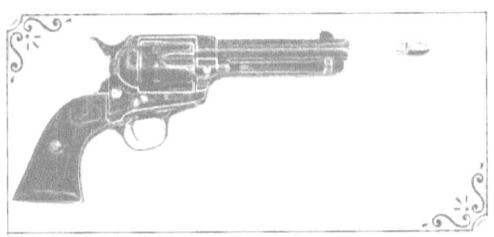

CHAPTER EIGHTEEN

-

The sun had disappeared over the tops of the mountains to the west and the moon was just rising over the eastern horizon. The air was beginning to cool down a little and the temperature was dropping at a steady rate.

Idandi climbed from his sitting position to a kneeling position and began to wail his death song. He didn't plan to die, but in case the gods frowned on him and decided it was his time to go to the great beyond, he wanted everything to be in order.

When the others heard Idandi singing, they got to their knees and began doing the same thing. It would soon be time to make their attack on the whites. They were tired, hungry and starved for water. Even as weak as they were, each one was eager for battle. After killing or taking the whites prisoners, they could celebrate and would have all the water they wanted to drink, plus, they would have their horses back and could eat one of the white men's horses. Their wailing filled the night air.

-

"What in the devil is that?" Mark asked - jumping to his feet at the sound of the Indians singing.

"Relax," Clay said. "They're singing their death songs."

"Death songs? Whose death songs are they singin' about? I don't want nobody singin' ah death song about me! Is that what they're doin'?"

Clay shook his head at their ignorance, but decided to explain. "It's not you they're singing about. Indians sing their prayers before going into battle, asking for bravery and courage, along with saying they are not afraid to die in battle as a warrior should, and if the gods will it, they will be happy to go to the great beyond, knowing they have fought well and earned the right to walk among the warriors who have gone before them."

"That's plumb crazy!" Mark said.

"Not to them it isn't," Clay said. "Actually, it gives them the courage to go into battle with more confidence than most white folks have."

"Heathens," Matthew said, spitting his contempt onto the ground.

Clay was sitting with his back to one of the rocks. "You boys can load your guns now. Once the singing stops, it won't be long before the dance begins."

He watched as they rushed over and began loading their pistols, then filling their pockets with extra shells.

First it was going to be the Apaches, and then, if they were the victors, he knew in his gut, he would have to face the Marlow brothers. He would have to use his rifle as much as he could and save his pistol for the shootout with them. It would be close up and fast. He sighed and leaned back against the rock to get some rest. He couldn't close his eyes and take a chance they wouldn't kill him, but he could rest. Seven to three. There was a chance they could come through this alive.

Suddenly, the singing stopped and Clay's nerves went on alert. He stood up and walked over to the pack and picked up the field glasses.

Standing next to the rock he had to take a chance and turn his back on the Marlow brothers, hoping they wouldn't try to shoot him until the attack was over.

"Can ya see'm? Are they comin'?" Matthew asked. His voice was nervous and a few notches higher than normal.

The moon was higher in the sky now and provided enough light for him to see that the Indians had slipped off into the darkness. The only thing left at their camp was the indentions on the ground where they'd been sitting.

Turning back to the Marlow brothers, Clay said, "Spread out. They're on the move and will try and surround us before they attack, so we have anywhere from a few minutes to a few hours before the show starts. Try to find a place where you can see a wide area. And remember, they're good at this and prefer close up hand to hand fighting, so be prepared."

As an afterthought, he said, "When this is over, I want those guns back and no trouble." He then walked over and kicked dirt over the fire and the area inside the rocks became dark, lit up only by the moon.

All three of the white men found positions behind a rock that allowed them to see a large area of the desert, but still gave them cover.

The problem wasn't being able to see the desert – the moon was bright enough to allow that. The problem was, especially for the Marlow brothers, they couldn't see any of the Indians.

The Apache's skin is much darker than a white mans and at night, they can lay on the ground and blend in with the desert - almost becoming invisible to the untrained eye.

Clay, being taught how to look at things by one of the Indians who worked for him back on his ranch in Texas, looked at the desert completely different than the Marlow brothers.

Clay's eyes looked at the entire area and made note of any changes. At first, he saw nothing and knowing a little about Indians, knew they would start from a good ways out and take their time crawling up to the rocks, making the impatient whites, nervous.

Matthew and Mark were both as nervous as a virgin on her wedding night and cursed the Indians under their breath for taking so long to attack.

It was close to two hours before Clay saw the movement of one of the Indians, who was very slowly, belly crawling up to the edge of the rock he was hiding behind. The movement was so slow and smooth he missed it the first time his eyes scanned the area. It was the dog that alerted him.

The dog came to his feet - a low growl emitting from deep in his chest and he stared in the direction Clay had just looked at, but passed by.

Turning his eyes back to where the dog was looking, Clay barely caught sight of the dark shape that moved not more than a few inches at a time.

Lifting his rifle, and just to make sure he didn't waste a bullet, Clay watched until the dark spot moved again, then sighted in on it and squeezed the trigger.

The sound of the rifle filled the night air as the dark spot moved upward slightly, then dropped back down onto the desert floor and lay still.

The sound of Clay's rifle shot opened the dance and prompted two of the Indians on the sides where the Marlow brothers were nervously trying to see into the darkness, to jump to their feet and come at them, screaming, knives in their hands.

The Marlow brothers were so surprised that for a moment they just stood there, watching as the Indians came over the tops of the rocks.

The one facing Mark leaped from the top of the rock, his knife raised for a killing blow.

Mark just stood there, unable to react; his mouth open – his eyes wide with surprise.

The Indian was in midair when the second rifle shot filled the night. Its bullet struck the Indian in midair and propelled him to the side of where Mark was standing. He landed near Mark's feet and the astonished Mark lifted his pistol and shot the already dead Indian three times before he came to his senses and looked over at Clay, who had turned his attention back on the desert and the other five Indians who were now coming at them, screaming their war cries.

Matthew, a little less startled than his brother and a man who killed more easily than his two brothers, reacted faster and more clear headed than Mark had. He shot the Indian who leaped at him and then quickly stepped aside and looked for more Indians to shoot. His eyes were ablaze with excitement and fear.

For a short period, the inside area of the rock fort was filled with four bloodthirsty Apache warriors, three white men, twelve nervous horses and one growling dog.

Clay shot at one of the nearest Indians, but missed and didn't turn fast enough to miss being stabbed in the left shoulder by Idandi, who had come over the rock behind him.

Idandi's eyes were wild with excitement as he jerked his knife back and made a swinging slice at the white man's chest.

Clay jumped back just in time, causing Idandi to miss by barely an inch, which made him growl and go into a fighting stance, his knife thrust out in front of him.

Idandi watched as the white man drew his own knife and also went into a fighting position, his eyes never leaving Idandi's eyes.

Out of his peripheral vision, Clay could see Matthew grappling with one of the warriors and saw another warrior knock Mark down and jump on top of him, his knife raised over his head for a killing thrust.

Just then, the Indian in front of him lunged and he barely sidestepped in time to keep from getting his belly sliced open.

Concentrating on his own survival, Clay didn't see the dog leap on the Indian who was about to kill Mark and sink his teeth into the Indians shoulder.

The Indian let out a bloodcurdling scream and rolled to his side, trying to loosen the dog.

The dog released his hold on the Indian's shoulder and leaped away, growling, ready for another attack.

Mark, still rattled from the near-death experience, came to his senses enough to pick up his pistol and shoot the Indian in the back, then rolled onto his knees and began to vomit.

At the same time, Matthew, after a hand-to-hand combat with the warrior who attacked him, and getting a knife wound to his stomach, raised his pistol and shot the young warrior in the face.

Clay faked a lunge, then swung his knife back, laying Idandi's chest open.

Idandi jumped back, surprised at the white man's knife fighting ability. He was about to make another move, one that would prove him to be the superior knife fighter when the dog rushed in and bit down on Idandi's left calf and tore a chunk of meat out of his leg.

Stifling the scream welled up in his throat; Idandi jumped away and took notice that he was the only warrior still alive. His brothers were all dead. They had lost the fight they thought would be so easy.

With blood running down his chest and leg, Idandi decided he'd had enough for this day and leaped over the rocks and disappeared into the darkness.

The dog started to follow him, but Clay called him back. He wasn't about to follow an Apache brave into the darkness where he might get himself killed, nor was he going to let the dog go, either.

Clay reached down and patted the dog on the head, which caused the dog to wag his tail and look up at Clay with what might be considered a smile.

Looking around, Clay saw Mark on his hands, and knees, still being sick.

Matthew was leaning against one of the rocks, breathing heavily. He was holding his stomach with his left hand. Blood was seeping between his fingers.

Clay walked over and stopped in front of Matthew, who handed over his pistol and watched as Clay stuck it in the waistband of his pants.

"Is it bad?" Clay asked of Matthew's wound.

"I don't think so, but I haven't had much of ah chance ta look," Matthew said with a slight grin. "Been kinda busy. How about you? Looks ta me like your shoulder is bleedin'."

Clay reached up and felt the wetness on his left shoulder, then flexed his arm.

"Don't think anything vital was cut."

"Is it over?" Mark asked, wild eyed and still shaking and trembling.

Clay and Matthew turned and looked at Mark who was now sitting on the ground with his legs spread wide open, the pistol in his hand.

"For now," Clay said. "One of them got away, but he's injured and won't bother us for at least a few days, if at all. You can't tell about Indians. Sometimes when they lose, they call it quits – but not always. Some of them just don't know when to give up. He might want revenge for what we did to his brothers."

Mark looked at Clay and asked, "You think this one will still want revenge?"

Clay scratched the itch on his nose, then said, "Can't say. We'll just have to keep looking over our shoulders for a while."

Mark got slowly to his feet, holding the pistol down by his side.

Clay saw the look in his eyes and said, "Don't be a fool. I'm twice as fast as you are. And I rarely miss. But it's your decision whether you want to take a chance or not. It's up to you to decide whether you want to live or die."

Clay could see that Mark was debating with himself whether to chance it or not.

Clay had just taken a step to the side - preparing himself for what might come when Matthew stepped between Clay and his brother.

"Give me your pistol," Matthew said to Mark in a commanding voice.

"Get outta the way, big brother. You're not givin' the orders this time. I don't plan on goin' back ta Texas ta hang any more'n you do. You shoulda' kept your gun, then it would'a been two against one and maybe one of us might'a got lucky."

"I don't think so," Matthew said; glancing over at Clay, then back at his brother. "I remember readin' about ah ranger named Brentwood who shot it out with ten mean shooters back in New Mexico and walked away without ah scratch."

Turning his head toward Clay, he said, "That was you, weren't it?"

Clay looked at Matthew, gave a sigh and nodded his head in the affirmative.

Matthew reached out his hand and Mark handed over his pistol. Matthew then turned and handed the pistol to Clay.

"Not today, Ranger. Not today," Matthew said.

CHAPTER NINETEEN

-

When the attack started, the Indian ponies bolted into the darkness, kicking up their heels as they ran away.

Idandi fled into the darkness in the direction of the horses and when he came up on them, limping and in bad need to get off his feet, the horses smelled the blood and shied away from him.

Idandi cursed under his breath, but spoke softly to the one closest to him and dragging his injured leg, moved close to the horse with the flared nose and wild look in his eyes.

The horse was confused by the soft words and the smell of blood, but in the end, stood still.

Idandi stroked the horse's forehead and rubbed his neck before, using ever bit of effort he could muster, to swing himself up and onto the horse's back.

Looking over his shoulder to see if anyone was following him, he saw nothing but the desert and the moon and stars.

Relieved, Idandi rode west toward the nearby mountain.

-

Clay looked at Matthew and said, "We'll need to be moving on soon. We'll make some coffee and have a bite to eat, then we'll get a few hours rest, but be ready to leave at first light."

While Clay was relighting the fire, Mark went to wake his brother, Luke and called out, "Matthew!"

Clay and Matthew rushed over and saw Luke, still in his sitting position, but dead – blood running from where his throat had been cut.

"One of them dirty heathens killed Luke while he was sittin' there sleepin'!" Mark yelled.

Matthew reached out and took Mark by the shoulders. "And we killed the injun that killed Luke, so I guess that evens things out."

Teary eyed, Mark turned on his brother and said, "No it don't. It ain't never gonna be even til all them dirty redskins is dead!"

Clay said, "I've got a shovel in my pack. You can bury him while I fix supper."

As Clay filled the coffee pot with water, he wondered what the rest of the trip would be like? He knew the dog didn't care much for either of the Marlow brothers and would warn him if either of them tried to slip up on him while he slept, but what if, somehow, they were able to kill the dog before he could make any noise? What sleep he would get would have to be done with one eye open, and they were still a long way from Texas.

-

Along the way toward the mountain, Idandi stopped and picked some white sage, prickly pear, desert passionflower and desert lavender – things he could eat and use to repair his wounds with.

As he swung up onto his horse's back, he smiled. The other horses were trailing a short distance behind. He knew when he found water and his wounds were bandaged so the horses would not smell blood, they would allow him to ride them.

It was close to two in the morning when the horse he was riding perked up his ears and lifted his nose into the air.

Idandi allowed him his head and smiled as the horse turned and headed up the mountain.

In a small grove of trees, the horse stopped next to a pool of water and lowered his head. As Idandi slid from his back, the other horses rushed up and began to drink.

Idandi hobbled over to the far side of the pool and knelt down and satisfied his own thirst. When he'd finished, he looked around to see where the water was coming from, but saw nothing and decided the pool must be fed from somewhere under the ground, which was not uncommon in these mountains.

By now Idandi was feeling the effects of his wounds and the loss of blood. He knew he needed nourishment for his body to regain some of its lost strength. He knew he needed to put medicine on the cut on his chest and the place on his leg where the dog had bitten him or he would not make it through the night.

First, he started a small fire and tossed the prickly pear into it to burn off the thorny parts. You couldn't eat prickly pear with the spear like thorns still attached; but with them burned off they would provide the temporary nourishment he so badly needed; plus, he could also use one of them to help heal the dog bite by tying it directly over the wound. Idandi smiled. The desert was filled with food and medicine if you knew what to look for.

The white sage would help soothe his stomach, which seemed to be very upset at the moment, while tea made from the desert passionflower would help him sleep, and last but not least, the lavender made a good lotion to help his dry and burned skin.

When he was finally able to lay down on the soft grass, he was feeling much better, physically. His stomach was full and he felt his energy returning, but not mentally. The thoughts of his dead brothers made him angry all over again.

Tomorrow he would find meat to eat and, in a few days, he would be able to travel again. He would find the white men and kill them, one by one. This he swore to the gods just before closing his eyes.

-

As the sun broke over the eastern horizon, Clay rousted out the two Marlow brothers and told them to relieve themselves, then grab a quick drink of water while he mounted the pack on the buckskin.

"Surely, we got time for some breakfast and ah cup or two of coffee, don't we?" Mark asked over his shoulder as he trotted toward the far side of the camp.

"We'll drink water and eat jerky in the saddle," Clay said, swinging the pack up onto the buckskin's back and cinching it in place.

"Hell, that Injun ain't gonna attack all three of us – not in the condition he's in," Mark pleaded from the far side of the rock emplacement.

Clay swung his saddle over the black stallion's back and began tightening it. "If the trail behind us is clear come noontime, then we can stop and fix a meal, but for now, we ride. Even if he is wounded, I want as much distance between us and him as we can."

With that, he made sure the fire was out and without another word, he stuck his foot into the stirrup and swung his leg over the black stallion's back and settled onto the saddle, and waited.

"You got any idea where we're headed?" Matthew asked as they left the rock fort and headed southeast.

"Tucson," Clay replied nonchalantly, "Shouldn't take more than a few days if we ride steady."

Clay didn't trust either of the Marlow brothers any further than he could throw his horse and motioned for them to ride ahead of him so he could keep an eye on them after giving them directions on which way to go.

"Ah few days, ya say," Mark threw over his shoulder.

Clay caught the remark and knew he would need to keep his guard up and not let himself slip into a deep sleep – at least until they could get to Tucson.

Clay knew the sheriff there and considered him to be a good man. He hoped he could put them in the Tucson jail for a couple of days so he could rest up. During the night, Clay had decided to take the train back to Texas if one was available.

If he remembered correctly, the Southern Pacific Railroad had a jail car he could lock them in while they traveled. There might be a charge, but it would be worth it to travel without having to worry about being shot, knifed, or clubbed by them, or having the Marlow brothers grabbing and making a hostage out of one of the passengers so they could escape.

"Any particular reason you want ta go ta Tucson?" Matthew asked, throwing the words over his shoulder and interrupting Clay's thoughts.

"Just keep riding in the direction you're headed," Clay answered, not wanting to disclose his reasons for going to Tucson. The least they knew about his plans the better it was for him.

The blistering sun climbed into the sky and once more heated up the desert, making traveling slower and slower.

Clay knew the Gila River was behind them and would be of no help, but there was a chance they could strike the Santa Cruz River and follow it down to Tucson.

Clay's biggest problem with this idea was the fact that unless there had been a goodly amount of rain, the Santa Cruz River would be just a dry riverbed. He could only hope for the best, otherwise he didn't have a clue on where any water holes might be and four days with what little water they had, would definitely not be enough.

When the sun was directly overhead, Clay saw a small clump of trees just off the trail they were riding and called a halt.

While there was no water to be seen, Clay knew the trees and small patch of grass couldn't grow without it.

After making a noontime camp, Clay took his shovel from the pack and looked around for a place to dig and decided near the edge of the grass should be a good spot.

"You boys walk over on the opposite side of the fire and sit down," Clay instructed the Marlow brothers before bending to his task.

"What'er you up to?" Matthew asked.

"I'm going to look for water for the horses and maybe some for us," Clay said as he pulled off his sweat-stained shirt.

Both men noticed the knife and gunshot scars on Clay's body and had second thoughts about trying to kill him. There were stories about other men who had tried... but on the other hand, neither of them wanted to hang, either.

"What makes you think there's water down there somewhere?" Mark asked, rubbing the back of his sunburned neck, trying not to think about the stories he'd heard about the ranger named, Brentwood and the fact that somewhere between here and Tucson he and his brother would try to find a way to kill him. Dying out here at the hand of the ranger seemed better than hanging and who knew, one of them might get lucky and kill the ranger.

"These trees, nor this grass grew without water, and it had to be nearby," Clay answered. "Look how green the grass is. I think there might be an underground waterway not too far down. Let's just hope I'm right."

The Marlow brothers looked at each other, then leaned back against a tree and watched as Clay dug.

Mark turned his head to his right and saw some fallen tree limbs. One of them looked to be just the right size to use as a club - one he could bash the ranger's head in with. The problem was, how could he pick it up and sneak up behind the ranger so he could get a clear shot at him without him noticing? None, at the moment, he decided, but he would keep an eye open for an opportunity. With his elbow, he nudged Matthew and nodded his head toward the pieces of wood.

Matthew looked at it and got the idea, then turned to his left and looked around at the fallen tree limbs near him, trying to spot one he could use as a weapon and saw two. He looked back at Mark and grinned, nodding his head toward the ones he'd found.

Unfortunately, at the moment, Clay was busy digging and missed what Matthew and Mark were up to. He'd just hit moist dirt and was anxious to go deeper, sure now that his hunch was right. After two more shovels filled with moist dirt, water began to seep into the hole. With a furry, Clay continued to dig and made the hole deeper and wider. Within another ten minutes of digging, he had a good-sized water hole that was quickly filling up.

Clay set the shovel aside and stirred the water around a little with his hand. It was cool to the touch and he took a handful and lifted to his mouth. With his tongue, he tasted just a drop of it.

He knew if the water was bitter or brackish they probably couldn't drink it. There was the possibility that it might even be poison.

The water tasted sweet, which caused him to smile. He then scooped up another handful and lifted it to his mouth, this time drinking it. It felt cool and sweet going down his throat and he looked over at the Marlow brothers and grinned. "We've got good water!" he shouted.

The Marlow brothers were dumbfounded. How did the ranger know so much about so many different things? It was going to be a shame to kill him after he had saved their lives several times now.

-

Idandi had risen with the coming of the sun and felt stiff and sore, but alive. After building up his fire, he made more tea and ate the last of the prickly pear, then rested for a little while. When he was feeling up to it he re-bandaged the bite on his leg and then took up his rifle and went, limping, into the forest.

Moving was slow and somewhat aggravating. The dog had taken a good-sized chunk out of his leg and it was very sore and painful to walk on. There would be a large scar, but scars meant he'd survived a battle and he would be held in high esteem for his bravery.

But for now, he needed meat and the only way he knew how to get it was to go out into the woods and hunt for it.

Not more than half a mile from his camp, Idandi came upon a small clearing that was filled with grass and flowers. It was an ideal place where game would come to graze. Idandi stepped in behind a tree, cocked his rifle and waited.

He'd been there only a short time when a small, pronghorn, even smaller than a white-tailed deer came hobbling into the clearing on three legs.

Idandi studied the small pronghorn and saw that it's left front leg was swollen and hung at a funny angle.

"Because you have broken your leg, you have come to save my life. Thank you for giving your life for mine," Idandi said.

And with that, he shot the young antelope.

It took Idandi more than two hours to carry the young antelope the short distance back to his camp. Even though it didn't weigh much, carrying it on his shoulders and trying to walk on his wounded leg was not only painful, but slow and tedious because he had to stop several times to rest his leg.

When he finally arrived back at his campsite, he dropped the antelope on the ground and bent down on his knees, thanking the gods again for providing him with the meat he so sorely needed.

-

The water had filled the hole, the dirt had sunk to the bottom and relatively clear water remained. They drank their fill, made coffee, filled their canteens and gave the horses a drink while their noon meal of beans and pan bread was cooking.

Clay was feeling good about himself and the Marlow brothers had complimented him on finding the water.

"I never would have thought about doin' that," Matthew commented. "You're a right smart fella, Mister Ranger."

Clay looked at Matthew, not knowing quite what to think about his friendly nature all of a sudden, so he just nodded his head, but kept a wary eye on him.

Mark jumped to his feet and hurried toward the woods. When Clay looked up, Mark called over his shoulder, "Nature's callin'."

Clay was pouring himself another cup of coffee when he heard a gagging noise and looked over at Matthew, who was holding his throat and gasping for breath. His face was beet red and his eyes were wide with fear.

Clay sat the coffee pot and cup down and rushed over to see if he could help Matthew. When he bent down, Matthew grabbed Clay by his hair and jerked his head down, banging it against his own head.

Before Clay could react, he felt a blow to the back of his head and everything went black.

CHAPTER TWENTY

Clay opened his eyes to something wet and slobbery licking his face and saw the dog standing next to him. The dog had dried blood mixed with the hair on his head.

When the dog saw Clay was awake, he stepped back and sat down on his haunches, wagging his tail.

Clay tried to move but found he was tied to a tree. Looking around, he saw that other than the dog, he was alone. The Marlow brothers were gone and had taken everything including his guns and horses.

He tried to remember what had happened and decided he'd been suckered by Matthew pretending to be choking and when he went to help, Mark had hit him over the head with a club of some kind. Looking around, Clay saw a large piece of wood laying nearby with blood on it, which confirmed what he'd been thinking.

Why hadn't they killed him when they had the chance? he wondered, which at this point was mute. He was alive and that was all that mattered. For now, he needed to figure some way to get himself untied.

Expanding his chest as much as he could, then exhaling as much as he could, caused the rope to loosen just a little and allowed him to move the rope upward just an inch or so.

After doing this a dozen times, he was able to get his hands under the rope and push it up over his head.

As he started to stand up a piece of paper fell from his lap onto the ground. He picked it up and saw that there was something written on it. He held it up to the light and read: "We let ya live cause you saved us ah couple of times. So now we figure the score is even, but if ya come after us we won't be so nice. Hopefully that Injun will come along and do it for us."

Clay folded the paper and put it in his pocket and looked around, but there was nothing to see, the camp had been completely stripped.

The sun was still low in the east, which meant he'd been unconscious all through yesterday and all through last night. They had nearly a full day's head start on him and they had the horses, food and water.

He knelt down and called the dog to him. "Hey ol' son, come here, boy."

The dog walked over and stood next to Clay while he examined the dog's head.

Clay led the dog over to the water hole and after a long drink, washed the blood out of the dog's hair as best he could, then washed his own head and washed his face with the cool water.

Clay was still unsteady on his feet and his head hurt something awful. He walked over and sat down and leaned his back against a tree. With a sigh, he closed his eyes and went back to sleep.

Sometime later he heard the dog growling and opened his eyes.

The first thing he saw was a pair of brown legs. Moving his eyes upward he saw the Apache brave standing some distance away.

The Indian had his hands on his hips and a leering grin on his face.

It was the same brave he'd fought during the attack; the only one to have escaped. He had a shirt on covering the knife wound Clay had given him and a bandage wrapped around his leg where the dog had bitten him. Clay watched him closely as he stood up - still a little unsteady on his feet and used the tree to brace himself.

Idandi watched the white man stand up and saw the rope still tied to the tree and wondered why his friends had tied him up and left him here, but that mattered little. The man was here and he, Idandi, would finally get the revenge he sought.

"Why are you so all fired bent on killing me?" Clay asked of the Apache brave standing across the grass from him.

Like most Indians, Idandi spoke Apache, Mexican and English, with the last being the lesser of the three, but still passable.

"You are the white man who killed our chief, He Who Did Not Die," Idandi said.

"I don't recall killing any of your people," Clay said with a questioning look on his face. "When was I supposed to have done that?"

Idandi didn't care for all this talking. He wanted to fight, to kill this white man, but out of politeness he said, "You drove our horses through our camp and during the stampede, our chief was killed. Now I am here to seek revenge for his death."

It was the longest speech he'd ever had with a white man and as far as he was concerned, the last one.

Reaching into his belt, Idandi pulled out a knife and tossed it into the grass in front of the white man.

Clay looked down at the knife and shook his head. He was in no condition to go head to head in a knife fight with this brave or anybody else for that matter. Turning to his side, Clay pointed at the lump and bloody spot on his head.

"I'm real sorry about your chief," Clay said, shaking his head. "It was not my intention to kill anybody, especially your chief. And I'm in no condition to do much fighting. I'm a Texas Ranger and those two men were my prisoners; at least they were until they bushwhacked me and left me here tied up, hoping you'd come along and finish me off. I got loose and was about to leave. Is there anything I can do for your people to keep us from fighting?"

Idandi looked at the white man standing unsteady on his feet and sighed. After a moment he said, "We are both wounded, so that should make us even. The only thing that will satisfy my people is your scalp hanging on my lodge pole. Now pick up the knife, or are you a coward; too afraid to face a wounded Indian?"

After a moment of staring at each other, Clay bent down and picked up the knife, knowing there was no other way. "I sure hope

I'm up to this, I can't keep living this way. If I live through this, this is definitely my last ranger mission," he muttered to himself.

As Clay stood up and stared across the grass at the waiting warrior, the dog eased up next to him and began to growl.

Idandi saw the dog move up next to the white man and heard the low growl coming from his throat and felt a moment of uncertainty. "I fight only you, white man, not your dog," he said pointing at the dog.

Clay looked down at the dog and said, "Sit." And to his surprise, the dog squatted down on his haunches, but kept his eyes on the Indian brave.

"Stay," Clay said and pointed his hand at the dog, then moved two steps away from him.

The dog sat there, but Clay could tell he wasn't happy about it. "This is between me and this brave here," he said to the dog, "and you're not invited to the dance, so just, stay!" Clay commanded. Then in a whisper he said, "If I lose, he's all yours."

The Apache warrior stood patiently waiting for the white man to declare he was ready to fight. But the truth was, he, himself, wasn't ready. His leg was not yet fully healed and it hurt to stand on it and the cut on his chest was scabbed over and red; but he had sworn revenge on the white man and his enemy was just a few feet away. He could see that the white man was in no condition to fight, either, but like it or not, one of them would die today.

Clay gave out a long sigh. He had no reason to kill this brave, if that was even possible in his condition, but he could see no way out of fighting him. The man wouldn't listen to reason – he'd already tried that.

Clay's head hurt from where they'd hit him and he guessed he might even have a slight concussion because he was having a hard time getting his eyes to focus.

"My patience is growing slim, white man," Idandi said, shrugging his shoulders.

Clay nodded his head and said, "So be it," then crouched in a fighting stance and motioned for the dance to begin.

For a minute or so, they circled each other, each looking for an opening that was slow to come, but when Clay staggered from losing his balance, Idandi struck, tearing Clay's shirt just above his belly button, then swiped the blade of his knife backward, aiming for Clay's throat.

With his left hand, Clay grabbed the Indian's right wrist, the one holding the knife and shoved upward, then stepped in, driving his knife toward the Indian's heart, but at the last moment, Idandi grabbed Clay's wrist and pushed it away. They wrestled around in a sort of dance like motion for some time, each man trying to break the others grip.

At the same time, they both jerked loose and stepped back, then once again began circling each other.

Each man sliced at each other repeatedly with as much effort as they could muster, but in their condition, both men were getting tired and gasping for breath.

Clay took a deep breath and decided this was not a good day to die. He had to do something soon before his energy was completely used up. If that happened he would die.

It was Idandi who made the next lunge and when he did, Clay sidestepped and stuck his foot out, tripping the Indian.

Off balance, Idandi fell face first onto the ground, and before he could roll over, Clay was on his back and grabbed a handful of his hair and jerked his head back.

Idandi felt the white man's knife press against his throat and knew he'd lost. He began to sing his death song, waiting for death to come.

Clay listened for a moment, then released his grip on the Indian's hair and stood up.

With a surprised look on his face, Idandi climbed to his feet and stared at the white man.

Clay looked Idandi in the eyes and said, "My name is Clay Brentwood and I have decided to let you live. You are a strong warrior and your people need you. When you get back, I would like you to tell your people about me and tell them I am their friend, and that not all white men are bad."

And with that, Clay looked at the dog and said, "Com'on ol' son, we've got some walking to do."

Idandi stood and watched the white man who called himself Clay Brentwood; walk away - the dog at his side.

As he stood there, something happened inside him he didn't quite understand. This was a man he had hated and wanted to kill, but now, he no longer did. Could there be friendship between a red man and a white man, he wondered?

Clay had gone no more than a couple hundred feet when Idandi called out, "White man."

Clay turned around and watched as the Apache brave walked up to him and held out his rifle and ammo belt, saying, "You will need these."

Clay reached out and took the rifle and ammo belt and said, "Thank you. But why are you giving me this?"

Idandi looked Clay in the eyes for a long moment, then said, "Give me your hand."

Clay held out his hand and watched as the Apache brave pulled his knife from its scabbard and cut a small slice on the palm of his own hand, then reached out and made a similar cut on Clay's hand.

He returned his knife to its scabbard and when there was blood on both palms, he joined hands with Clay.

"One day soon I will be the new leader of the mighty Chiricahua people and my name will be known throughout this part of the land. Our blood has mixed. Clay Brentwood and Idandi of the Chiricahua are now blood brothers." Idandi reached up and removed a necklace from around his neck and placed it over Clay's head. "You can now travel through Idandi's land in safety. If any of the Apache or Comancheros try to harm you, you can tell them you are Idandi's blood brother and show them your scar and my necklace. They will allow you to go in peace. If someday we should meet again, we will share a meal and speak of this time, Clay Brentwood."

With that, Idandi turned and walked over to his horse and swung his leg over its back and rode away without looking back.

Clay stood and watched Idandi until he became nothing but a small dot on the horizon. He wondered what it took for him to do what he'd just done. Apache braves were proud men. Was it because he had let Idandi live? Or was it because he thought of Clay as brave. The Apache honored bravery. He wasn't sure why he'd changed his mind about killing him, but for whatever reason the young brave seemed to feel a kinship between them. Although this Idandi, as he called himself, hadn't said anything, Clay leaned toward the fact that he was the first white man to ever show him kindness.

Clay shook his head. Now he had a half-brother from the Comanche people and a blood brother of the Chiricahua Apache people. He guessed that was not a bad thing, not a bad thing at all.

Clay had been walking for a little over an hour and his feet were hurting; boots were not made for walking long distances, especially in the desert where his feet sunk into the sand with almost every step.

Clay heard what he thought was the sound of a horse running and he spun around, rifle at the ready, expecting to see an Apache brave charging down on him, but what he saw, caused his heart to pound.

Clay was standing dead still with a grin spread across his face as the black stallion ran up to him and stopped just short of stepping on him and laid his head across Clay's shoulder.

Clay put his arms around the horse's neck and hugged him, tears welling up in his eyes. "Where in the world did you come from, big fella?"

Clay stepped back and rubbed the horse's forehead, noticing he had on neither bridle nor saddle. "Did you run away when they tried to catch you? Is that what you did, Midnight?"

The black stallion snorted and shook his head up and down as though he knew what Clay had said and was responding.

The dog seemed almost as excited to see the big horse as Clay was. He jumped up and down making little yipping noises.

Clay grabbed a handful of mane and swung up on the black stallion's back and urged him forward by guiding the horse with his knees and feet. The dog trotted along beside them as if his world was right again.

Clay rubbed the stubble of whiskers on his face, then combed his hair with his fingers before slapping his hat back down on his head. As he rode along, he stared at the Superstition Mountains far in the distance, wondering if the Marlow brothers had gotten that far, yet?"

It wasn't long before the blistering sun beat down on the desert like a furnace blast from a Pennsylvania steel mill.

Clay's sweat stained shirt stuck to him like a second skin. His eyes burned from the salty sweat running from his forehead. The glare of the sun made his eyes ache and from time to time, caused him to blink to get them back in focus. He pulled the brim of his hat a little further down on his forehead to help protect his eyes.

As Clay rode along, his mind began to stray. What if, he wondered, instead of trying to track down the Marlow brothers and arrest them, again, and try to take them back to Texas - what if he just got his horses and other property back and left them out here in the desert, afoot?

Clay knew he was just feeling sorry for himself, but he couldn't help it. His head hurt, along with almost every other muscle in his body. He was tired of chasing outlaws, getting shot at – having hand-to-hand knife fights and living daily like an animal. He was ready to say, "To hell with it," and go home – home to his ranch back in Texas where his biggest worry would be getting yelled at by his housekeeper, Mrs. McIntyre, for tromping mud into her clean kitchen.

The money they paid rangers for chasing down outlaws wasn't worth the effort. Hell, he paid his foreman more than he made as a Texas Ranger.

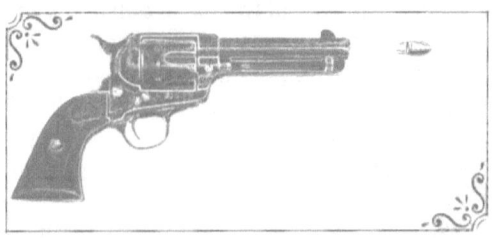

CHAPTER TWENTY-ONE

-

After tying the ranger to the tree, Matthew and Mark loaded the packhorse and tried unsuccessfully to get a rope on the black stallion, but couldn't come close. In fact, the big horse had lunged at Matthew with barred teeth and came close to biting his face.

After close to an hour, they gave up and left, wanting to be far away when and if the ranger woke up. The last they saw of the ranger's horse, he was just a small dot on the western horizon. They could care less where he was headed as long as he was nowhere in the vicinity when the ranger woke up, if in fact he ever did?

On their second day of traveling Matthew glanced over his shoulder and sighed. "I don't reckon we need ta worry no more. I don't see hide nor hair of 'im comin' up behind us. Nor that injun, either. I reckon they's done in."

"I still think you should have let me kill him while we had the chance, Matthew," Mark said to his brother as they rode across the desert in the direction of Tucson.

Matthew couldn't explain why he hadn't killed the ranger and was almost having second thoughts, but in the end, he heard himself saying, "I cain't explain it but killin' him whilst he is unconscious like that just didn't seem right, especially since he saved our bacon more'n oncet. No, we'll wait, and if'n that Injun don't kill him and he comes lookin' for us, and he's standin' on his own two feet, well that's altogether different and we'll fill'im with so much lead it'll take half ah dozen men ta tote him away."

"So, what are we gonna do in Tucson? We ain't got no money. I searched the ranger and he only had two dollars in his pocket," Mark said, not realizing that hidden in the pack on the buckskin horse was several thousand dollars. Clay never went anywhere these days without money, but kept it hidden and used it only sparingly.

Mark reached into his vest pocket and pulled out one of the dollars he'd taken from Clay and handed it toward Matthew. "Here, I'll share with ya."

Matthew shook his head and said, "Naw, you keep it. Sides, I plan on us havin' money jinglin' in our pockets by the time we get ta Tucson."

Mark looked around at the vast country surrounding them and said, "I don't see no bank ta rob. Hell, I don't even see ah town nor a farm or nuthin' – so how do you reckon we'll have any money when we get ta Tucson?"

Matthew took his time and bit off a chaw of tobacco and wallowed it around in his jaw until it felt comfortable, then spit a stream of brown juice off to the side. "Last night whilst you was sleepin', I was still wide awake and walked off, out away from the fire, and that's when I seen it."

"Seen what?" Mark asked, his eyes growing wide, looking around as though he expected to attacked any time.

"The light," Matthew responded, nonchalantly.

"Light? What light?" Mark asked, even more curious now.

"I'm purty sure it was light comin' from somebody's fire, but it was ah long ways off," he said, pointing toward the direction they were traveling.

"What's ah fire light got ta do with us havin' money?" Mark asked, scratching his ear.

Matthew spit another long stream of tobacco juice off to the side again, this time aiming for a small lizard, but missed. "If'n it's somebody headed west, theys' probably got money on 'em ta pay for supplies and other things. And if'n we get lucky and there's several folks, you know like ah family in ah wagon goin' ta maybe, oh I don't know, California or somewhere, why who knows how much money they'll have?"

"And if they got ah couple of pretty young gals travelin' with 'em..." Mark said, letting his words hang in the air.

Matthew thought about that for a few minutes and decided it wouldn't be such a bad idea if they had women folks with 'em, young or old, didn't matter none ta him ah woman was ah woman as far as he was concerned.

By early afternoon the Marlow brothers could see a dust column in the far distance, a little to the right of the direction they were traveling.

"Wonder if'n that's ah wagon or men on horses?" Mark asked, looking toward his brother, who was also studying the dust column.

"Could be either one," Matthew said, spitting his chaw out onto the desert floor which was immediately attacked by ants. "But I'm leanin' toward ah wagon or maybe two of 'em."

"What makes ya lean that direction?" Mark asked, looking back and studying the dust column a little closer.

Matthew bit off a new chew and wallowed it around for a minute or so before explaining his reason for thinking the way he did.

"Look at the column real close like, little brother and tell me what ya see," Matthew finally said.

Mark looked at the dust column as he wiped sweat from his face and eyes. "All I see is ah big ole column of dust comin' our direction."

"And that's all you see?" Matthew asked.

Mark took another look, then shook his head and said, "Yeah, what else is there ta see?"

"Did you happen ta notice the speed the dust column is travelin'?" Matthew probed.

"Well, it sure ain't movin' as fast as ah tornadie," Mark replied. "What's speed got ta do with it, no how?"

Matthew spit out a long stream of tobacco juice at another small lizard and this time the juice landed squarely on its back, causing it to turn and run away, spittle flying into the air.

"Well now, if'n it was men on horseback, they would be movin' at ah faster pace and the dust cloud would reflect that little fact, but it ain't movin' fast atall. As ah matter of fact, it's moving kinda slow, like ah wagon would make."

Suddenly Mark's eyes got wide and a grin spread across his face. "Ah wagon train that might have females with it?"

"I ain't sayin' it's no wagon train. The column is too small for that; maybe one or two wagons at the most."

Mark's grin disappeared and was replaced by a frown. "You suggestin' it might be freight wagons with no women on board?"

"I ain't suggestin' nuthin'. What I am sayin' is, we check it out afore makin' any stupid conclusions," Matthew said, after spitting again, then wiping his lips on his shirtsleeve.

"And just how do ya pursume ta do that, big brother? Just ride up to 'em and say, we've come ta look ya over. Got any money and women folks with ya?"

Matthew sighed. "Your brain cain't be no bigger than ah pea," he said shaking his head. "Sometimes I wonder how you ever lived this long."

"Don't start on me!" Mark yelled. "I don't half'ta..."

Matthew held up his hand and Mark closed his mouth.

Mark looked at Matthew with contempt and said, "Well, I'm waittin'."

Matthew shifted his chew to the other side of his mouth, then pointed. "See that small mesa yonder. I figure we'll find ah way and ride up the backside and hide behind the rocks on top and have ah look see when they get close."

Mark's eyes looked at the small mesa ahead of them, then at the dust column and saw the dust column would pass right by the mesa.

"You're right big brother, I probably would never have thought of that."

Matthew turned and rode toward the mesa, knowing his younger brother didn't have sense enough to come in outta the rain, let alone, do any figurn'.

With the horses tied to small scrub trees on the backside of the top of the mesa, the Marlow brothers duck walked up behind two of the boulders on the front side and looked down.

In the near distance they saw two wagons coming in their direction. The wagons were being pulled by oxen, which accounted for them moving slow.

From where they were crouched, both Mark and Matthew saw an older man with long white hair and a long white beard, and a young boy sitting on the seat of the lead wagon. The young boy was around seven or eight and had bright red, curly hair. The older man was showing the boy how to hold the reins.

A man in his mid to late twenties was on horseback and riding up front as though he was scouting the way. He also had red hair from what they could see below his hat.

Another man, maybe a year or so younger, was riding on the right side of him, closer to the mesa. Both young men were armed with pistols riding against their legs and each had a rifle stuck in the long gun boot attached to the saddle.

Following, in the second wagon, was an older, more sophisticated looking man sitting on the seat, dressed in a dust covered suit - his head nodding like he was about to fall asleep.

Trailing behind, on horseback, watching their back trail, was yet another man in his mid to late twenties and resembled the man in the suit, only much younger; maybe the older man's son.

In this part of the country you could see for miles and therefore didn't need to do a lot of watching to see if anyone was approaching, so their vigil was lackluster and the young man pulling up the rear guard was rocking back and forth on his saddle and also seemed to be about to fall asleep.

"Looks like easy pickin's ta me," Mark whispered in Matthew's direction.

Matthew grinned at his brother and whispered back, "Since I'm the best shot, I'll take the lead riders and you take the one in the back. Once the young ones are out of the way, the old men shouldn't be hard ta deal with. They'll probably just give up."

Mark nodded his approval and lifted his rifle to his shoulder.

There were two things the Marlow brothers weren't taking into account; one - the downward angle of the shots and two - the sunlight reflecting off their rifle barrels.

As the Marlow brothers raised their rifles to their shoulders, the lead rider of the small wagon train just happened to glance up at the top of the mesa they were approaching and saw the sun reflect off the rifle barrels and assumed the worst.

"Ambush!" he yelled and turned his horse aside just as the sound of several rifle shots filled the air.

Both wagons were pulled to a halt and the two men and the boy jumped off to the backside of the wagons, while the man bringing up the rear, raced his horse up behind the rear wagon and jumped down, bringing his rifle with him.

Matthew's shot missed its mark as far as Mark's had and the two brothers looked at each other and frowned.

Not to be denied a kill, the two brothers turned their attention to the oxen pulling the front wagon and shot both of them, but had to hide behind the boulders when lead from the men below struck the rocks near their faces, throwing chips in all directions.

"Who the hell is shootin' at us?" the man in the dusty suit yelled.

"More'n likely some outlaws thet want ta steal whatever it is they think we have," the man in the bib overalls said, checking his fifty-caliber buffalo gun, while glancing around the end of his wagon, looking for somebody to shoot at.

"Anybody hurt?" the redheaded man asked as he checked to make sure his rifle was fully loaded.

"Looks like we're all okay," The man in the suit said.

The small boy ran over to the red headed man and asked, "Are we going to be all right?"

Glancing at the top of the mesa, the red headed man said, "Looks like there's only two of 'em up there. We can wait til dark, then ease on up the trail with somebody walkin' next ta the oxen, leadin 'im. I'll take the front wagon."

"But papa, they shot the oxen pulling the front wagon," the boy protested.

The young man looked at the fallen oxen and shook his head.

"We'll just have to take one of the oxen from uncle Ephram's wagon. It'll be slow but better'n stayin' around here and gettin' shot at," the red headed man said.

Throughout the afternoon, there were gunshots back and forth between the men on the mesa and the men behind the two wagons, but their bullets found no one from either side, although, the big buffalo gun did a lot of damage to the rocks the Marlow brothers were hiding behind, splitting one of them in half, sending them scurrying for better cover.

The blistering sun beat down on Clay with a vengeance – like maybe what hell would feel like. His clothes were drenched with sweat and his eyes hurt from glaring at the heat waves that danced in front of him.

Before long, both man and horse had their heads bent low, suffering from the one hundred twenty-degree temperature. The only thing keeping Clay going on was catching the Marlow brothers and getting his buckskin horseback, along with knowing they would meet the hangman when he got them back to Dallas. He knew they would want him to testify at their trial and he had plenty to say.

-

After a great deal of thought by Matthew, he decided they were just wasting their ammunition and decided to move to the back side of the mesa and make some coffee and possibly fix something to eat.

"With their oxen dead, they'll still be there in the morning, especially if'n one of us takes ah shot att'em from time ta time."

Mark and Matthew had just made their way to where the horses were tied when Mark looked off to the north and said, "Matthew, there'd somebody comin'."

Matthew reached into the pack and pulled out Clay's binoculars and put them to his eyes.

"Damn!" he exclaimed.

"What is it?" Mark asked

"It's that damn ranger!" Matthew replied.

"Well, how'd he get loose?" Mark asked like he couldn't believe his ears.

"Now, how would I know that?" Matthew said, then spit into the dirt.

"Where'd he get ah horse?" Mark asked.

Matthew shook his head from side to side frustrated at his brother for asking so many questions, especially ones he didn't know the answers for.

Matthew looked through the binoculars again and said, "Looks ta me like he's ridin' that black horse of his'n and carryin' ah rifle."

"Well now how did he come ta be ridin' that horse? Last time we saw 'im he was goin' west like his tail was on fire. And where did he get ah rifle?"

Matthew ground his teeth together, then said, "I don't know that either. Suppose you go down there and ask him."

"Are you crazy? He'd most likely shoot me on sight!" Mark gasped.

"Hand me my rifle," Matthew said. "I tole him in that note I left, if he was ta get loose and come lookin' for us, I'd kill 'em this time and that's just what I'm gonna do."

Clay had been hearing gunshots for some time and was looking ahead of him to see if he could see who was shooting at who. It could be Indians attacking a wagon train, or wagons carrying silver ore, or most anything. It might even be the Marlow brothers doing what they did, robbing people; and maybe this time the victims were shooting back.

It was getting late in the day and the shooting had stopped around twenty minutes ago, making Clay wonder if whoever it was had called a halt for the night or one side or the other had won the shootout.

Just as Clay leaned forward and patted the black stallion on the neck, he felt a sharp pain on his right shoulder as a bullet tore his shirt and ripped a knife-like gash across the skin.

Because of several years of being shot at by outlaws and Indians, Clay dove off the left side of his horse and rolled over and over, barely being missed by more shots.

Clay rolled behind a boulder and lay there panting as several bullets hit the large rock he was now hiding behind.

Clay looked back over his shoulder and smiled, the black stallion was well away from the action and still running, with the dog not far behind.

If he hadn't leaned forward when he had, the bullet would have hit him in the chest instead of grazing his shoulder. Another close call.

Clay scooted to the far side of the rock he was hiding behind, took a deep breath and peeked around the side, taking a quick look at the top of the mesa to see if he could see anyone.

He saw the late evening sun gleaming off of something metal, possibly a rifle barrel, but he wasn't sure.

After checking his wound and found that it was superficial, he dabbed it with his neckerchief until the bleeding stopped, then leaned back against the rock.

His first instinct had been to return fire, but what if he didn't? What if he let them think he'd been mortally injured? Would they leave him alone or would they come down to check? He doubted it. Whoever they had been shooting at should be important enough to keep them on top of the mesa.

Just then, he heard two more shots - one coming from the top of the mesa and the other from the far side of the mesa, possibly from down at the bottom. The shot from the top sounded like a thirty caliber, but the loud boom from the rifle below sounded more like a fifty-caliber buffalo gun.

He quickly discounted an ore wagon or a wagon train. Both would have returned fire with more than one rifle.

Clay rolled and lit a cigarette and blew the smoke into his neckerchief to keep it from being seen from the mesa, alerting them that he was still alive. Even though it was dusk and what little smoke he would make would be hard to see from that distance, why take a chance?

By the time he'd finished his cigarette, the moon was coming over the eastern horizon. Clay rolled onto his stomach and belly crawled to the side of the rock and looked at the desert between him and the mesa to make sure no one was coming to see if he was dead. Only when he was sure he was alone did he let his eyes travel upward.

At the top of the mesa he could see the glimmer of a small fire. By now it was too dark to see more than a few feet and guessed they were having supper.

Clay thought about waiting until they'd gone to bed, then try and sneak up on them, but decided this was not his best choice. They might take turns keeping watch in case the people in the wagons tried to climb the mesa and sneak up on them. Besides, he wasn't completely sure it was the two imbeciles called, Mark and Matthew Marlow - and if he was wrong...

In another few minutes, full darkness had come and Clay made his decision. The sky was filled with stars and the full moon was bright enough for him to see the outlines of his horse some distance to the north.

He turned and began to belly crawl toward his horse, hoping he didn't come face to face with a scorpion, a rattlesnake or a Gila monster. From time to time, he glanced over his shoulder to make sure he wasn't being observed, which he might have been had he stood up and walked or run.

He'd crawled close to two hundred yards before the dog ran over and began to lick him on the face. "Good to see you, ol' son," he said and patted the dog on the head.

He crawled a few feet farther, then climbed to his feet next to the black stallion. Looking back, he could barely see a glimmer of the firelight at the top of the mesa and decided they couldn't see him, even if they were looking.

"So far, so good," he said as he swung up on the black stallion's back and rode him even farther away before turning him to the southeast, giving a wide berth to the mesa. The dog trotted along beside him. In the moonlight the mesa stood out like a huge castle.

Close to two hours later, and on the far side of the mesa, Clay could see the outline of two large wagons in the moonlight off to his right and pulled the black stallion to a halt.

Clay sat there for several minutes deciding what to do next. If he approached them from this angle, they might think he was one of the outlaws and open fire on him. But if he went farther on and came back toward them from the south, he stood a better chance at them not thinking of him being one of the men shooting at them, and palaver with him about the situation. If they were in fact victims, he wanted to help them and at the same time, capture the Marlow brothers.

The moon was much higher in the sky when Clay stopped his horse and called out in a loud whisper, "Hello the camp. I'm a friend and would like to come in," he said, hoping he was right.

"Step down and walk real slow like with yer hands in the air," a voice from his left said.

Clay was surprised they knew he was close and had him covered, but he couldn't worry about that, now. He stepped down and raised his hands shoulder high and said to the dog, who was standing next to him, growling deep in his chest. "Easy ol' son."

The dog immediately stopped his growling but stood facing the area from where the voice was coming from.

"Heard ya comin' awhile back. Seems you weren't tryin' ta sneak up on us, but what I'd like ta know is, what'er ya doin' out here this time ah night?"

"It's kind of a long story which I'd be happy to tell over a cup of coffee if you happen to have some," Clay said, trying to sound jovial.

"Start walkin'," the voice from his left said.

When Clay got close to the camp, he could see a small, shaded fire next to one of the wagons.

"That'll be far enough," another voice said, and Clay stopped, reaching down and patting the dog on the head. "Easy, boy."

The dog relaxed and squatted down on his haunches, but did not wag his tail.

The unsaddled black stallion stopped just behind Clay and rubbed its nose against Clay's back, which did not go unnoticed by the men next to the wagons.

Clay watched as two men approached him. One of them was wearing well-worn bib overalls and carrying the buffalo gun he'd heard earlier.

A young man in his twenties, holding a pistol pointed at him, came up to him slowly and relieved him of his rifle.

The other man, the one with the buffalo rifle stepped closer and asked, "What's yer business here, mister?"

The man appeared to be close to sixty or so, Clay observed, but didn't have the swaddle of an outlaw. Clay relaxed some. He looked like a man who'd worked with his hands for most of his life and was maybe just protecting his property and the people around him.

"Before we go any further, I need to show you something," Clay said, reaching slowly for his vest pocket.

Both men raised their weapons and trained them on Clay's chest. The one with the buffalo gun said, "Be real careful, mister."

Clay nodded, then very slowly, he pulled his badge from his vest pocket. "Clay Brentwood, Texas Ranger."

A voice from close to one of the wagons said, "Texas is ah mite fer piece from here. What's ah Texas Ranger doin' this fur from home? And why does he come up on folks in the middle of the night?"

"Like I said, it's a long story – best told over a cup of coffee, if there's any to be had?"

After a long moment, an elderly man in a dirty suit said, "Com'on in and sit and tell your story, but it better be a good one."

Just then, a small, redheaded boy walked up and stood next to the young man with the pistol and asked him, "Why doesn't the horse have a saddle, papa?"

"The man looked down at the boy and said, "I hope that's part of the story the man is gonna tell us," he said, then looked at Clay. "It will be, won't it?"

Clay looked at all of them and said, "Yes, that will be part of it."

The man in the suit spoke the first names so far and said, "Patrick, get the man a cup of coffee while Ben tends to his horse.

Clay looked at the young man who approached him and said, "Maybe I'd better do it. He tends to get ornery with folks he doesn't know."

The young man called Ben nodded his head and led them over behind the second wagon where the oxen were tied and eating hay.

Clay reached down and picked up a handful of hay and held it out to the black stallion. The big horse stepped closer and took a mouthful.

Clay patted him on the neck, then looked at Ben and said, "He'll be ok now."

Ben looked at Clay with a question in his eyes and asked, "You not gonna tie him to the wagon wheel?"

Clay grinned. "As long as I'm nearby, he won't go anywhere."

Just then, the small boy called Patrick, walked up with a piece of meat in his hand and looked up at Clay. "Will it be alright if I feed this to your dog, Sir?"

Clay looked at the dog and saw the desire in his eyes, but wasn't how he would react to the young boy feeding him.

He rubbed the dog's head and said, "It's okay. Go on over there, but be nice, he just wants to feed you."

The dog looked up at Clay and for the first time since coming into the camp, he began wagging his tail. He walked over and gently took the meat from the boy's hand, then went off to the side and lay down, and ate the meat.

"Well I'll be horn-swaggled," the old man in the bib overalls, said. "It's like them animals understand everthin' you say."

Clay nodded, "Guess that'll be part of the story, also. Now, about that cup of coffee?"

CHAPTER TWENTY-TWO

-

The man in the suit introduced them as the Hacker family, or what was left of them, stating they were coming from Nogales, on their way to San Francisco, California. He said his name was Ephram Hacker and they too had a story to tell. "Ben there, is my son. The man in the bib overalls is my brother, Elijah and the other young man; the one with the red hair, he's Elijah's son, Justin. The boy is Justin's son, Patrick. And last but not least, that young man standin' next to the wagon is Elijah's other son, Jeremiah," Ephram said, nodding his head.

"We were attacked by those men on top of the mesa. They missed hittin' any of us, but killed two of our oxen. We plan to sneak out of here later, after they go to sleep, with one oxen pulling each wagon - maybe sometime after midnight."

About then Patrick noticed the bloodstain on Clay's shirt and Ephram said he had some medicine in the wagon, and something to bandage it with.

Clay sat drinking coffee and for some reason he couldn't explain other than he felt comfortable among these people, told his story from the time his home had been raided by the Beeler gang and left nothing out.

"And that's why I came in from the south," Clay finished up with.

"I'll get ya ah plate of food," Jeremiah said.

While he was eating, Clay's mind thought back. For a man not yet thirty, he had suffered far more hardships as a ranger than he liked to remember. The burning in his shoulder reminded him of all the gunshot wounds, knife scars, times he'd been severely beaten – even once nearly being frozen to death. Then there had been all those long days in the saddle in every kind of weather a man could think of, along with trying to get a decent night's sleep on the cold, hard ground.

With all the people who'd tried to kill him, it was hard to believe he was still alive. So far, he'd been dammed lucky and as he wiped his plate clean with his biscuit, he wondered how much longer his luck would hold out?

It was funny - he had never wanted to be a Texas Ranger, or a lawman of any kind. He had always considered himself to be a quiet, gentle man who wanted nothing more than a good paying ranch, a loving woman by his side and maybe a couple of kids – possibly a son for him and a daughter for his wife.

After putting his plate and fork in the pan of dishwater sitting next to the fire, he lit a cigarette and allowed his mind to think of better things than chasing outlaws. Even though he'd lost his wife to the Beeler gang of cutthroats, he still had their ranch, which he was glad he'd decided to go back to and try to rebuild. He had approximately ten thousand acres of good land a few miles west of Seymour that had a river running through it. He was introducing white-faced cattle to the area and they were prospering. He caught, broke and trained wild horses that he sold to the army and nearby ranchers. He had as good a crew of men working for him as any rancher could want. So why was he unhappy? Because over the past few years, he'd spent little time there, that was why.

While he was a strong believer in justice, being a Texas Ranger was beginning to take its toll on him. His biggest problem was, he was good at his job and had built a reputation as a man who got the job done.

To keep from being wrongfully hung, he'd agreed to be a ranger for two years - but those two years had come and gone some time ago and here he was still out chasing outlaws.

Last year, after that ordeal with a hired killer the papers called, The Chameleon, he'd decided to once for all, hang up his star, but like every other time he'd tried to quit the rangers, Bill McDaniel, his boss and head of the rangers, would talk him into just one more job.

And now, here he was, out in the middle of the Arizona desert, wounded again, sitting with some people who wanted nothing more than to find their way to San Francisco, California, while the two outlaws he'd been chasing, were not far away and wanted to see all of them, dead.

The boy interrupted his thoughts. "You sure got a nice dog, Mister Brentwood."

The dog was sitting next to Clay, wagging his tail, while the boy stood next to the dog, patting him on the head and scratching his neck.

"He's not exactly mine," Clay stammered. "I found him with an arrow in his leg and pulled it out and put some medicine on the wound, and well, ever since, he's been following along wherever I go."

"What's his name?" Patrick asked.

Clay was caught by surprise. A name had so far, never been an issue. And after a minute, he said, "Well now, I guess I've never given it much thought. The only thing I've ever called him is, dog, or ol' son."

Patrick smiled and exclaimed, "Ol' Son, that's a good name!"

"Then, Ol' Son, it is..." Clay said with a grin.

While patting Ol' Son on his back, Patrick looked up at Clay and asked, "What about your horse? Do you have a name for him?"

Clay grinned. "I do. Have you noticed how black he is?"

Patrick looked over at the black stallion and then back at Clay and said, "Yes sir, I have. He looks as black as a starless night."

"That's right," Clay said, "And that's why I named him, Midnight."

"Boy, that sure fits him all right," Patrick beamed.

Just then Justin walked up and said, "Patrick, it's time you said goodnight and get in the wagon. It's well past your bedtime."

With a sad look on his face, Patrick said, "Alright, papa." And after taking his time about it, he said reluctant good nights, then climbed into the wagon.

They all made their way over next to the fire and poured coffee for themselves, then hunkered down next to the rear wagon.

As Clay sat down and leaned back against the wheel of the wagon, Ephram asked, pointing toward the top of the mesa, "You plan on going up there after them two?"

Clay took a sip of the hot coffee, then said, "That's my plan. Are you still planning on trying to sneak off while they're sleeping?"

Justin spoke up and said, "That's part of our plan, but not all of it. We've been talkin' and, well, I've decided I'll go up there with you."

Clay started to protest, but Ephram raised his hand and said, "Now hold on, ranger. We've given this some thought and I think you should hear us out before you say, "no."

Clay let out a breath of air and nodded his head. "I'm listening," he said, feeling like he was talking to his boss, Bill McDaniel.

CHAPTER TWENTY-THREE

-

One ox each had been hitched to a wagon and stood quietly while the men in the wagons waited for a signal to begin moving out.

Justin Hacker was climbing up the front of the mesa where the wagons were, while Clay and the dog climbed up the backside.

Justin was the first to reach the top and hunkered down just below the rim and waited, checking his pocket watch from time to time.

As planned, Justin gave Clay an extra forty minutes to get around the mesa and up that side.

In the moonlight, Justin's watch showed ten minutes to three in the morning. He nodded his head, then took off his hat and waved it.

Elijah and Ephram saw the signal and began shouting "Yee Haw!" at the oxen and slapping the reins against their backs.

The sound of the men yelling and harness jiggling filled the night air as the oxen began pulling the wagons slowly forward.

Hearing the noise, both Matthew and Mark jumped to their feet and grabbed their rifles.

"Sounds like they're tryin' ta escape!" Mark yelled as they ran for the front side of the mesa.

They were only half way across when Clay and the dog climbed over the top and saw the two outlaws scurrying toward the opposite side.

"Hold it right there!" Clay yelled as Ol' Son ran to the far side of the Marlow brothers and began easing closer to them.

Both brothers recognized Clay's voice and stopped. They stood there wondering if they could turn and kill the ranger before he could kill them?

They heard a growl to their left and looked over and saw the dog's barred teeth in the moonlight.

Still hesitating, Mathew whispered to Mark, "If I take the dog, can you take the ranger?"

"You should take the ranger, you're faster," Mark said.

"But the dog is on my side," Matthew reminded his brother.

"Maybe we could switch sides?" Mark asked.

Matthew sighed. "No, we can't switch sides, now do as I said. After I shoot the dog I'll turn my rifle on the ranger that hopefully you'll have already put lead into."

"But..." Mark started to say, but was shut up when Matthew continued.

"No buts," Matthew hissed. "When I say, now, we go."

Before Matthew could say anything else, they heard Clay's voice say, "Don't be stupid. You try what you're thinking and you're both dead men."

Matthew thought for a second, then said loud and clear, "Maybe you're right. Now might not be the best time, but maybe somewhere between here and the hangman, we'll have ah chance ta escape."

Whispering to Mark, Matthew continued, "When I say, now, we go."

Matthew took a deep breath and was about to make his move when Justin climbed up over the ledge and pointed his rifle at them.

"I think the ranger has the right idea. Drop your rifles and you'll live ta see another day," Justin said in a casual, but commanding tone that caused both men to drop their rifles on the ground and raise their hands in surrender.

"Where'd he come from?" Mark asked of his brother.

"Reckon he just dropped out of the sky," Matthew hissed.

"Huh?" Mark said, then grinned. "You're just funnin' me aincha'?"

Matthew just stood there as the two men and the dog came close.

Justin collected the two rifles and handguns before Clay herded the Marlow brothers back to where the horses were tied.

When the buckskin saw Clay, he nickered and Clay walked over and patted her on the neck, then pulled off the rope she was tied with and turned her loose.

Reaching into his pocket, he pulled out a small, wrinkled apple and said, "Look what I brought for you..."

The buckskin took the apple and stood there, chewing contently.

-

At the bottom of the mesa, over breakfast, thanks and goodbyes were said all around and Clay watched as the wagons headed slowly west.

When they were well on their way, Clay turned back to the Marlow brothers, who were tied to their horses and the horses tied to the pack on the buckskin.

"I won't make the same mistake twice. You try that gagging trick again and I'll just let you die."

With that, he touched his feet to the sides of the black stallion and headed toward Tucson, with the packhorse and Marlow brothers following along behind. Looking down, he saw the dog wasn't with him. He was a bit sad, but not surprised. The boy and dog had taken quite a shine to each other. He would miss him and the extra protection the dog provided, but as they say, "Life goes on."

Clay had gone a little less than a mile when he heard a horse running hard and pulled up and turned around.

Justin and the dog came alongside and stopped.

"You didn't have to bring the dog back. If he wanted to stay with Patrick that was his choice."

Justin looked down and for the first time, noticed the dog. "I didn't bring him back. I guess he made that decision on his own."

"Then what are you doing here?" Clay asked.

Justin rubbed his hand on his pant leg and said, "Once I get Patrick and the rest of 'em settled in California, maybe I could come ta Texas and put in for ah ranger job. If I did that, do you think you could put in ah good word for me?"

Clay grinned and nodded his head. "Not only would I put in a good word for you, you could take my place. I'm planning on retiring when I get back and turn these two over to the sheriff in Dallas. Only thing is, you'd have to move to Texas."

Justin reached out his hand and they shook hands. "Much obliged. I'll give that some thought. I'd stay and help but I've got ta see ta Patrick."

"Thank you. I'll be fine," Clay said. "When we get to Tucson I've got a plan that will make the rest of the trip seem like a holiday."

When Justin turned and headed back toward the wagons and his people, the dog stayed next to him. Clay looked down and asked, "You sure, Ol' Son?"

The dog yipped and wagged his tail, then ran on ahead and turned its head and barked, as if to say, "Well, come on."

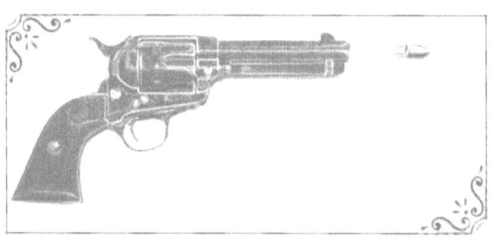

CHAPTER TWENTY-FOUR

-

The ride to Tucson was uneventful. There had been enough rain in that part of the country so that Clay found several pools of water in the Santa Cruz River - enough to make the trip comfortable.

Clay seemed to never let up his vigilance and try as the Marlow brothers did, they could never find an opening that would allow them to kill Clay and make their escape.

As they rode into Tucson, Clay in the front, with the dog at his side and the Marlow brothers trussed up, following behind on horses that were tied end to end with lead ropes, people stared at the newcomers and made comments.

Reining in at the sheriff's office, Clay grinned when he saw a tall, lanky man around forty open the door and step out onto the sidewalk.

The sheriff stood there for a moment, looking at the three men and the dog, not recognizing any of them, although the two men tied up did resemble faces he should know, maybe from a wanted poster. He'd have to check.

Looking back at the man on the black stallion, he said, "Somethin' I can do for you, mister?"

Clay was surprised his friend didn't recognize him, then remembered he hadn't had a bath or shave in some time and his clothes were ready to be burned. And on top of everything else, he guessed he looked like he'd been dragged through a hog wallow and probably smelled like it, too.

"It's been some time, and while I don't much look like I did the last time we crossed paths, we used to be friends, Rance," Clay said with a grin.

Rance Logan grinned and shook his head from side to side. "Clay Brentwood, you ole son-of-a-gun. You look like hell. Get down and tell me what you've been up to. You want me to lock those two in a cell?" he asked, pointing at the Marlow brothers.

Clay lifted his hat and wiped the sweat from his forehead on his shirtsleeve and said, "I would take right kindly to that offer and maybe before you ask too many more questions, I can see about getting cleaned up some. I'll be happy to tell you all about it over a steak and some beer, my treat."

"Where you gettin' money fer that. When I went through yer pockets, you only had two dollars on ya," Mark said matter-of-factly. "And I've got that."

Rance looked at Clay and asked, "You let the likes of him get the drop on you?"

Pulling the Marlow brothers off their horses, Clay said over his shoulder, "Like I said, over a steak and some beer."

After making sure the Marlow brothers were safely behind bars, whining and complaining about needing a bath and something to eat, Clay took the horses down to the livery and paid the man there to take care of them, then went over to the hotel and rented a room for the night. After putting his bags in the room, he went to the barbershop where he could get a bath, a haircut and shave for two dollars.

The barber started to complain about the dog, but Clay raised his hand and said, "Where I go, the dog goes."

The barber looked at the two of them, then shrugged his shoulders in defeat.

Just before climbing into a tub of hot, steamy water, he told the barber to burn his clothes and ask the man from the mercantile store to come over.

Two hours later, dressed in a fairly decent suit and new boots, Clay and the sheriff were sitting in the hotel bar and restaurant, drinking cold beer while Clay summed up his story about the Marlow brothers and the dog, which Clay had taken back down to the livery and left there with the horses, promising to come back for him before he went to the hotel.

They had just finished their second glass of beer when the barman told them a table was ready for them.

Over steak dinners, Clay told the sheriff in no uncertain terms, "This is definitely my last ranger job. Once I get these owlhoots back to Dallas and under lock and key, I'm going home and I might not ever leave the ranch again."

They had switched to coffee with their meals and the sheriff raised his coffee cup and said, "I surely do hope that comes true for ya. You've earned the right, but I hardly think you'll never leave the ranch again."

Clay grinned at his friend and said, "Well. there is a gal back in Tennessee I was planning on dropping in to see when McDaniel talked me into hunting down the Marlow brothers. After resting up some, maybe I'll take a trip.

Rance and Clay went back a long way to when they both lived in Wichita. Rance knew Martha and had attended their wedding. He also knew of her death and said, "That's good. Martha wouldn't want you spendin' the rest of your life alone."

Clay nodded his head, remembering standing next to her grave and talking to her about it, then said, "Did I mention, I now own my own train?"

Rance looked at Clay with his jaw hanging open. "Train? What's this about a train? How in the world did you come ta own a train? This is definitely a story I want ta hear."

That night, for the first time in quite a while, Clay slept like a man who had not a worry in the world, which right then, he didn't. The dog was curled up asleep on the floor next to the bed and the Marlow brothers were locked safely in jail. Tomorrow, he would see about train tickets to Dallas.

The Marlow brothers had been allowed to clean up in a water trough out behind the jail and then taken back to their cell and locked in. An hour or so later they had each been given a large bowl of stew and a pot of coffee.

Mark complained that he wanted a steak and maybe a beer or two, to which the sheriff said as he placed the bowls of soup in the cell. "Eat, don't eat, makes no difference to me. As far as drinks go, in my jail you get a choice, water or coffee with your meal. Which will it be?"

Matthew tried his magic of offering the sheriff a bribe to let them go, to which the sheriff walked back into his office, laughing like he'd just been told the funniest joke he'd ever heard.

In the first place, he had never ever taken a bribe and he'd been offered a few from men who actually had money.

Secondly, Clay was his friend and he would never betray him.

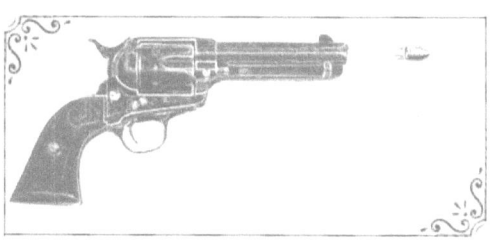

CHAPTER TWENTY-FIVE

-

The following morning, Clay got up early, had another bath and shave, then met his friend, the sheriff, for breakfast at the hotel restaurant.

"You need to watch those boys real careful like," the sheriff said. "Last night the oldest one, Matthew, I think he said his name was, tried to bribe me. Offered me a thousand dollars apiece to let him and his brother out of jail."

"Hopefully you turned them down," Clay said with a grin.

The sheriff took a sip of coffee and two bites of his breakfast before answering, letting his friend sweat a little before finally saying, "Of course I did. In the first place, I don't take bribes. Second, I didn't believe they have that kind of money, and third, I'm doing fairly well from a few investments I've made over the years, thanks to your attorney back in Wichita."

Clay's eyes lit up with surprise. He wasn't aware Rance even knew his attorney and said so. "Rance, you old son-of-a-gun, I didn't know you knew Blackstone! And you've been making investments all this time. Well good for you."

The sheriff grinned and leaned back in his chair. "You introduced him to me about five years ago, remember? You were back there buying some cattle and I was passin' through on my way out here. I didn't have any money at the time, but later I wrote a letter to Blackstone and I now own stock in your bank and several other enterprises you're involved in. I figure if they're good enough for you..."

Clay grinned and said, "In that case, breakfast is on you."

Later, Clay booked passage on the Southern Pacific Railroad back to Dallas for himself and his horses, and paid for the Marlow brothers to be locked in a jail car, along with paying a man who worked for the railroad, extra money to guard them.

When the horses were loaded and the Marlow brothers safely locked in the jail car, Clay said goodbye to his friend, then boarded the train for their trip back to Dallas.

By his calculations, with stops and layovers, Clay figured it would take close to five days for them to get back to Dallas, if there were no delays, which was a whole lot easier than riding horseback and trying to keep two bloodthirsty owl hoots from killing him while he slept out on the trail. He was suddenly beginning to appreciate the comforts of traveling by train.

Dressed in his new, gray suit, starched white shirt, new black hat and boots, Clay was rewarded with smiles from women, young and beautiful, to ones who had seen better days.

Several of them stopped to pet the dog and make small talk, while batting their eyes at him and making obvious invitations for later.

Several were tempting, especially one who reminded him of Loralie Benson. She had long red hair and big blue eyes and a figure that enhanced her clothes to the limit.

But in the end, Clay decided he needed to stay focused on the trip. He had criminals back in the jail car that would need constant watching. Yes, he'd hired a man to keep an eye on them, but he was in his sixties and not the most reliable, as far as Clay was concerned. The railroad only kept him on because the man had worked for them for a long time and felt they owed it to him.

Later in the day, Clay walked along with the porter, who took them their supper. When they entered the jail car the old man was sitting up next to the bars of the cell, playing checkers with Matthew.

Clay wasn't sure he liked the old man being that close to them, but decided since the keys to the cell were at the opposite end of the car, they couldn't do much.

"Hope you don't mind, Ranger," Matthew said. "It gets kinda borin' just sittin' here and I like playin' checkers."

Mark stood up from the bunk and walked over and asked, "What'ya bring us for supper. I sure am hungry. Think I could eat ah horse."

Clay had pulled the cell door keys off the peg where they hung and said, "Step back to the rear of the cell and turn around."

Mark looked at his brother and both of them sighed, but went to the back of the cell and faced the wall while Clay opened the door and allowed the porter to sit the food on a small table inside the cell.

The porter was tall and skinny and anxious to get this over with. He had never liked coming to the jail car. It made him nervous and he gave a sigh of relief when he was once again headed back to the dining car.

Clay hung around to talk to the old man whose name was Henry Nickels. "They giving you any trouble?" he asked.

"Not that I can't handle. The young one, he's ah bit of ah whiner, but I just let it slide by. The older one, he's the talker of the two and not a bad checker player."

Clay nodded toward them and said, "Don't let them fool ya. They're slicker than grease on a doorknob – killers, both of them."

For the next three days, everything was quiet and Clay was feeling much better about the old man, but on the morning of the fourth day when he went with the porter to take them their breakfast, the sliding door was standing wide open, the cell was empty and the old man was laying on the floor with a broken neck.

Even though there was no one there to harm him, the porter dropped the tray of food and ran for the dining car, screaming like he'd been struck by lightning.

Clay walked over and pulled the emergency stop cord and a few moments later felt the train brakes bring the train to a screeching stop. They were making their way through the mountains and the train had to slow down from time to time to climb the steep grades.

When Clay pulled the emergency stop cord, they just happened to be on a stretch of flat land between the hills.

Clay jumped down on the ground and looked around for the car that held his horses and saw two other cars with their doors wide open, which gave him a bad feeling.

As he was walking toward the first open boxcar door, the engineer came hustling up to him and asked, "You the one who pulled the emergency cord?"

"Yes," Clay answered, as he continued to walk toward the open door of the box car.

The engineer started to say something but the dog stepped in between him and Clay and began to growl, barring his teeth.

Clay reached down and patted the dog on the head and said, "It's all right, Ol' Son. He's just blowing off steam."

Turning away from the engineer, Clay continued on.

Chasing behind him, but giving a wide berth to the dog, the engineer yelled, "Well you'd better have a damn good reason! I've got a schedule to keep!"

Clay looked in both box cars and saw they were empty. Somehow Matthew and Mark had overpowered the old man, killed him, got access to the keys, made their way to the cars that held the horses and escaped without anybody seeing or hearing anything.

"We have to go back a ways," Clay said to the engineer, a fat, balding man who looked older than he was.

"What? Are you nuts? The only way I'm goin' is straight ahead, mister!"

Suddenly he noticed the open boxcars and looked in. "Who opened them doors and let the horses out?"

Clay reached into his pocket and pulled out his ranger badge and showed it to the engineer. "Clay Brentwood, Texas Ranger and I need you to back this train up until I can find where my prisoners got off."

The engineer swelled up and said, "This ain't Texas mister and you ain't got no authority here! Where's Henry? What happened to him?"

"He's dead. He got stupid and my prisoners killed him and stole the horses, now get a move on, we're wasting time."

"No sir, I ain't goin' back. I've got ah schedule ta keep. Them prisoners are your responsibility, not mine. And you'll be held accountable for Henry's death, you can be sure of that."

"Maybe this will help you change your mind," Clay said as he drew his pistol and stuck it in the man's face.

"I'll be makin' ah report to my superiors about this! You can count on it!" the engineer said as he turned and headed for the engine, with Clay and the dog right behind him.

People gawked at them through the windows and Clay saw the face of the red headed woman. Her eyes were wide with excitement.

A little over an hour later, Clay told the engineer to stop the train, and when he did, Clay got off and looked at the marks on the ground where the horses had landed after jumping from the slow-moving train.

The engineer, the man who shoveled coal, and a multitude of people from the train who had gotten off out of curiosity, stood looking at Clay and the hoof prints.

They were at the bottom of a mountain where the train had begun to slow down before starting its climb, and behind them the desert stretched away as far as Clay could see. Clay sighed, they had beaten him again and he wasn't sure what he could do about it. They had all the horses and he was afoot. By now, they were miles away and getting farther with every minute.

Clay was about to get back on the train with the hope they reached a town soon where he could buy a couple of horses, restock his packs and head out.

"This is definitely my last ranger job," he muttered as he started for the train, but stopped short when the dog began jumping around and barking, then lit out around the caboose.

Running down to the end of the train, Clay rounded the caboose and stopped. In the far distance, he could see a dust column coming toward him and the dog running toward the dust cloud.

The people from the train had climbed back aboard, but watched in awe through the windows as the black stallion and buckskin mare ran up and put their heads over Clay's shoulders while the dog ran circles around them, barking and jumping around.

With tears in his eyes, Clay hugged both horses and said, "They just can't keep you two tied down, can they..."

After getting his gear off the train, and restocking his pack as best he could from supplies from the dining car, and buying every apple they had, Clay handed the engineer forty dollars to see to Henry's burial.

By now the engineer had calmed down enough to keep his temper in check, but still didn't like the ranger. The man had messed with his schedule and gotten one of their own, killed.

The last they saw of him, Clay was sitting astride the black stallion watching the train disappear down the tracks.

Clay looked down at the dog and said, "Well Ol' Son, looks like we've got to start all over again.

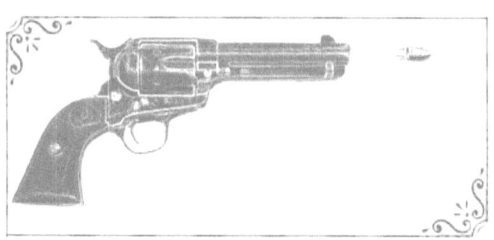

CHAPTER TWENTY-SIX

-

The engineer could hardly wait to get to a telegraph office where he could wire his friend in Albuquerque who owned the newspaper there.

The telegram was a condensed story, but enough for the editor of the Albuquerque newspaper to fill in the gaps and embellish what he didn't know.

The story spread like wild fire and by the time McDaniel, head of the Texas Rangers, read it on the front page of the Austin newspaper, the story had been blown all out of proportion and made Clay look like a bumbling buffoon.

McDaniel slammed the paper down on his desk and grabbed up the last telegram he'd received from Clay, stating the Marlow brothers were locked safely in the jail car owned by the Southern Pacific Railroad and was headed back to Dallas.

"What the hell happened?" he sputtered out loud to himself as he slapped his hat on his head and headed for the Austin newspaper.

The editor of the Austin newspaper looked up and gulped when McDaniel came storming into his office.

After ten minutes of stern interrogation by the head of the rangers, the editor finally admitted to putting his own slant to the story to help sales, which didn't help McDaniel's anger.

"You have to understand, Bill," the editor said. "I sell newspapers to make my living and people don't want dull, unexciting stories. They want sensation, and that's what I try to give them."

"Try doin' it without lying," McDaniel said. "Now, hear me and hear me good, I want a retraction printed stating the story was nothing but a pack of lies told by an engineer with an inflated imagination. And I want it on the front page of tomorrows paper."

The editor just sat there, stunned and looked up at McDaniel who glared back at him with such intensity that he thought McDaniel was going to hit him.

When the editor didn't readily agree, McDaniel continued. "If you don't print that story the way I just said; I'll see you tarred and feathered, and run out of town on a rail!"

The editor knew the ranger meant what he said and he was so scared all he could do was to nod his head in agreement.

The following morning, while drinking his coffee, McDaniel read the story on the front page of the paper and shook his head. It said pretty much what McDaniel had told him to say with the exception that the editor claimed after extensive investigation on the newspapers part, he, the editor, had dug up the truth and knowing his readers would want to know the facts, had reprinted the story, hoping his readers would understand.

Bill shook his head and said, "Well, at least he finally got the story straight."

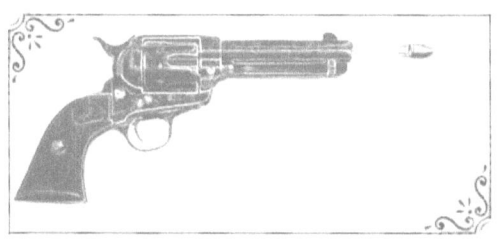

CHAPTER TWENTY-SEVEN

-

Clay Brentwood felt like a beaten man when he rode into Tucson for the second time in a month.

Rance Logan had just stepped out of his office on his way to the cafe down the street when he saw his friend come riding toward him looking tired and worn out.

He waited until Clay had stepped down and dropped the reins of his horse before he said anything.

"Heard what happened, or more precisely, read the story in the newspaper. They weren't very kind to you for letting them escape," Rance said, shaking his head.

Clay shrugged his shoulders. He couldn't care less what other people thought. He'd underestimated the Marlow brothers from the beginning and his self-blame was more than enough.

"Don't worry about it too much my friend, I screwed up, too."

Clay looked at the sheriff and asked, "What are you talking about? Have they been here?"

"Here and gone," the sheriff said. "Before I knew anything about it."

Over lunch, the sheriff related how the Marlow brothers had come into town, beat up the owner of the mercantile store, dressed up in fresh clothes, stole his money and boarded the west bound train for San Francisco.

"By the time I found out about it they were long gone."

"And you're sure it was them?" Clay asked.

"From the description the owner of the mercantile store, Lewis Miller, gave me, I was pretty sure it was them, but confused by the fact that the last I knew, they were locked in the train jail car that was headed for Dallas. What happened?"

Clay told him the story, leaving nothing out and when he finished, the sheriff looked at him and said, "Wow. That's sure not the way the newspapers are telling it. Wonder how they got it so wrong?"

"It's my guess the engineer was getting even with me for making him back the train up and throwing him off his schedule," Clay said with a shrug.

"Well he sure did a bang-up job of it," the sheriff said with a grin.

It wasn't something he needed to worry about right now, Clay decided. "Guess I need to catch the next train headed to San Francisco," he said with a sheepish grin.

"Reckon so," the sheriff said. "But the next one don't come through till tomorrow morning, probably somewhere around ten."

"That should give me time to get cleaned up, again," Clay said.

The hotel clerk gave him the eye when he checked in, but said nothing.

Of course, the barber and the owner of the mercantile were glad to see him again.

In his room, Clay checked the money pouch he kept hidden in the pack and saw he was still all right, money wise, but if he didn't get the Marlow brothers back to Dallas, soon, he would have to wire for more.

-

Mark sat in the dining car, smoking a cigar and savoring a glass of good whiskey – much better than the rotgut he was used to drinking.

He'd had a bath and a shave and was wearing a suit of clothes they'd stolen from the mercantile store back in Tucson, and as far as he was concerned, he looked dapper, like one of them travelin' salesmen. He chuckled at the thought of robbing the store in broad daylight in the town where the ranger's friend was the sheriff – and right under his nose, too.

He almost laughed out loud at the thought of the ranger finding the jail cell empty and that ole man dead. Stupid old man had fallen for the gaggin' trick.

He wondered if the ranger would finally give up and go on back ta Texas with his tail between his legs, or would he stubborn up and come after them, again.

Mark took a sip of whiskey and said to himself, "No use worrin' about it right now, we're safe here on the train and if'n he comes ta San Francisco, well, we'll worry about that then."

Mark looked up in time to see the widow lady, Maybelle Jarvis coming down the aisle.

He jumped to his feet, bowed slightly and offered her a seat.

Sitting down across from her, Mark waved at the porter and when he came over, ordered a bottle of champagne."

"Champagne. Oh my," Maybelle Jarvis exclaimed. "Champagne makes my head spin and who knows what I'll wind up doing?" she said, giving Mark a come-hither look.

Mark had seen her shortly after he and Matthew had boarded the train. The porter told him he'd heard she was a rich widow from Denver on her way to San Francisco.

Mark had deliberately bumped into her, causing her to drop her purse and after picking it up and apologizing, they had struck up a conversation.

Wanting her to think highly of him so he could get close to her, Mark let it slip that he was in the shipping business out of San Francisco and was on his way home.

Mark knew he didn't have the slightest bit of knowledge about ships or how to run a shipping business, or any other business for that matter, but she didn't know that.

He paid her compliments about her youthful beauty and she said he was just being polite, but to continue, it would get him whatever he wanted.

When the champagne was gone, she said she was feeling dizzy and needed to lie down and asked if he would mind escorting her to her stateroom.

Mark was excited with the prospect of not only having this woman to do as he pleased with her, but when he'd finished relieving her of her money and jewelry, he just might strangle her slowly. Matthew would be proud of him when he turned up with all that cash and jewelry.

He and Matthew would get off at the next town, then catch the train the following morning and nobody would suspect a thing. His plan was foolproof.

Inside her stateroom, the widow lady became less than lady like as she lifted Mark's hand and placed it against her chest.

Mark felt an electric shock run through him and suddenly he was like a school boy, ripping and tearing at his own clothes,

Mark had just gotten down to his drawers when she screamed and the door burst open. A man entered, took one look and pulled a pistol and pointed it at him.

"He was trying to rape me," the woman said.

The man cocked his pistol and said, "Prepare to meet your maker."

Mark felt the panic run through him and he said, "Please, no, it's all a mistake. She brought me here."

"That's not true," she said. "He followed me here from the dining room and burst in with the intent of having his way with me and he touched me inappropriately."

The man looked at Mark and said, "Give me one good reason why I shouldn't blow your head off, right here and now?"

"I've got a little money. You can have it all if you don't shoot me," Mark said, almost crying.

"How much money?" the woman asked. "My honor has been impugned."

Mark thought about the stolen money they had in their stateroom. He wasn't sure how much there was, but guessed over three hundred dollars.

"I've got three hundred dollars back in my stateroom," Mark said, hastily.

"Three hundred? That's all?" the woman said. "I thought you said you owned a big shipping company?"

Mark swallowed and said, meekly, "I was just tryin' ta get ya ta like me so you would invite me back here to yer room."

The woman looked at the man and said, "Well, I guess three hundred is better than nothing at all."

The man waved his pistol toward the door and said, "One false move and you're a dead man."

When they entered the room, Matthew jumped to his feet and stared at the strange man and woman, noticing the gun in the man's hand.

He looked at Mark who was pale as a ghost and asked, "What's goin' on? Who'er these people?"

The man pointed his pistol at Matthew and said, "He owes us three hundred dollars and we're here to collect, now fork over the money or I start shooting."

"Pay him, Matthew," Mark cried. "He means it. He'll shoot us both."

Matthew looked at the man and said, "Before I give you all the money we have, what did he do that makes you think he owes you three hundred dollars?"

"He impugned my honor," the woman said.

Matthew nodded his head, understanding now what was going on. Mark had been taken in by a couple of con artists who made their living off of idiots like his brother.

After a moment, Matthew nodded his head at the woman and said, "I'm very sorry for my brother's actions. I'll get the money."

With that, Matthew reached into their travel bag and pulled out a pistol and shot both the man and the woman, then turned the pistol on his brother.

"You idiot, you were hoodwinked by ah couple of con artists. I swear - I can't leave you alone for a minute. I should shoot you and get it over with."

"I'm sorry. Please, I won't act stupid again, honest I won't," Mark pleaded.

Matthew sighed and put the pistol back in the bag, then looked at Mark and said, "As soon as it gets a little darker, we throw 'em off the train, but first, we see how much they've stolen from other suckers."

"I said I was sorry," Mark said with a scowl.

"You search the man, I'll search the woman," Matthew said, kneeling down next to the woman and jerking the necklace from around her neck.

The man had close to six hundred dollars in cash and a gold watch that Matthew thought he should have, and the woman had a little over nine hundred dollars in her purse along with her jewelry.

Matthew let out a long, low whistle. "Little brother, what started out ta be stupid on your part, turned out ta be the biggest heist we've ever made."

Mark smiled - happy that his brother was not mad at him anymore.

Along with the jewels and money, they found the key to the man and woman's stateroom and when they investigated, Matthew realized he and the man were the same size and the man had a suitcase full of nice clothes, along with another five hundred dollars in cash, a gold cigar holder and several expensive tiepins.

After packing the woman's clothes in her traveling chest, they dragged it down to the end of the car and threw it off the train.

Matthew took the man's luggage as his own and when they left the man and woman's stateroom, it was empty and looked like they had simply gotten off the train, somewhere.

Throwing the bodies off the train was the hard part. Matthew kept watch while Mark dragged each one down to the end of the car and tossed their body off where they were unlikely to be seen for some time. The man went into a river as the train crossed the bridge and the woman went into a deep ravine.

CHAPTER TWENTY-EIGHT

-

After a lot of discussion, both Clay and the sheriff decided the Marlow brothers would probably head for San Francisco. From what Clay had heard the city was wide open, which would be to their liking.

"They might even grab a ship going to Alaska or some other place," Rance said, "and just plumb disappear."

Figuring he wouldn't need them, Clay boarded his horses at the livery in Tucson, then, after a major discussion with the man behind the ticket counter, bought train tickets to San Francisco for both him and the dog.

"He won't be taking up a seat, and he'll sleep in the stateroom with me," Clay had argued, but the man behind the counter wouldn't budge.

"I'm sorry sir, but the Southern Pacific Railroad is very firm about this." the man who sold the tickets had said; so, Clay had buckled under and purchased a ticket for the dog, secretly smiling inside. It would be something to talk about when he got back... if he ever got back.

Before Clay and the dog boarded the train, the sheriff looked Clay in the eyes and said, "You be real careful out there. I hear they have women working in the bars who get a man drunk, then men come and take him away and when he wakes up he's a deck hand on some ship headed for China or South America, or one of them other foreign places. Maybe by the time you get there, them Marlow brothers might be learnin' a new trade – either scrubbin' a deck, or shanghaiing innocent men to be sold to the ship owners. I'm sure they'd just love to see you on your hands and knees, scrubbing a deck."

Clay scratched his neck. "You might be right, but I don't have any other choice - except to let them go and we both know I'm not about to do that - not after what they've put me through."

"Wish I could go with you, but..." Rance said, letting his words trail off.

"I know," Clay said, "and you'd be welcome, but you've got obligations here and, in all honesty, it's up to me and no one else."

-

Once again Clay was dressed in a new suit, this time a black one. His stateroom was a mite cramped for both him and the dog, but it was the only one available and much better than them trying to sleep sitting up in a seat.

The dining car was crowded and Clay was asked to share a table with a man who said he was a businessman from south Texas - going to San Francisco on business. The man was not only tall, but also broad shouldered and looked like he could pull a tree right out of the ground with his bare hands. He was well groomed and his suit was of the expensive kind. He had a winning smile and a very personable attitude Clay thought, but guessed the man would be completely different if you got on the wrong side of him. It would be kinda like going head to head with an angry buffalo.

The porter brought a piece of meat for the dog and set it under the table so he wouldn't block the aisle.

When the man asked about the dog, Clay told the story of how he'd come to have the dog and all the times the dog had been a tremendous help, then finished by saying, "I guess he's my dog now, but he's free to leave if that's what he chooses to do."

After that, they talked about Texas and cattle, and when they finished eating, the man who introduced himself as Frank Lubber suggested a drink in the lounge car. Clay said, Clay Brentwood, rancher, Seymour, Texas. Sounds good."

Over glasses of whiskey, the man asked Clay if he was a poker player?

"Oh, I play a little now and then for fun, but if you're talking serious money, I don't think I'm of that caliber. Why do you ask?" Clay asked with a grin.

"Fella from New York who goes by Sam Rider, a businessman like me, is going to San Francisco on business, but fancies himself a poker player and has set up a game for tonight, with serious money on the table. But we need one more player – thought you might want to join us," the man said.

"Just as Clay was about to refuse, again, a young man no older than twenty, wearing a brown suit with a diamond stickpin in his cravat, stopped next to their table. He had sandy red hair, a pencil thin moustache, bright blue eyes and pearl white teeth that showed in his wide grin. "Poker game? Did I hear someone mention a poker game?"

The big Texan looked up and grinned. "You ah poker player, son?"

"Well, I don't like to brag and I'm not quite ready to admit to being a professional player, yet, but I will grant you, I'm not too bad as long as you stick to stud or draw. I don't play those fancy - anything is wild kinds of games."

"Just straight poker, I'm told," Frank said, standing up and introducing himself, then said, "There's a thousand dollar buy-in. Still interested?"

"What time, and where?" the young man who introduced himself as Randy Baker from St. Louis, Missouri asked with a wide, toothy grin.

Clay introduced himself and studied Randy with interest. He seemed a bit too young to have the kind of money that was mentioned.

"Run out of poker players back in St. Louis, did you?" Clay asked with a grin.

Randy Baker looked down at Clay and for just an instant; Clay saw something in the young man's eyes he didn't like.

"No, nothing like that. My father owned several businesses back there and just plain worked hisself to death. He died a year ago and me being the only heir - I inherited it all. But I'm not much of a businessman. I want to travel and enjoy life while I'm still young. So... I sold everything and for the past few months I've been traveling around playing poker and seeing all the big cities I've read or heard about. I hear San Francisco has some big poker games going on day and night, along with exotic oriental women."

Clay nodded as though he understood perfectly, but still had that nagging feeling. The young man's story seemed a bit too pat, and he spouted it out like an actor delivering his lines.

So far, Clay had neglected to mention he was a Texas Ranger and decided to keep it that way, at least for the time being.

Clay tried passing the evening away sitting in his stateroom, reading, but the rumble of the train and the clickity-clack of the rails distracted him. He got up and went out to one of the passenger cars and looked out of the window, but it was too dark to seen anything.

After pacing around for a while with the dog staying close by his side, Clay found himself at the door of the private car where the poker game should by now, be in full swing.

He knocked on the door, then tried the knob, but it was locked.

He was about to turn and go back to the lounge when the sandy haired young man, who called himself, Randy Baker, opened the door and said, "Mister Brentwood! If you're looking for a seat, you can have mine. They've just about cleaned me out."

Clay and the dog stepped into the room and Clay chuckled and said, "No, I was just bored and thought if you didn't mind, I would watch for a while."

Before anyone had a chance to say ya or nay, the sandy haired young man pulled a pistol and pointed at the men at the table, then threw the door wide open and yelled, "Come on in, boys!"

Two young men scrambled down the ladder from the top of the car and stepped inside. Both were wearing jeans that had seen better days, run down boots, faded shirts; sweat stained hats and their neckerchiefs pulled up to hide their faces.

Both were pointing forty-four handguns at them.

The dog, who was standing next to Clay, had a low growl rumbling in his chest.

"Do something with that dog or he dies right now," Randy said.

Clay reached down and stroked the dog on the head and said, "Quiet."

The rumble in the dog's chest stopped and he sat down on his haunches, but didn't like it. Clay could feel him trembling under his hand.

"Now, if you gentlemen don't mind, we're in a bit of a hurry; so, here's what I want you to do. First, I want you to lay any weapon you may have on you, on the table real easy like. We don't want to shoot anybody, but if you even look cross-eyed, one of us will put a hole in you big enough to drive this train through. Then, when you've done as I've asked, I want you to put all your money, and I mean all of it, on the table, then Mister Brentwood here will put it into this sack.

With that, the young man pulled a small cloth bag from his pocket and tossed it in Clay's direction.

Clay caught it and looked at the young man, then said, "Not me. I don't want anything to do with this."

Clay looked at the young man who called himself Randy and said, "I suggest you drop your guns, turn around and raise your hands in the air. You're under arrest."

The sandy haired young man, snickered and said, "Right." Then his eyes got serious and he said, "You supposed to be some big lawman, or what?"

Still holding the bag in his left hand, Clay reached into his vest pocket with his right hand and retrieved his badge and held it up so they could all see it. "Clay Brentwood, Texas Ranger," he said.

As one of the other young men started to raise his pistol the dog leaped from his sitting position and grabbed the man's wrist in his teeth and took the young man to the floor.

At the same time, Clay tossed the bag in their direction and two shots rang out so fast it almost sounded like one, long shot.

When the smoke cleared, two of the three young outlaws were standing there, holding their gunshot wrists, their pistols laying on the floor while the other one was still at the mercy of the dog – blood was running from his wrist.

"Turn him loose," Clay said and the dog released the man's wrist and came back and sat down next to Clay, wagging his tail, but still eyeing the three outlaws.

"Now, like I said, turn around and put your hands in the air. You're under arrest for attempted robbery."

When the young outlaws were locked in the baggage car, Frank Lubber invited Clay back to the private car, and when he got there, they sat him at the table and placed a drink in front of him.

Sam Rider, the man from New York and owner of the private car sat down across from Clay and said, "I know I speak for all of us when I say we're glad you were here. They would have cleaned us out and I have a feeling they would have shot us so no one could identify them later."

"That sure was some bit of shooting," one of the others piped in.

"Yes, it was, but we can talk about that later," Sam said as he pushed a pile of bills across the table at Clay. "There's five thousand dollars; our gratitude for what you did. You saved us more than you probably realize."

Clay looked at the money, then up at Sam and said, "Thank you, but I don't want or need your money. I'm just glad I was here and could help."

Sam eyed him and said, "I wasn't aware rangers made enough money to turn down a five-thousand-dollar reward."

"They don't," Clay said, "but I'm not a full-time ranger. I only help when they need an extra hand. I'm a cattle rancher. I have a good-sized spread a few miles west of Seymour, Texas, just below the panhandle. I mainly raise Herefords, but have some Hereford, longhorn mix."

"You raise Herefords in Texas?" Sam asked as though he couldn't comprehend the thought.

"I do," Clay said. "Brought over a bull and ten cows from England a few years back, and when they were prospering, I bought a thousand head. I now have close to five thousand head of some of the best beef you can find anywhere in Texas, or anyplace else for that matter."

"Well, I'll be damned," Sam, said. "We may be able to work something out after all. I own three slaughterhouses – one in New York, One in Kansas City and one in Wichita. And if your beef is as good as you say it is, I'll buy all you can supply."

After everything that had happened lately, Clay couldn't believe his good luck.

Clay looked across the table and said, "They're ever bit as good as I said. If you're going to be in Texas any time soon I'd be obliged if you'd stop by so I can show them to you."

"My business in San Francisco shouldn't take more than a week, then I'll be headed back east. I could stop in Texas and have a look. And if I like what I see, we'll work out a price. How long will it take you to drive them to Wichita?"

Clay grinned and surprised them all when he said, "Not long at all. I have my own train."

Frank slapped Clay on the back and said, "You sure are full of surprises, yes sir, you sure are."

A few hours after sunrise, the train stopped in a small, whistle stop of a town where normally they only picked up coal and water, but waited until Clay tried to turn the outlaws over to the sheriff, but he would have nothing to do with it.

"Sorry, ranger, but I ain't even got a jail, just a back room at the general store. And we ain't got no judge neither. You take 'em on up to Phoenix, sheriff there'll take 'em off your hands, I'm sure."

Clay didn't mention what he'd gone through with the sheriff up in Phoenix, but instead, shook the sheriff's hand and said he understood.

Back on the train, Clay related his story about the Marlow brothers without leaving anything out, and then asked for their opinion about what to do with the men who tried to rob them. Obviously, he couldn't turn them over to the sheriff in Phoenix without stirring up some old trouble.

Frank Lubber grinned and said, "Stay out of sight and let me handle it."

Clay had the curtain drawn in his stateroom but peeked out of the window and watched as Frank Lubber, Sam Rider and two other men escorted Randy Baker and his fellow would-be holdup men off the train and took them up to where the sheriff was standing on the platform, observing the new arrivals.

After a short conversation, the sheriff waved his arm and two deputies came over and took the young outlaws away.

Frank Lubber and the others had just boarded the train and Clay felt it start to move. He let out a sigh of relief and was about to step away from the window when one of the deputies came running back onto the platform, waving his arms, talking excitedly and pointing toward the train as it slowly moved forward.

The sheriff drew his pistol and started for the train, motioning the deputy toward the engine.

Clay left his stateroom and sprinted down the aisle toward the other end of the car and just as he opened the door, the train came to a stop.

The sheriff was almost running as he hurried through the passenger cars, looking at each and every passenger, frightening most of the ladies.

In the cars that held staterooms, he opened every door and looked over the occupants, his eyes wide with anticipation, creating screams from several of the women who were not fully dressed.

"Where you hidin' him?" the sheriff asked Frank Lubber when he opened Frank's stateroom door and found him reading the newspaper.

"Who?" Frank asked, trying to look surprised.

"You know damn well who. Clay Brentwood, the ranger!" the sheriff screamed.

"Oh him. He got off at that whistle stop east of here. We thanked him for what he'd done and offered him a reward, but he wouldn't take it. He said he was just doing his job. He said he had other business to take care of and asked us to deliver those three outlaws to you with his compliments. Did we do wrong?" Frank asked.

The sheriff looked at him for a minute, then stalked from his stateroom and left the train.

When the train was beyond sight of the train station, Clay climbed down from the top of the train and went back inside his car.

When he entered his stateroom, Frank and Sam were waiting for him.

"Where did you disappear to? We've looked everywhere for you," Frank said.

"Not quite everywhere," Clay said with a grin. "You didn't look on the roof."

CHAPTER TWENTY-NINE

-

The two-day trip to San Francisco was mostly uneventful. The most exciting thing that happened was at one of the small towns when Clay let Ole Son off to go do his business. Ol' Son spotted a rabbit and almost missed the train when it left. If Clay hadn't been hollering and whistling for him, he surely would have. As it was, Ole Son had to run alongside and leap onto the platform, where Clay grabbed him by the scruff of the neck and kept him from falling back off.

Ten miles out from San Francisco, Clay yelled for Sam and Frank to climb up on top of the train and see the view.

All three men sat on the roof of the train, staring in awe. San Francisco spread out in front of them with the bay and Pacific Ocean beginning where the land stopped. Where the business part stopped, houses dotted the hills, stretching out for miles.

Tall ships with their sails furled were rocking back and forth in the bay and black smoke rose from factory smokestacks. San Francisco was teaming with business from large manufactures to small mom and pop stores.

"It's going to be a grand city someday," Sam said with conviction.

"Looks like it's well on its way," Clay said, studying the wharf area as best he could from such a long distance away.

"She still has a long way to go," Sam said. "The crime rate down on the docks is even worse than New York, they say," Sam declared.

Clay looked at the bay area and wondered if that's where he'd find the Marlow brothers? Or would they have already moved on?"

When they got closer, Sam pointed and said, "See that large ship out in the bay - the one with three masts? I believe that's the one I came to see and possibly purchase."

"You plan on going into shipping along with the meat packing businesses?" Frank asked.

"There's big money in shipping these days," Sam said, at which Frank began to laugh.

"What's so funny?" Clay asked.

Frank wiped the tears from his eyes and said, "I think that's the same ship I'm here to look at. I plan to ship out of Houston.

-

Fog was beginning to roll in as they stepped down from the train, and by the time they hailed a horse drawn cab to take them to a hotel, it was so thick they couldn't see ten feet in front of them, although the cabbie seemed to be having no trouble.

"How can you see in this thick fog?" Sam inquired.

"Your first trip to San Francisco?" the cabbie asked over his shoulder.

"Is it always this thick?" Frank wanted to know.

"Comes in most every day around this time," the cabbie said as he pulled up in front of the Palace Hotel and yelled, "Whoa."

The hotel was built in 1875 and reputed to be the largest, most luxurious and costly hotel in the world. During this time San Francisco went by several names including, Paris of the west. It was also viewed by many to be the wickedest town on the North American continent.

When the three men entered, they stopped and stared at the huge lobby with its grand furniture, high ceilings and giant chandeliers. People dressed in their finery were coming and going in all directions.

Clay was about to turn and leave. This was too fancy, and not where he would find the Marlow brothers, he was sure.

Sam grabbed him by the arm and asked, "Where are you going?"

Clay shook his head; "This is a little too nice for the men I'm hunting. I need to find a place a little closer to the wharf. Plus, I'm sure having a mongrel dog in my room would be frowned on."

Sam nodded his head knowingly and said, "At least stay and have supper with us. I insist."

Clay looked at his watch and said, "It's still a bit early for supper. How about I find a place to stay and meet you in the bar around seven."

"Seven it is," Sam said, then shook Clay's hand.

After shaking Frank's hand, Clay turned to leave and Sam called out to him. "Don't forget – seven o'clock. I want to know more about those cattle of yours."

The cabbie would only take Clay to within a block of where the Chinese part of town began.

"I don't go any farther, Mister. And unless you're looking for more trouble than you can handle, a man like you shouldn't either."

"You mean because of the way I'm dressed?" Clay asked.

"That's exactly what I mean. That's a rough bunch of cutthroats down there and if they see you, dressed the way you are, they'll be fighting over who gets to rob you. You want my advice, go back up on the hill where you belong. It ain't safe during the daylight hours, and when it gets dark – well let's just say, a man like you will wind up scrubbing decks on some ship headed for who knows where."

Clay thought for a moment, then decided the man may be right. "Take me back to the Palace Hotel," he said.

One night in a fancy hotel might do him good; plus, he would be having supper with a very rich man who he could do a lot of business with if he played his cards right, so to speak.

The hotel clerk was reluctant to allow Ol' Son into the hotel until he found out he was of royal blood from Siberia and had survived an attack by Indians who planned to eat him. Clay even showed the clerk the arrow scar on Ol' Son's leg and the place on his head where he'd been clubbed.

"I'm looking for a good veterinarian to have him looked at and then a place where I can get him groomed. He's not used to looking like this," Clay said, shaking his head.

"We have a very good dog groomer right here at the hotel. I'm sure she would take very good care of him and you could pick him up in the morning looking all fresh and clean."

It cost Clay four dollars, and when the lady learned he was of royal blood, she promised he would look like a prince by the time Clay picked him up tomorrow morning.

Clay still had plenty of time before he was to meet with Sam and Frank, so he sent his clothes out to be cleaned. His room had its own bathtub, which he took advantage of.

Sam and Frank had a glass of whiskey waiting on him when Clay walked up and sat down at the bar.

Both men were surprised to learn that Clay had changed his mind and was staying at the Palace.

But when Clay told them the story about Ole Son and his heritage, they both burst into fits of laughter.

"This is one trip I'll never forget," Frank said, after ordering another round.

By the time the sun came up, Clay was up, bathed, shaved, and had finished his breakfast. He was having his second cup of coffee when the lady appeared with Ol' Son.

Clay could hardly recognize him. He was spotlessly clean and his coat was soft and shiny. He ran over and put both front paws on Clay's lap and yipped at him.

Clay gave the woman the four dollars plus a dollar tip. "His majesty never looked so good," he said.

The groomer beamed and said, "He really is a prince of a dog. And by the way, he's had his breakfast, so don't let him con you out of more food."

Ol' Son was eyeing the small portion of steak still left on Clay's plate.

Clay had the cabbie stop at a general store a few blocks from the wharf and bought some Levis, boots, a wool shirt, and western hat. Before changing into them, he took them out in the alley and scuffed them up some. After what the cabbie had said last night, he wasn't about to go walking around in new clothes.

In his new, but now, dirty clothes, Clay and Ol' Son walked down along the store fronts, glancing in from time to time, but didn't stop until he got to the bay.

The bay stunk of sewage and filth. The bars were open twenty-four hours a day and Clay could understand why it was called the wickedest town in the west or anyplace else for that matter.

In the first bar he came to, a place called The Hangout, Clay stepped through the door and stood looking around. A pretty, young, Chinese girl sidled up next to him and said, "You buy me a drink, I show you a good time."

Clay took one look at her and the hair on the back of his neck stood up. His mind was suddenly filled with visions of him on his hands and knees, scrubbing the deck of a ship far at sea.

"No thanks," Clay said and turned to leave and had not yet reached the door when two rough looking men who smelled of whiskey walked up on each side of him and grabbed his arms and began hustling him towards a side door.

Clay reacted by jerking loose from the man on his right, then sending his right fist into the nose of the man hanging onto his left arm.

The man let go of his arm and staggered backward, blood gushing from his broken nose, covering the front of his sweat stained shirt.

Clay whirled to face the other man but didn't need to hurry. Ol' Son had the man flat on his back and had his barred teeth close to the man's throat – a deep growl emitting from his mouth.

The man's eyes were wide with fright. He was afraid if he tried to move, the dog would latch onto his throat with those mean looking teeth and not turn loose until he was dead.

Based on what he'd heard, Clay knew what these two were up to. They planned to load him up with booze or dope of some kind, then sell him to one of the ship captains and he would wind up a deck hand, never to be heard from again, but they would find shanghaiing him would not be as easy as they thought.

Clay looked down at the man who was being guarded by Ol' Son and said, "If you want me to call off my dog, then you need to answer a couple of questions. If I get the answers I want, I'll call him off. Otherwise...."

Clay let the word trail off, allowing the man on the floor think what he might.

The man looked at Clay and said, "You... you call off your dog, and... and I'll tell whatever you want ta know, mister."

Clay turned and hauled the man with the broken nose to his feet and dumped him next to his friend.

Next, he reached down and laid his hand on Ol' Son's back and said, "Good boy, now come over here and sit next to me, but keep an eye on them."

Once Ol' Son was sitting next to him, Clay pulled his pistol and pointed it at the two men and said; "Now here's the thing. If I don't get honest answers from you two, I'm going to turn my dog loose on you, one at a time. Then when I think he's had enough fun, I'm going to shoot you in your knees and wrists. You'll be useless cripples for the rest of your miserable lives. Any questions so far?"

Both men shook their heads, no.

Clay nodded his head. "Alright, then. I'm looking for two men and I need to find them right away. Their names are Matthew and Mark Marlow, and I think they may be hanging around down here somewhere – probably up to no good and causing trouble of one sort or another. Do either of you know where I can find them?"

When they just stared at him, Clay looked down and said, "Ol' Son."

"Wait a minute!" the one with the bloody nose yelled. I ain't seen 'em taday, but I did last night. They was down ta the Bloody Bucket – ah couple of blocks from here. Spendin' money on liquor and whores. Near beat ah couple of'm ta death, they did. And when the owner got himself all lathered up, the one called, Matthew ups and gives him some money, he did. Nows they's bosom buddies, they are."

Clay nodded his head and said, "A little advice. You boys need to find yourselves a new profession, but just in case you don't – you ever come after me again, you won't find me being so nice. I promise, you'll wind up dog meat."

With that said, Clay turned and once again headed for the front door, calling over his shoulder, "Ol' Son."

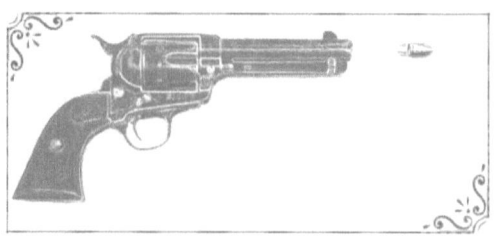

CHAPTER THIRTY

-

Clay looked through the dirty window of the Bloody Bucket and saw a few early morning customers, but neither of the Marlow brothers was there.

Turning, Clay could see the loading docks down the road a short distance and headed in that direction.

The sun was shining with just a few small puffer clouds floating around to break up the blue of the sky.

The docks were alive with activity – men loading ships – other men unloading ships – small boats being rowed out to the ships anchored in the bay.

Clay was killing time – watching the activity, when out of the blue, he heard his name being called.

"Clay? Clay Brentwood? Is that you?"

Clay turned and saw Justin Hacker walking toward him. They grinned and shook hands.

"What the devil you doin' here? Last I saw of you, you was headed back ta Texas with them two jaspers that tried ta way-lay us," Justin said, reaching down and scratching Ol' Son behind the ears.

Clay reached up and pulled off his hat and wiped sweat from the inside. "Howdy, Justin. Kind of surprised to run into you down here, but now that I think about it, you did say your father and uncle were looking to open a store of some kind, and this seems to be where the activity is."

"Yeah, yeah, I'm looking for some properties for them to look at," Justin said, "but   back to my original question. What are you doin' here?"

Clay scratched the back of his neck and said, "It's a long story."

Justin grinned and said, "Com'on, you can tell me over a piece of pie and a cup of coffee. There's a nice little restaurant just up the hill."

"With the prettiest waitress I've ever seen?" Clay asked with a grin.

"You'll see for yourself," Justin said.

The pie was delicious, the coffee was hot and black, just the way he liked it and the waitress was a very pretty young woman of twenty, who got a twinkle in her eyes every time she looked at Justin.

"So, you think they're here? And maybe prowlin' around down on the docks?" Justin asked.

"I'm told they were in the Bloody Bucket last night, having themselves quite a time."

"That's as rough ah place as you'll find down there, I'm told," Justin said. "You plan on goin' down there tonight?"

"I don't see that I have much choice. If that's where they are, that's where I have to go."

"Maybe you should have some company," Justin suggested.

Clay looked at his new friend and said, "I can't let you do that. First of all, if I find them down there, it's probably going to get nasty and I won't subject you to that. And second, you're a civilian. This is lawman's work."

Justin scratched the tip of his nose and smiled. "Now, let me explain a thing or two to you Mister Texas Ranger who is a long way from Texas. First, I'm no stranger to a knockdown, drag out. I spent a good bit of time working on the docks back in New York City. I was also ah sparin' partner for a professional fighter and I'm from a border town called, Nogales. Maybe you've heard of it?

If not, I can guarantee you, it's a rough place ta grow up in. Now, second, and what I propose - you could deputize me. You're going to need somebody coverin' your back, my friend."

Clay looked Justin Hacker in the eyes and saw determination staring back at him. He knew having Justin there, along with Ole Son, just might even up the odds tremendously, and the man had said he was thinking about becoming a ranger, hadn't he? This might let him see what being a ranger was all about.

"Raise your hand and repeat after me - I Justin Hacker..." Clay finally said.

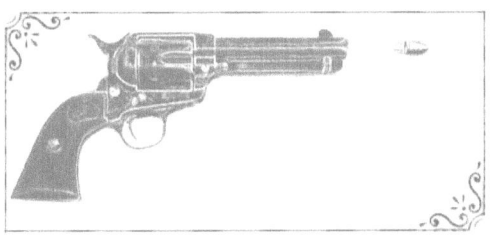

CHAPTER THIRTY-ONE

-

Around nine o'clock that night, Clay left Ol' Son on the sidewalk outside the Bloody Bucket when he and Justin went inside to look for the Marlow brothers. The place was packed with men of widespread backgrounds. There were farm boys, cowboys, prospectors and men from the ships, some of the sailors setting their feet on real ground for the first time in six months or more, along with men from dubious other walks of life. They were drinking rotgut, watered down whiskey and vying for the attention of the harlots who roamed the room and in general, as rowdy a bunch as you'd find anywhere.

Along with the drinking, there was gambling with the house taking in much more than they gave back, but even so, the suckers were lined up three deep to give their money away.

They watched several fights break out over this or that woman who intentionally instigated a riff between the men – mainly drunken cowboys and young men from town.

Bully Boys as some called them, bouncers by others, men who worked for the Bloody Bucket, waded in and beat the men into unconsciousness with clubs, then dragged them away toward the rooms at the back.

"Those boys will wake up tomorrow with a huge headache and wonder why they're locked up in the hold of some ship," an old man standing next to them said, shaking his head.

"Happen a lot?" Justin asked.

"Ever time ah ship is about to leave for China or somewhere. The captains are always in need of crew. Some of the men can't adapt to life at sea and die. Their bodies are dumped overboard out in the middle of the ocean someplace. Others are beaten to death for some stupid infraction, and some jump ship as soon as they're close enough to land. Men who can't even swim jump overboard, figuring it's better to die trying than the treatment they get on board the ships."

"You sound like a man who speaks from experience," Clay said, motioning to the bartender to bring the man another drink.

The old man had watery eyes and sun wrinkled, leathery looking skin. He looked at the drink, then lifted the glass to his lips and took a sip. "Twenty-one years," he said. Believe it or not, I used to be a bank clerk, back before I was shanghaied."

"And now?" Justin asked.

The old man looked at the drink, then gulped down what was left and motioned for the bartender to bring him another. "Boson's mate on the, Shangri-La. Never had the guts to jump ship. Would you believe I'm only forty?"

Clay stared at the man he thought was at least in his sixties and said, "I'm sorry."

The man looked at Clay for a moment then reached out his hand and said, "Marcus James Connors."

Clay shook the man's hand and introduced himself and Justin, along with telling Marcus why they were there.

Marcus nodded his head and said, "You know, I think you missed them by maybe an hour or so. Not positive it was them, but it sure sounds like'um. The older one tried to get one of the women to go upstairs with him and she refused. Made him mad and he slugged her in the jaw, then kicked her when she went down. He grabbed her by the hair and began draggin' her upstairs, kicking and screamin'."

He took a sip of his drink, then continued. "Big mistake. The Bully Boys watch out for the girls here and jumped on him like ah pack of wolves jumpin' on ah deer. And when the other one jumped in, the one they said was his younger brother, the Bully Boys hauled both of them out the back door."

"Any idea where they might be now?" Clay asked, motioning for the bartender to bring Marcus another drink.

"More than likely they're..."

This is as far as he got when they heard a loud commotion coming from the front door. Ol' Son was growling and someone was yelling, and before Clay could get to the front door, he heard Ol' Son yelp.

Bursting through the front door, Clay looked down and saw Ol' Son laying on his side on the sidewalk with blood running from his head. Standing in front of Ol' Son was one of the Bully Boys. He was scowling and raising his club to strike Ol' Son a second time.

"Don't even think about it," Clay warned the man.

The man turned and stared at Clay through eyes that showed meanness out of control.

"Stay outta this, mister, less'en you want your brains bashed in, too," he bellowed.

Clay was standing in front of a man who stood at least six feet six inches tall and had to weigh close to three hundred pounds. The man's face was heavily scarred and his nose looked as though it had been broken several times. The club he was carrying looked more like a fence post than a club.

Clay glanced at Ol' Son and wondered how he'd survived being hit by the big man.

"I'm not telling you again," Clay said as men crowded around. "You try to hit my dog again, you'll answer to me."

The Bully Boy looked at Clay, a man half his size and said, "Take your mongrel dog and get outta here, mister. I ever see either of you around here again, I'm gonna break both of you up so bad you'll never heal."

Clay was indecisive as what to do. Right before this happened, he was about to learn what had happened to the Marlow brothers and it bothered him to just walk away. He wasn't too keen on fighting this mountain of a man who thrived on beating people to a pulp, either. Truth be known, the man had probably killed his share of opponents.

Clay looked back toward the bar and saw the place where the old man had been standing was now vacant and he was nowhere in the crowd around him.

"Let's take the dog and get outta here," Justin said, stepping up close to Clay's side. "The man ain't worth the trouble that will come to us. The other Bully Boys would love ta jump in and have ah go at us and I don't hanker scrubbin' decks."

Clay looked from Ol' Son, who looked back at him with pain in his eyes, then to Justin, and finally back to the bouncer.

"Take your friends advice and leave, little man. You wouldn't last five minutes against me," the man said with an ugly, smirkish grin.

Clay looked at the big bouncer and said, "That club make you feel big and mean, does it? My guess is, you don't like to fight a man face to face. You'd rather come up behind them and bash their heads in with that fence post you're carrying, like you did the Marlow brothers a couple of hours ago."

The bouncer looked at Clay and everyone could see the anger building in his eyes. He didn't like being accused of being a coward, especially by a man half his size. He could hear smirks coming from the crowd that had now grown to close to a hundred; including the prostitutes and men coming down the street.

"I don't know who you are, mister, or what your association with them two is, and I don't care, cause you're about ta join 'em."

And with that, he swung his club at Clay's head.

Clay was expecting this and stepped under the swing and drove his right fist into the man's midsection, expecting him to double over.

Instead, Clay's fist met hard muscle and the man didn't even grunt. Realizing he needed room, Clay sidestepped and then went down the two steps and into the street. When he got to the center of the street, he turned and motioned with his hands for the bouncer to follow him.

"Put that club down and come out here and face me man to man, you big tub of guts. Or are you afraid of a man half your size will embarrass you in front of all these nice folks?"

Justin raced up to Clay and said, "Are you nuts? That man kills people just for the fun of it."

Clay unbuckled his pistol and handed it to Justin. "If I don't make it, make sure Ol' Son gets to a veterinarian."

Justin sighed and said, "I think you're crazy, but just so you'll know, you don't come out of this alive, I'm gonna shoot him."

By now, two more Bully Boys who also worked for the Bloody Bucket had come up and heard Clay's challenge.

"You don't need a club ta take that one, Surge," one of the others said. "I'll hold it for ya."

"When you're finished, we'll dump what's left of him in the back room with those other two."

"Scrubbin' decks for the next several years will make him wish he'd never tried ta buck us," one of the others yelled.

The three bouncers all laughed as the one called, Surge, handed his club to his friend, then shrugging his shoulders and cracking his knuckles, made his way out into the street.

Clay watched as the mountain moved toward him and tried to figure how he was going to defeat this man. Being smaller and quicker had to be an asset, he hoped as he began to circle, looking for an opening, knowing he couldn't let the man get his hands on him. The big monster of a man would crush the life out of him.

The big man kept coming, unconcerned about the smaller man in front of him.

Concentrating on the bouncer coming toward him, Clay stepped on a rock and was thrown off balance. He saw the fist coming but couldn't move fast enough. An explosion went off in his head and he felt himself being lifted off the ground.

Clay landed on his back in the street, and for a moment the pain in his head blinded him.

Before he could get to his feet, he felt the bouncer's hands grab him and lift him high over his head, and then once more, he felt himself flying through the air.

He landed against the side of a wagon and the wind was almost knocked out of him. He slid down to the street and lay there, trying to breathe.

Through a fog filled brain, Clay saw the big man coming for him, again, and with all the strength he could muster; he grabbed the wheel of the wagon and hauled himself to his feet, gasping for breath and trying to clear his head.

Surge was in no hurry. The little man was all but done for – a condition he would remedy very quickly. A little action always got him excited and his thoughts at the moment were on Candy, the big brunette prostitute he favored.

Clay shook his head and watched the man come. Taking two deep breaths, he stepped away from the wagon and once again, motioned for the big man to come to him.

A roar of encouragement came from the crowd, which made Surge turn and scowl at them.

One of the other bouncers yelled, "Look out!"

When Surge turned back toward his opponent, he saw the fist coming toward his face, but was too slow to duck out of the way.

Surge heard his nose break, and not for the first time. Next, he felt his head rock back when Clay's second blow slammed against his jaw.

Surge took a step backward, shook his head and grinned. "That all you got, little man?"

Clay followed Surge's backward movement, and when he got close, instead of trying to punch him, Clay leaned sideways and kicked the big man on the knee with the side of his boot.

The crowd heard the bone break and Surge felt his leg begin to buckle.

Surge reached for Clay, but felt his hands being pushed away, then felt a fist being smashed against the side of his head, then another to his already broken nose.

The last thing he remembered was landing on his back and everything going black.

When it was evident the Bully Boy had been bested by a man half his size, the other Bully Boys decided it was time to intervene and stepped into the street, beating their clubs against the palms of their hands.

"Clay!" Justin shouted and tossed Clay's pistol in the air.

Clay caught it and suddenly the Bully Boys were facing two men with guns pointed at them.

"Back off!" Clay shouted.

For a long moment the air was filled with tension as they stared at each other.

"Get your mongrel dog and get outta here," one of the Bully Boys growled. "We see your ugly faces around here again, it ain't gonna be pretty."

Clay tossed his pistol to Justin.

While Justin held the Bully Boys at bay with a pistol in each hand, the crowd parted to allow Clay to walk up onto the sidewalk and lift Ol' Son into his arms.

"That was some fight," Justin said, glancing over his shoulder as they made their way up the hill. "How are ya feelin'?"

"Like I butted heads with a Longhorn steer," Clay said with a grin.

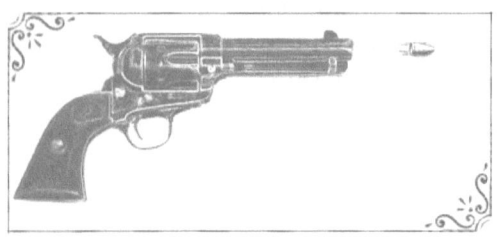

CHAPTER THIRTY-TWO

-

Ol' Son was resting in a cage at the veterinarian's office. His wound had been treated and the doctor had requested Clay leave him, at least for the night.

"I think he may be suffering from a concussion and I'd like to keep an eye on him for a day or so. In truth, he's lucky to be alive."

Clay agreed and told the doctor, "Do whatever needs to be done."

The veterinarian looked at Clay and said, "I'm no people doctor, but I think I can patch you up so you'll also live to fight another day."

Bruised and in pain from head to toe, with Justin's help, Clay checked out of the Palace Hotel and into a smaller one, not far from where the Hacker's had rented a house.

The man who ran the hotel wasn't happy at Clay wanting a tub of hot water so late at night, but eyed the extra money and the battered man in front of him, and nodded his head.

Justin said he'd see him in the morning for breakfast and left.

After soaking in the tub for close to an hour, Clay dried himself off and fell into bed, asleep by the time his head hit the pillow.

Over breakfast, Justin took a look at Clay and suggested he take a couple of days to get back on his feet. In the meantime, he'd try to find out what happened to the Marlow brothers.

Reluctantly, Clay finally agreed. After all, Justin reminded him, he was an official deputy and would be working under Clay's direction.

Normally, Clay was not a man who could spend his time lollygagging around, but when he got back up to his room, he pulled off his clothes and climbed back in bed. He slept straight through the day and all night.

The following morning, Clay climbed out of bed at the crack of dawn. He was still sore from being slammed into the wagon and onto the ground, but would not allow himself to spend another day in bed. He had a job to do; plus, he needed to check on Ol' Son.

He was just finishing his breakfast when Justin came in and dropped down in the chair across from Clay.

"How you feeling?" Justin asked

"Much better," Clay lied. "You find out anything?"

"No," Justin admitted, "but I did get some information from the woman the older brother, Matthew, slugged. She's still sportin' a bruised jaw by the way and had trouble talkin'."

"But she did?" Clay queried.

"Like a songbird. She hates him. Said he cost her not only a doctor bill, but several nights work."

"And out of the goodness of your heart, you gave her some money," Clay said with a grin.

"Twenty dollars, which was almost ever cent I had."

"Make out a bill and I'll reimburse you. I'll turn it in and get my money back when I get back to Texas," Clay said, knowing full well he probably wouldn't. He was still owed for a stack of other vouchers he'd turned in.

The waitress brought Justin coffee and asked if he wanted breakfast?

She was a woman in her fifties who looked as though she'd worked hard all her life and it was trying hard to not let it catch up to her. Justin felt sorry for her.

Justin smiled that woman pleasing smile of his and said, "Darlin', just lookin' at you is breakfast enough for me."

Her face turned the color of a ripe tomato and she grinned from ear to ear. Clay guessed she rarely got a compliment and was loving this one.

"Go on with ya, now," she said swatting him lightly on the shoulder. "What would you do if I took ah fancy to yer fine talk? You'd run like ah scared rabbit, I'm bettin'."

Justin grinned and handed her a dollar tip, then flashed his deputy badge and said, "On the ground is my heart, broken inta ah million pieces, lass, but as much as I hate to, darlin', duty calls and I must leave ya."

The woman smiled and tucked the money in her pocket and as she left, she said, "Thank ye kindly fer both the compliment and the money. You've somewhat renewed my faith in men."

Clay looked at Justin Hacker and decided he was not only a man to ride the river with, but a man who made life interesting no matter where they went.

Wiping his mouth and standing up, Clay said, "Com'on lover boy, we've got work to do."

"And now ain't that just what I tole the fine lady?" Justin said in his Irish brogue.

The first thing they did was go to the veterinarian's hospital and speak with the doctor.

"I think he's going to be fine. He's tough," the doctor said, opening the door to the cage and allowed Ole Son his freedom.

Ole Son stepped gingerly out of the cage, then ran over to Clay and looked up at him, his tail wagging furiously.

Clay squatted down and hugged Ole Son, wondering how, when and where he'd grown so attached to him.

After paying the doctor's bill, they left and headed toward the wharf.

They'd gone close to three blocks before either of them spoke.

"I think they're still in one of the rooms at the back of the Bloody Bucket," Justin said.

"You saying they haven't been taken to a ship, yet? How do you know?" Clay asked.

"She said normally they would have, but the ship they'll be sold to, the Bombay, isn't due in for ah week or so from now," Justin said, shrugging his shoulders.

By now they had gotten down to the docks and Clay sat down on one of the many benches and stared out at the bay and counted six ships floating in a leisurely manner. In the distance, still far out on the ocean, he saw what appeared to be white sails and wondered if that was the ship the Marlow brothers was being sold to, then shook his head. Justin had said at least a week from now which gave him some time to figure something out.

Ol' Son eased up and laid his chin on Clay's knee and looked up at him.

Absently, Clay reached out and scratched the dog's ears, being careful not to touch his wound.

"So, what's the plan?" Justin asked. "Are you gonna try and rescue 'em or are you gonna let 'em be sold inta slavery?"

Clay rolled and lit a cigarette and smoked half of it before he answered. "Not sure," he said. "The ranger side of me says I'm bound to take them back to Texas to stand trial, but the civilian side of me, the side that wants them to suffer for what they've put me through, and all the people they've hurt, tells me slavery might just be the right punishment for them. Hanging would be too quick."

Justin leaned back and put his hands behind his head, then stretched out his legs and crossed them. "Let me know what you decide," he said, pulling his hat down over his face and closing his eyes.

Clay watched the people coming and going for close to an hour before he came to a decision. Leaving them to the Bully Boys would be true justice, and allow him to go home; and he would have chosen that route except for that damn vow he'd sworn to when he took the rangers oath.

He nudged Justin with his elbow and when Justin pushed his hat back up onto his head, Clay said, "Not sure how, yet, but I am going to steal them away from their kidnappers and take their sorry carcasses back to Texas."

"That so," Justin said as he sat up straight and stretched. "Do I still get to come along as your deputy?"

"Clay smiled and said, "I was kinda hoping you'd want to. Got any ideas how we should go about it?"

Justin thought for a moment, then said, "Since they work until all hours of the night and into the wee hours of the mornin', I reckon we should do it durin' the day when they're restin'. Seems like the easiest way to me."

Clay nodded his head in agreement. "Maybe you could get your lady friend, the one Matthew beat up on, to tell you which room the Marlow brothers are being held in. I'd hate going in there having to look into each and every room to find them."

"I suppose I could do that, but it won't be easy. The Bully Boys know what I look like and if they see me snoopin' around, well I guess I don't have ta tell ya what will happen."

The girls each had their own room above the saloon and gambling hall and the young lady in question had given Justin her room number.

The sun was indicating it was somewhere between two and three o'clock in the afternoon when Clay, Ol' Son and Justin crept up the back stairway of the Bloody Bucket and eased into the dark hallway.

Clay stationed himself in the middle of the hallway and looked in both directions while Justin made his way to room 206 and tapped lightly on the door. Ol' Son sat next to Clay and waited to see what was going to happen.

Justin was in the young prostitute's room for only a couple of minutes and then came back out, making his way quietly to the back door and the stairs.

In the restaurant where the pretty waitress worked, Justin ordered coffee then said, "She said they've moved 'em. She said you got 'em spooked. They're afraid you might try ta bust 'em loose, so they set ah trap for ya."

"What kind of trap?" Clay asked.

"They put out the word and told folks if you come lookin' for information, you're ta be told they're bein' held in room 105," Justin said, rolling his eyes.

"And they'll have someone in there waiting with a gun, probably a shotgun, and when I come in they'll fill me with lead and claim I broke in with my gun in my hand. Claim it was self-defense."

"Somethin' like that," Justin agreed.

Clay took a sip of coffee and asked, "Did she happen to say when they'd be taken to the ship?"

"She said they're ah mite tight lipped on that account, and she's afraid to ask too many questions. She's worried about causin' them ta think she might be in cahoots with us and make her life worse than it already is."

Clay nodded his head in understanding. "Can't say I blame her."

For the next five days, they roamed the waterfront, asking questions to no avail.

Just the mention of the Bully Boys was like putting a padlock on their mouths.

By the end of the fifth day, they had exhausted every angle they could think of to find the Marlow brothers. At Justin's suggestion, they stopped at a saloon a few blocks away from the wharf area.

They were standing at the bar, having a beer when Justin looked at Clay and said, "Feels like we've been chasin' our tails and gettin' nowhere don't it."

Clay sat his glass on the bar, wiped the foam from his lips and nodded his head in agreement. "It does. They've got everybody too afraid to talk, and we're running out of time. The ship is due in day after tomorrow some time, and I'd bet my last nickel they'll hustle them out there faster than a racehorse out of the gate."

"So, what'er we gonna do?" Justin asked. "Finally admit they're gonna get their just due and you go on back ta Texas?"

"I've still got two days," Clay said, raising the glass of beer to his lips.

CHAPTER THIRTY-THREE

-

Their break came when Clay was almost ready to quit the search and go back to Texas without the Marlow brothers. It also came from an unexpected source.

Clay and Justin were both physically and mentally tired from trying everything they could think of, including bribery, to learn the whereabouts of the Marlow brothers, but had come up empty handed.

They dropped into chairs at the restaurant where the pretty waitress worked and when she saw them, she rushed over and poured coffee, then pointed toward the menu behind the counter where a large sign advertised the special of the day – fresh salmon.

"I haven't tried it yet, but everyone who has, said it was delicious," she beamed.

"Why not," Clay said half heartily. "And the same for the dog."

"And what about you, handsome?" she asked of Justin.

Justin smiled and said, "Ahh, darlin', just hearin' ya talk about it makes me heart go pitter-patter with wantin' it. I do believe you could talk the devil inta changin' his ways."

She looked at Clay and said, "Don't you just love the way he talks?"

Before Clay could say something smart, Marcus James Connors, the boson's mate from the Shangri-La walked in and sat down in a chair opposite Clay and Justin and said, "I'll have what they're havin'. And give the bill ta Mister Brentwood there."

Marcus looked like he'd been dragged through a river and then down a dusty road. His eyes were bloodshot and he looked like he needed a week's worth of sleep.

The waitress looked at Clay who glanced at the boson's mate and said, "Why not? Sure, put his meal on my tab, also."

When she'd gone, Clay looked at Marcus and said, "You didn't just happen by here, did you?"

Marcus wiped his mouth across his mouth and said, "No, I didn't."

Clay could feel the hair on the back of his neck stand on end.

Ole Son must have sensed the change in Clay because he stood up and began to growl.

Clay reached out and stroked his neck and said, "Easy boy. Everything's fine."

Ole Son looked at Marcus, then up at Clay, who nodded his head. Satisfied everything was all right, he dropped down on his belly and rested his head on his paws.

"I hope whatever it is you have to say is worth the price of the meal," Clay said.

Marcus poured a cup of coffee from the pot the waitress had left and took a sip before speaking. "I think information on the men you seek should be worth a fish dinner, don't you, Ranger?"

Both Clay and Justin sat up straighter and stared at Marcus.

"If you know where they are, I'd sure appreciate hearing about it," Clay said.

"Thought you might," Marcus said, taking another sip of coffee. "Good coffee," he said after drinking half a cup.

It was all Clay could do to keep his patience in check.

Justin wasn't quite that strong and blurted out, "Well, man, where are they, and why are you just now bringin' the information to us?"

Marcus rubbed his chin and said, "I'm just now bringin' the information because I just learned it. And since we're weighin' anchor first thing in the morning, I feel safe enough tellin' ya. I'll be gone and far away from the Bully Boys."

Still, Clay waited for Marcus to continue.

Marcus poured himself a little more coffee, took a sip and said; "They think I'm an old man so they don't mind talkin' around me."

He took another sip of coffee, smacked his lips and continued. "I was in the Bloody Bucket, havin' ah farewell drink or two when I heard two of the Bully Boys talkin' about movin' the Marlow brothers out to the ship as soon as it gets dark."

"But the ship isn't due yet," Justin said.

"Came in bout an hour ago," Marcus said, rubbing the back of his hand against his left eye. "Must'a had good wind."

"You wouldn't happen to know the location where they're holding them, would you?" Clay asked.

Marcus looked at Clay and shook his head. "Not the actual address, no sir. But I do know they'll be transportin' six of 'em," He said.

"How will they get them down to the docks?" Justin asked.

"Most anybody who's been here for any length of time knows that," Marcus answered with a grin. "Prison wagon. They haul their captives down to the dock in ah prison wagon, then turn 'em over to the sailors from the ship, who row 'em out to the ship in ah small boat and then load 'em aboard."

"What keeps the captives from jumping out of the boats and escapin'?" Justin wanted to know.

"Cause they're either so drunk or doped up they could care less about what's happenin' to 'em," Marcus said as though he was talking to a schoolboy.

Justin noticed the implication that he was stupid and felt a rush of anger that quickly passed, due to the situation.

"So, what you're saying is, we need to grab them before they're given any booze or dope," Clay said. "Otherwise, we'll have to throw them over our shoulders to haul them away – and it's hard to fight the Bully Boys with dead weight hanging over your shoulder."

"Somethin' like that, if you ain't already too late," Marcus said as the waitress brought their dinners.

The dinner was as the waitress had said and they all told her so. Standing up, and fishing in his pocket, Clay left a large tip.

Outside, Clay looked at Justin and said, we need horses or a buggy, and we need to find a house with a prison wagon sitting nearby," Clay said.

"If it was me, I'd check out the stables. They won't take the wagon near where the prisoners are until they're ready ta move 'em," Marcus told them.

"And by the time the wagon gets there, the prisoners will already be in no condition to resist," Clay muttered.

"Probably ain't never been anything but," Marcus declared.

"What are you talkin' about?" Justin asked.

Clay jumped into the conversation. "What he means is, they're much easier to control if they keep them drunk or doped up until it's time to move them, right?"

"That would be my guess," Marcus answered.

"So, what do we do?" Justin wanted to know. He was frustrated that they couldn't just waltz in and grab them away from the Bully Boys and disappear into the night.

Clay scratched the back of his neck and said, "What we need to do is find out where they're being held. I figure it'll be a whole lot easier snatching them from a house somewhere, than it will be trying to grab them from the prison wagon down on the dock where there will be a whole bunch of men who don't care for the idea of us taking them away."

Justin got two of his horses from the stable and he and Clay rode up and down almost every street in San Francisco, barring Nob Hill, where the elite lived.

Justin looked around and said, "It's gettin' dark and I think we should get down ta the docks. Didn't Marcus say they was gonna take 'em down there as soon as it gets dark?"

As they rode toward the house where the Hackers were staying, Clay rolled and lit a cigarette – and after a minute, he said, "I guess you're right, we should."

"Then what are we waitin' on?" Justin wanted to know. He was anxious to get this done with. He was getting ideas concerning a certain waitress.

Clay blew a smoke ring, then said, "Problem is, there's only two of us and the dog – and we don't know how many of them there is. I don't want to go in there blasting away with our guns. That would be murder, but I don't see any way to catch them by surprise. No, we've got to come up with a different plan, one where nobody gets killed if we can help it."

As they stepped down, Elijah and Ephram Hacker came walking down to meet them.

"Any luck?" Ephram asked.

Justin brought them up to date and as they stood there in the moonlight, Elijah grinned and said, "I jest got an idea."

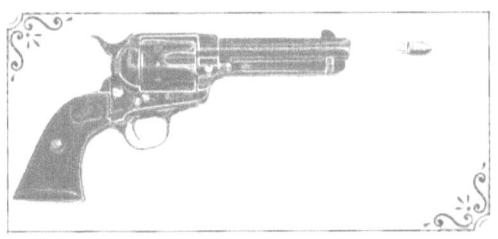

CHAPTER THIRTY-FOUR

-

From the shadows, Clay and the Hackers watched as the prison wagon rolled to a stop on the dock where at least a dozen heavily armed men stood. The men driving the wagon stepped down, but didn't unlock the door. They were waiting for the boat from the ship to dock before bringing the prisoners out.

In the distance, they saw a large, double ender boat being rowed by two burly men and when it tied up to the pier, Surge, the Bully Boy who Clay had made look bad, walked over and opened the door after looking around to make sure no one was going to show up and cause trouble.

Surrounded by six armed guards, with another six looking around at the crowd of people who came to watch the men being hauled away - they pushed and prodded the prisoners toward the waiting boat.

The way they staggered and stumbled along, it was obvious they were under the influence of something.

As they neared the boat and the waiting sailors, Clay, Justin and Elijah raised a rifle to their shoulder and began firing just over the Bully Boys heads.

Their reaction was instant. Several of them began returning fire, but not knowing what direction to shoot at. The rest of the guards herded the prisoners into the waiting boat and the two sailors began rowing with all their strength.

As soon as the return fire started, Clay and the Hackers backed into the shadows and left, allowing the Bully Boys to shoot at an empty space.

Getting on horses that were nearby, Clay and the Hackers rode hard for half a mile then reined in and looked down at Marcus.

"Everything ready?" Clay asked.

"Just like Mister Hacker ordered," he said as he watched them step down from their horses and tie them to the nearby hitch rail.

Down at the water's edge, three boats waited with two men in each one.

"You bring the money?" Marcus asked as Clay walked up next to him.

"You said, fifty dollars for each of you," Clay said, reaching into his pocket and pulling out a wad of money.

"And cheap enough it is ta ask ah man to risk his life over ah few worthless no goods like the ones we're goin' after," Marcus snarled.

From where they stood, they could see the backside of the Bombay and saw that all hands were on the port side, watching for the new prisoners to come aboard, leaving the starboard side, empty and unprotected.

As they climbed into the boats, Clay reminded them, "We wait until the prisoners are aboard before we make our move."

"I'll be on that short pier, there," Marcus said pointing back along the shore.

While the prisoners were being rowed out to The Bombay's port side, Clay and the others were rowing toward her starboard side.

As the three boats came along the starboard side of the ship, the sailors quickly tied their boats to the Bombay and waited.

It seemed like an eternity before Justin nudged Clay and pointed.

Clay turned his head toward the pier where Marcus was supposed to be and smiled. In the darkness, he saw a small light moving from side to side.

Turning to the others, Clay whispered, "It's time. They're on board."

The sailors were the first to climb quietly over the starboard railing and ease themselves onto the deck. Clay was next, then turned and lifted Ol' Son onto the deck, followed quickly by the others.

The captain, a portly man dressed in his nightshirt, stood looking at the newest members of his crew.

Turning to his chief boson's mate, he said, "You know what to do with them, and I want no trouble out of them."

"Aye, aye, Sir," a burly looking man of around forty said, and before he could give an order, they heard, "Hold it right there!" come from the far side.

"What's this?" the captain asked turning toward the men who had boarded his ship.

Clay stepped forward and said, "We've come to relieve you of those men," he said, pointing at the Marlow brothers and the others.

"Like hell you will," the captain yelled. "I paid good money for those men and by Gawd, you'll have to fight to get them!"

Turning to his crew he yelled, "Throw these no goods off my ship, and be quick about it."

Clay made a quick count, there were ten of them and twenty-eight of the Bombay crew.

With a yell, the crew of the Bombay drew their weapons and charged; a few of them who had only short knives, also had belaying pins in their other hand.

-

On the dock, one of the Bully Boys touched Surge on the shoulder and when he turned around, the man pointed toward the Bombay and the ruckus that was going on.

"So that's how they're doin' it," he said, wiping spittle from his mouth on his shirtsleeve and running toward a rowboat tied up to the pier. "They're afraid ta face us, so they wait til the prisoners are on board the ship, then sneak aboard and attack the sailors, hoping they can tak'em from 'em and make us look like ah pack of fools."

"Where are you goin'?" one of the other Bully Boys called, Halverson, asked.

"Why out ta give 'em ah hand. Ain't you gonna come along? We can't let 'em get the upper hand on us, can we? We got ah reputation ta uphold."

Surge and three of his cohorts jumped into the rowboat and began making their way out to the ship.

The tide was coming in and water washed over the gunnels of the small boat forcing one of the Bully Boys to scoop water out of the boat with his cupped hands. As he did, he looked up at the stars and said, "Lord don't let us sink. I can't swim."

"Put yer backs inta it boys. We wanna get there before it's over. I want that one they call, Brentwood."

As it was, Clay was having all he wanted. He didn't want to shoot anyone, but when he was faced with two of them – one swinging a long knife and the other one a belaying pin, he had to make a choice and shot the one with the long knife.

Instead of coming on, the one with the short knife and belaying pin, ducked behind a large crate and threw the belaying pin at Clay, then raised his arm to throw his knife.

The belaying pin hit Clay alongside his head, knocking him to his knees and when he went down the man took aim at Clay's chest. But before he could bring his arm forward, Ol' Son leaped on him and bit down on his wrist.

The man screamed with pain and doubled up his other hand into a fist and smashed Ol' Son alongside his head, knocking him loose and when he fell to the deck of the ship, the man kicked Ol' Son in the side, sending him sliding across the blood-stained deck.

During the melee, the captain ran for the passageway going down below and when he was inside, he closed and locked the doors from inside, then turned and went to his cabin and again locked the doors. Safely inside, he took up a shotgun and sat in the corner, trembling. He was only tough when he had men around him that would protect him. What was going on topside was something he couldn't control, and he wanted no part of it.

The crew of the Bombay were a tough lot; raw boned and willing to fight because they were afraid not to. The more blood they saw, them wilder they became, but they were also not trained soldiers and wreckless, which became their downfall.

Ironically, most of the blood covering the deck belonged to the crewmen from the ship.

The two old Hacker brothers stood back to back and had picked up cutlasses from fallen sailors to offset their pistols and were holding their own.

Justin saw Clay go down and headed in his direction but was waylaid by a man who looked like a tree trunk. The man swung his cutlass with all his might and Justin felt the tip tear a slice across his stomach, and before he could get his pistol lifted, the man was on top of him, smashing the butt of the big knife against Justin's head.

Justin grabbed the man's hand and held on, doing his best not to black out, but was fighting a losing battle. As everything went black, he felt the man's weight lifted from him and the last thing he heard was a growl coming from Ol' Son's throat and the man screaming.

Ol' Son ripped a chunk out of the sailor's shoulder and his attack knocked him off of Justin. The man swung his fist and hit Ol' Son in the ribs, sending him back across the deck with a yelp.

Elijah Hacker saw his son go down and saw the dog try to help, but the sailor trying to kill Justin was coming to his feet, looking around for his long knife.

As the man got to his feet, Elijah yelled, "Hey!" and when the man turned in his direction, Elijah swung his sword with both hands and all his weight behind it.

The man's head was severed and rolled across the deck, but the body stayed erect for a while longer before toppling over like a felled tree.

Elijah felt like being sick, but choked it back as he rushed over and lifted Justin's head and said, "Wake up, son, we still got fightin' ta do."

Blood was coming from the side of Justin's head and Elijah quickly wrapped his bandanna around it to stop the bleeding as Justin opened his eyes and shook his head.

"Easy son," Elijah said. "You've got ah mean head wound."

Justin said, "I'm okay, pa," then shoved his father to the side and shot the sailor who was about to drive a boat hook into his father's back'

Clay opened his eyes and looked around. His head hurt something awful, but he was able to get to his feet, and what he saw made him groan, "Ah hell," he said when he saw Surge and his cronies come climbing over the railing of the ship.

Surge stopped and looked down at the Marlow brothers who were slumped down on the deck, drunk and trying their best to stay out of the fight.

Surge saw Clay and grinned. "You want these two?" he yelled, then slammed the butt of his pistol down on both their heads, rendering them unconscious. Then he reached down and grabbed one in each hand and lifted them and tossed them over the side of the ship.

Clay couldn't believe what Surge had just done. They were gone, just like that - and after everything that he had gone through - it was over in the blink of an eye, leaving him still fighting for his own life and the others with him.

After throwing the Marlow brothers overboard, Surge turned back and waded through the throng of dead bodies and blood. He was headed for Clay, and when he got close, he yelled, "I'm gonna enjoy killin' you, ranger man."

Clay still had a cutlass in his hand and watched as Surge picked one up from the deck and immediately swung the blade at Clay.

Clay stepped back and parried the thrust, then made a counter thrust that just missed Surge's chest.

For what seemed an eternity, they swung their swords at each other, both connecting - making small cuts here and there, from time to time.

Both men were bleeding from at least a half dozen places on their bodies – and both men were getting tired; their arms were aching and the big swords felt like heavy weights at the ends of their arms.

Blood was running into Clay's eyes from a cut on his forehead and as he stepped backward to get out of the way of another thrust by Surge, he slipped on the bloody deck, then tripped over a fallen body and went down.

Surge saw his opportunity to end it and lunged at Clay, raising his sword over his head for the deathblow, only to feel excruciating pain in his side.

Ol' Son had climbed back onto his feet and saw Clay go down. Although he was in a great deal of pain, his only thought was of Clay and he leaped toward the man who was about to kill his master and clamped his teeth onto the man's stomach.

Clay was trying to get back on his feet, but without much luck and saw Ol' Son latch onto Surge's stomach.

Surge looked down and saw the dog's jaw locked onto his stomach and instead of stabbing the ranger; he swung the sword at the dog and felt it strike bone.

Ol' Son released the man and fell to the deck next to his severed right front leg.

"No!!!" Clay screamed, as he steadied himself against the railing of the ship. Out of rage at what Surge had done, Clay drew his pistol and shot Surge in the gut. Then shot him again, and again.

Surge dropped his sword and looked at Clay as though he didn't understand.

Clay was on his feet now and leveled his pistol at Surge and pulled the trigger.

The force of the shot caused Surge to stagger backwards and bump into the railing.

Clay's last shot knocked Surge over the railing and Clay heard his body hit the water.

By now, what was left of the Bombay crew had given up. Their number was down to nine.

Both sides had wounds, but only one of the men with Clay had been killed - the oldest sailor of the group. His friends wrapped him in a piece of canvas and took his body with them when they left.

Clay bent down next to Ol' Son and wrapped his neckerchief around the stump of Ol' Son's leg, then picked him up and cradled him in his arms.

Both Elijah and Ephram would carry scars to remind them of this day along with stories to tell. Ephram helped load Ol' Son into one of the rowboats, and then told Clay, "I'll go with you and help with the dog."

Once again, the veterinarian was awakened in the middle of the night and when he saw who it was, he shook his head. But when he saw that Ol' Son had lost his leg, he rushed him into the surgery room.

"Couldn't put his leg back on," he told them two hours later, "but I believe he's going to pull through. He can get around on three legs, but no more fighting, you hear?"

Clay looked down at Ol' Son who was looking back at him, and said, "I can guarantee that, Doc; yes, sir, I can guarantee that."

-

It took two full pages of the newspaper to tell the story and shortly thereafter, both Clay and Justin were offered jobs as US Deputy Marshals by the head of the marshal's office there in San Francisco. Clay gracefully declined, but Justin told the man he might be interested.

When Justin's younger brother, Jeremiah, and his cousin Ben, heard about what had happened, they said they were sorry they weren't there to help.

Justin told them both to be thankful they were out of town. "I've been ah scrape or two, but nothin' like that one. We're all, lucky ta be alive."

Clay sent a wire to his boss, Bill McDaniel, explaining the Marlow brothers were dead, and would file a full report when he got back.

Clay stayed around San Francisco while both he and Ol' Son healed up enough to travel, then he thanked the Hackers for all their help and promised to keep in touch. "You decide to take that US Marshals job, you come by my place. I'll have a good horse for you. My thanks for all your help."

Justin shook Clay's hand and said, "I just might take you up on that."

Three weeks later, Clay drove a buggy through the gates of his Mexican style hacienda in Texas and came to a stop – the black stallion and the buckskin trailing close behind.

The people who worked for him came running up, cheering and jumping up and down – they're voices blending together as they all told him how glad they were he was back.

Juanita Hernandez, one of the young daughters of Jose Hernandez, the ranch blacksmith, ran up to the buggy and stared at Ole Son, then looked at Clay and asked, "Why is there a three-legged dog sitting on the seat next to you, Senor Brentwood?"

Clay grinned and spoke to all the people standing next to the buggy, "This is the newest member to our family. His name is Ol' Son. He's been through hell and high water. And he saved my bacon on several occasions, so I brought him home with me to sorta retire. He's gonna need a whole lot of special attention from all of us."

Everyone nodded their heads in agreement, indicating they would.

His housekeeper, Mrs. McIntyre was standing on the porch with tears streaming down her cheeks. She was smiling and wondering what to fix for her boss's homecoming supper.

Juanita climbed up on the wheel and began to pet Ol Son and laughed when he licked her on the cheek.

Riley, one of his foremen, a long, lanky drink of water, walked up and scratched Ol' Son on the ear and said, "Welcome to the family, Ol' Son."

Ol' Son licked Riley's hand and wagged his tail.

Riley looked up at Clay and asked, "What about you, boss, you plannin' on retirin' too?"

Clay looked at him for a long moment, then grinned and said, "You bet I am. No more rangering or chasin' outlaws for me."

Riley nodded his head, and then got a questionable look on his face that Clay noticed.

"What's that look mean?" Clay asked.

Riley pulled a piece of folded yellow paper out of his shirt pocket, unfolded it and then handed it to Clay. "Came just this mornin'."

Clay knew instantly that it was a telegram and he'd come to dislike telegrams... They were usually from Austin, which meant bad news, like another ranger job.

Clay took the telegram from Riley, then held it up to the light so it was easier to read.

To his surprise, it wasn't from McDaniel, head of the Texas Rangers, as he had expected, but even so, it still made him shake his head as he read –

**HORSE RUSTLERS STEALING MY STOCK [stop]
NEED YOUR HELP [stop] LORALIE**

THE END

FROM THE AUTHOR

Thank you to all my readers. Your reviews and requests for more Clay Brentwood books is an inspiration to me. I'll keep writing them as long as you keep requesting them...

Jared McVay

MEET THE AUTHOR

At the current time, Jared McVay lives in Oregon where he writes his books,

does storytelling, book signings, speaking engagements, and gets in a little fishing from time to time.

Before becoming a novelist, Jared was a professional actor – stage, film and television, and a ghostwriter for screenplays.

As a young man he worked as a cowboy, a rodeo clown, a lumberjack, barker for a carnival and a truck driver. During the 1950's he rode the rails as a hobo and during the 80's, a blue water sailor. He spent his military time in the US Navy Sea Bees, where he learned his electrical trade as a power lineman, then spent ten years as a lineman for Kansas Gas & Electric. But it was his love of entertaining people that led him into acting and writing.

Jared has five children, eleven grandchildren, fifteen great grandchildren and four great, great grandchildren.

When not writing or talking about writing, or answering e-mails from his fans, you can find him enjoying life with his girlfriend, Jerri.

THANK YOU FOR READING!

If you enjoyed this book, we would appreciate your customer review on your book seller's website or on Goodreads.

Also, we would like for you to know that you can find more great books like this one at

www.SixGunBooks.com

Stories so real you can smell the gunsmoke.™